# DARING WIDOW

*Those Notorious Americans, Book 2*

## CERISE DELAND

# COPYRIGHT

Jo-Ann Power writing as Cerise Deland

W. J. Power Publisher

Photographic art: Period Images

Graphic designer: Wicked Smart Designs

**ISBN-13: 978-0-9908943-6-0 Digital**

**ISBN: 978-0-9908943-7-7 Print**

❀ Created with Vellum

# PROLOGUE

**September 11, 1877**
**Rue des Abbesses**
**Montmartre**
**Paris, France**

Remy skimmed his hand across the page. With an arc here, a shadow there, his impression of the line of dancers blurred, sharpened. A rush to capture their expressions and exertions in graphite flitted through his imagination. All were impressions to develop later when he was alone tomorrow morning as he drank his coffee.

He cocked his head, stopping to consider his sketch. Not bad for midnight and a liter of wine. He liked the idea of painting a chorus line, the women laughing, hoping for a few men to seek them out backstage. Remy had made one of these women famous and sought after last spring when he debuted a portrait of her alone in the dressing rooms, her long red hair falling to her shoulders, her hand to her pert breast. Pretty thing, she'd retired from the cabaret line to one *comte's* love nest in the Rue Moncey.

Remy was a connoisseur of bodies. Their form. Their function. The supple flow of muscles beneath the obliging skin. The toned ones that showed dexterity. The thin ones that showed their poverty.

The fat ones, the gross ones, whose gluttony had induced an effluence of flesh. The crippled ones. The children, too pale, too pocked to have ever been a heavenly cherub. The deprivation that deformed the perfection of their birth and left a wreck prone to disease and catastrophe. All showing the disease that could kill and the charm that could enchant.

Remy folded his foolscap sketch pad and tucked his graphite into the special pocket in his waistcoat that he'd designed so it didn't mark his clothing. He hailed the *garçon* to deliver another flask of *vin rouge* for him and his friend.

"No, don't," said Julian Ash, the Marquess of Chelton. "I'm ready to leave. You appear to be too."

"You're right. I'm done for tonight." Andre Claude Marceau, Duc de Remy, Prince *du sang*, and the English marquess had been friends for years. Fellow *bon vivants* since their mothers had introduced them eight years ago, they traveled the city together whenever Julian's business brought him to Paris. Though Julian was five years Andre's junior, they shared a view of the world that accommodated them as aristocrats with land and a greater desire than skill for administering it. That was why Julian applied his nighttime activities to gambling and Remy himself to the pleasures of molding bodies. In bronze or marble, graphite or pen, Remy called himself an artist. More than that, he styled himself a lover of bodies.

Human bodies. Strong or weak, lean or well-fed. A man, now and then. A child, less often. But women. Ah, the female of the species lured him as no other fascination. And tonight's bevy of women at this *cabaret* could appeal for perhaps another five minutes.

"I like Sabine there." Remy lifted his chin toward the woman who pranced onto the riser, her glossy cheap red satin skirts hoisted to her waist.

"Her charms are——" Julian choked on a laugh. "Abundant."

"*Certainly.*" Sabine, spicy dish that she was, loved to display her copious charms. In particular, she was adept at the new sensation in this northern arrondissement of Paris, the *cancan*. She drew an audience——and embellished her salacious reputation——by her acrobatic skill to kick high and yet keep time with the three musicians. More than that? Well, few could say her best offering was her long Gallic face. Nor her curvaceous legs. *Non*. What attracted attention to her was the thick curly black hair at the junction of her thighs.

Remy considered what it would be like to make love to Sabine. "She provides a good cushion for the romp, would you say?"

"I will pass, thank you." Julian downed his glass. "I bet you have too."

"You know me too well."

"Time to go to Tourelane's," Julian said.

"You've a desire to lose more money to the *marquis*?" Remy asked him. Julian was a gambler who had motivation to play, but not the persistent skills that could embellish his meager coffers.

Julian stood, straightening his white shirt collar and sapphire waistcoat. His dark good looks cut a fine figure in his black evening clothes. A few ladies cast their greedy glances down his elegant form. "A man must try."

Patrons were clapping in time to the raucous music, leering, laughing and pointing at Sabine and her distinguishing charm.

"Agreed. We can find better amusement."

Remy stood, waved their *garçon* over and pressed a few francs into his hand.

"*Monsieur le duc, merci,*" the waiter began. "You and *le Marquis* have not finished your wine."

"Take it for yourself, Henri. Tell the owner I said it is yours. With my regards." Remy put his top hat on his head, adjusting it to the wealth of tawny curls he could never seem to tame.

"Sabine will finish this number but we have a new dancer you may like better." Henri liked his money from Remy and wished to keep him here drinking.

"*Non,* Henri. *Le Marquis* and I have another engagement. *Pardon e moi.* We'll see you soon."

The man bowed with small deference. "*Merci, a bientôt. Merci.*"

"You overpay him," Julian remarked with a smirk. "Again."

"He's good. Knows what we like."

As Remy turned, an ostrich plume caught his eye. A flash of platinum hair followed. Pink lips. Skin of cream topped with cheeks that spoke of strawberries. The colors of her, the health of her, the wealth she wore were complements to the symmetry of her long winged blonde brows, the perfect oval of her face and the wide lush sweep of her mouth.

He paused. "Who is that, Henri?"

"*Pardon? Que?*" The waiter followed Remy's line of sight.

"The lady with the white feather in her hat?" Remy cursed the flickering gaslight that gave him nothing more of the champagne blonde with the expressive brows and kissable lips. "The one with the dark-haired woman in blue and the tall blond man? There."

"I'm certain I do not know, *Monsieur*, but I can inquire and—"

"No, *merci,* Henri. That—" That would be improper. And he'd learn who she was. Well dressed, expertly coiffed, she was graceful as she crossed the room and took a table with her escort and her companion. "That won't be necessary."

Julian had already made it to the door. Pushing aside the heavy red velvet drape covering the entrance, he raised his brows at Remy as if to ask what the delay was.

He'd just seen an angel.

But he'd find her again.

Watch her.

Memorize her.

Draw her.

He smiled. And if he were fortunate, he'd do more.

# CHAPTER 1

**September 12, 1877**
**Rue Haussmann**
**Paris, France**

Marianne Roland inhaled the brisk clean air of Paris and grinned at her cousin Lily Hanniford who climbed in to sit beside her in their family town coach.

"I'm glad we left without waiting for Madame Chaumont. We were lucky to avoid your father's wrath!" She couldn't believe her Uncle Killian had not gone into one of his famous tirades. Their escapade last night to go to the *cabaret* was such a fabulous adventure. But downright scandalous. No lady should ever be caught attending a performance of nude dancers. But because their French *comtesse* who was their companion in Paris was late this morning for their dressmaker's appointment, she and Lily had quickly escaped the man to their carriage. "He was kind, too, after he saw that terrible cartoon of you in the English gossip sheet."

"He hated it more than I did."

"That cartoon was awful."

"That woman looked nothing like me," Lily said with a scowl. "He made me hook-nosed and skinny!"

Marianne winced at the memory of lovely Lily portrayed as a cowgirl atop a bull drawn from dollar signs. The artist had done his best to make her appear ugly. And absurd. All in the effort to discredit Americans who visited Europe and brought their families and their millions with them.

Well, Uncle Killian had earned his fortune. He'd worked hard and long, running blockades during the American war between the states and later in manufacturing. He deserved to enjoy his riches. He also wished to enjoy them without a tinge of ridicule and he'd asked for Marianne and Lily to cooperate with him in that. Time and again, her uncle had warned them both to be careful and not create a scandal while abroad. In the few weeks they'd been in Paris, both of them had been perfectly behaved until last night when Lily's avid suitor, Lord Pinkhurst, agreed to take them to the cabaret in Montmartre.

"When we go to London," she told Lily, "I'm sure he'll have a few harsh things to say to the publisher of that rag."

"And in the meantime, you diverted his attention with that discussion about singing and dancing in the chorus line. You were splendid." Lily shivered in delight. "My heart is still pounding wildly. I thought he'd die of apoplexy when you told him you liked how the ladies did the *cancan*."

"Those were no ladies, my dear."

"So true," Lily said with a chuckle.

Marianne smiled. It was always sublime to see Lily laugh. She was younger than Marianne by nine years. But they'd formed a friendship borne of shared joys and sorrows. The loss of Marianne's aunt, Lily's mother, soon after Marianne had arrived to live with the Hanniford family in Baltimore, had been the first that bound them closer. Their mutual respect for each other made love all the easier.

"But when you admitted to singing with the patrons? That was outrageous!" Lily shook with laughter.

"He even expected that of me. Did you notice?"

"I did." Lily sank back into the cushions.

"Besides, I sang only with the other patrons," she said suppressing a grin. "That's surely acceptable, wouldn't you say?"

"Ha! To others, not to Black Hanniford, the robber baron of New York and Baltimore." Lily often referred to her father by his less than noble monikers. She was proud of him, despite some people's accusations that he was a ruthless businessman.

"Still, he didn't punish us."

"Papa knows you so well that punishment would not change you."

"Or you."

Lily tipped her head to and fro. Her little red velvet toque wobbled on her lustrous dark hair. "True. Two peas in a pod."

"He could tell I'd like to learn how to do that *cancan*." Marianne gave her cousin a sly look. "But I'd never raise my skirts like that."

"Oh, definitely not," Lily added. "Especially without any drawers!"

Marianne put a hand to the lace bodice of her mint green walking dress. But the memory of the dancers' black lace garters and silk stockings had her grinning. "Oh, but of course, I'd wear drawers. That is, if I could and still kick that high."

The two of them sputtered in laughter.

"No, honestly," Lily recovered herself first. "I think if Papa were older, you'd have given him a heart attack with that admission."

"Well, it was only right to do so." Marianne dug a handkerchief from her reticule and wiped a happy tear from the corner of her eye, then cleared her throat. "Uncle Killian likes the truth. I only wish to please."

"Still. You promised him you wouldn't return." Lily's dark brows knit together.

"I'll honor that," she said in truth.

Lily gave her a skeptical glance. "Even if you don't want to?"

"What your father has done for me deserves my compliance." Marianne shifted in the plush squabs of the family carriage. Her uncle had offered her hope and hearth when she'd had none. She would never forget that or be ungrateful for his kindnesses to the poor Confederate widow who'd lost everything in a cruel war. But someday, she'd leave her uncle's nest and be totally independent. "Someday I may go back to Montmartre. Not soon."

Lily's pale blue eyes danced in glee. "When you have a lover to escort you?"

"Which is doubtful." Marianne patted Lily's gloved hand in reassurance, knowing her cousin teased her. "I haven't found a soul yet who'd please me. It's been so many years since Frederick died. Honestly, I said I'd take a lover just to make you laugh." *But one would definitely brighten my days and nights.*

"But if doing that made you happy—"

"I'd still not do it, Lily. I'd never hurt any of you and taking a man to my bed would cause a scandal that even I would not know how to live down."

Lily squeezed her hand.

"And you? You have no regrets about what you just said to your father?" Marianne asked Lily to be certain of the twenty-year-old's intentions about marriage.

"None. You know Papa." Lily tossed her dark curls, appearing satisfied with her bargain. "He loves a wager."

Marianne lifted a brow. "One he can win."

"I promised I'd stay for one year and look for a husband, but that's my time limit. I won't be made fun of. That cartoon of me on that bull made me look like a fool."

Marianne recalled the ugly sketch and hated the man who used his art to insult people.

Lily set her gaze out the window. "I don't intend to be put up on an auction block."

*No young girl does. Nonetheless it happens, too often, for one reason or another.* "Uncle Killian wouldn't do that to you."

Former blockade runner, factory owner and American buccaneer Killian Hanniford wanted a British lord or a European nobleman for his oldest daughter. Most likely for his younger one, too. And if he could find one for his niece on whom he'd settled a large inheritance equal to his daughters', he'd do that too.

Lily fidgeted. "It's not so much what he would do as what I would feel. I agreed to come to Europe for the fun of it, but I won't be corralled into taking a man I don't care for. Especially if he seems to like me for Papa's millions."

"No one is forcing you to take any man. We'll go slowly and enjoy the opportunities before us. All of them."

Lily glanced at her and Marianne wiggled her brows.

Then Lily challenged her with narrowed eyes. "There you go again. Implying naughty things."

*Like having a man without all the folderol of marriage bonds?* "As if you don't want to experience a few risqué activities?"

"Well, last night was definitely fabulous," Lily said smug as a bug, folding her gloved hands in her lap.

"Astonishing." They'd left the dinner party they'd attended with an English nobleman who had an eye for Lily. Lord Pinkhurst was a charming fellow and he sought favor with her cousin by assisting her in escaping to Montmartre and a scandalous cabaret. The raucous show consisting of female dancers had amazed Marianne not only for the women's agility to kick their legs above their waists but also because they wore no drawers. Marianne, however, had found something else much more fascinating. Someone else, actually. A man. A most virile and captivating creature.

"I'll admit I want new gowns," Lily went on while Marianne smiled recalling her favorite moments of last night's adventure. "From Worth."

"Of course." Marianne's marvelous male specimen had sat in one corner of the dim cafe with a male friend. Dark though the room was, his huge form caught her attention. It wasn't merely his shock of bright blond hair strictly combed, slicked back to his nape that held her, handsome as a god though he was. It was more. His formal evening frock coat, open to a crisp white, if loosely tied stock showed him to be a gentleman. His numerous rings—three or four—twinkling on his long fingers marked him as a man of wealth. But his hands were her focus. They were large, massively boned, as was the rest of him. But long, elegant and agile. Deft, his fingers swept across his bound sketchbook, his graphite stokes forming impressions she longed to see.

"And of course, I want new lingerie from...what is the name of that designer?" Lily rattled on.

"Piderot."

"Yes, that's the one."

In her reverie, Marianne saw her giant stand again, felt her heart leave her chest at his height and his beauty. She bit back her self criticism for how she'd looked away when her eyes couldn't get enough of his power and might. She'd never seen a man so tall or commanding. He shocked her with his size, his health, his stamina. His broad shoulders and thick muscular arms seized her will power, as if she were a fawn frozen in a bear's sight. He was a man of consequence and presence. And if that were not enough to fascinate her, he possessed this other occupation, so unusual in so raucous a place as the cabaret. How could a man so large do so delicate an act as draw? And care to draw women? Have the skill to draw them dancing? Marianne felt her blood warm at such evidence of his sensibilities. A man like that was one a woman would never wish to leave. Unless she was mistaken and he was an artistic dilettante...and a brute.

"Are you listening to me?" Lily touched her hand.

"Absolutely." Tearing her mind to the topic, Marianne focused that they were on their way to the famous House of Worth for a fitting. They would later to look at silky night-gowns and peignoirs. Such a feast of the senses was surely meant for some other fortunate woman, it always seemed to Marianne. *Not me.* "I like new clothes, gowns, lingerie as well as any woman. I'll order something no one else will ever see. Something frothy."

"Mmm. You mean transparent."

Marianne gave her a wicked look. "Deliciously so."

Lily chuckled. "You are very bad."

"It will be only for me."

"Don't be ridiculous. Eventually you'll want someone to see it, see you. You'll want someone to love." Lily eyed her. "Papa urges you, too, to find a good husband."

Marianne struggled with that. "I am aware. But it's more difficult to marry off a jaded war widow thirty years of age than a lovely ingénue of twenty."

"Almost twenty-one." Lily sobered, her pale blue eyes boring into Marianne's. "After what you endured during the war, you deserve to be happy. To have a husband again who walks with you through the years would be a blessing."

*I doubt it.*

The carriage turned into the Rue de la Paix and Marianne

breathed a sigh of relief. This conversation was one she always tried to cut short. "I've searched for a man I might care for as a husband. But I haven't found one. Indeed, I found more comfort in my nursing."

Lily squeezed her hand. "They loved you in that rebel hospital in Virginia, I'm sure. I know they did in Corpus Christi. Among all your patients, I wonder you didn't find a man to love."

"I was too busy tending them to think of marrying any of them." *My own wounds from the war were too raw to think of taking another man to my bed.* "And you discovered you liked the work, too. So there. We both benefitted from the nursing."

After Marianne had gone to live with the Hannifords, she'd volunteered at hospitals in Corpus Christi and Baltimore. When Lily grew older, she went with her. Uncle Killian had not liked it, but Lily was insistent that she go. It became more Lily's calling than Marianne's. For that, Marianne prided herself that she'd helped Lily find a vocation she liked. For herself, she struggled to define what precisely her interest was in medicine. Saving others from disease and disability and death was a noble cause. She felt gratification that she'd offered it to those in need—and she tried not to dwell on the fact that what she needed was something more or something else. And she postponed the time when she must declare to herself what that was.

"Here we are," Lily said, scooting forward on the velvet squabs. "I hope Madame Chaumont has arrived or at least sent a message here to our *vendeuse*."

"She's never been late before," Marianne said. "I fear she's ill."

"We'll soon know," Lily said, gathering her skirts.

The Hanniford coachman slowed the horses to a halt. The conveyance idled and the groom was at the door, swinging it wide for them.

Lily took the groom's hand and stepped down and out into the sunshine. She smiled up at Marianne while she adjusted her big hat that trembled in the sharp breeze.

"*Merci beaucoup*, Robert," Lily said to their French groom.

"Uncle Killian says we're not to say thank you too often, if at all," Marianne reminded Lily as she brushed the folds of her skirts, then watched their coach drive away. "He says Europeans believe servants are not to be even noticed."

"Well, I'm an American." Lily looped her arm through Marianne's. "We're different. What do you say?"

A din rent the air.

Women in front of them scrambled to flee the sidewalk.

One screamed.

"Good heavens," Lily said, looking to and fro. "What's happening?"

"There!" Marianne pointed to a large black carriage that careened this way and that along the street.

"A woman's inside!"

"I hear her," Marianne said as the public hackney passed them in a crazy swerve that barely missed two pedestrians. Up on the box, the burly coachman attempted to control the wild horses, yelling at them.

Two men, one dark and one blond, pushed through the throng. Marianne gasped. She recognized them both from last night. The tall blond was the one from the cabaret. He was a whirl of motion as he ran and caught up with the coach, grabbing the rims of the box and swinging himself up beside the panicked driver.

His companion meanwhile ran like the wind to catch up with the runaway animal. The poor horse bared his teeth in fright and turned a corner to a side street off the boulevard.

Marianne picked up her skirts and hurried along the walk.

"Wait!" Lily yelled after her. Where are you going?"

"To see—" *That man.* "A woman. It might be— Oh, Oh, Lily! It's the *Comtesse.*"

The huge Frenchman handed the woman out of the carriage into the street. Supporting her, he spoke to her softly. He was solicitous, an arm around Chaumont's waist, leading her to support herself with one hand to his chest, her hip touching his.

Marianne caught up to them—and halted.

His sky blue eyes seized hers. She was riveted. So near, his features in light of day were a palette of appealing manly hues. His eyes, large and almond shaped, were indeed the color of the cerulean heavens. His complexion was flawless, tinted by exposure to the sun, while his hair, no longer slicked back but wild, curled around his ears and caressed his nape. The color was golden. And he, in his fullness, was imperial.

"Are you in pain?" Lily asked Chaumont as she hurried closer. Then she turned to the lady's rescuer. "Monsieur, if she's hurt her neck or back, she must not stand."

"Do you have pain, *Madame?*" the man cajoled the lady in his arms.

"Pain?" The *comtesse* offered a small smile to Lily, a hand going to the crown of her head. She patted her lank curls, her eyes dazed. "I—I don't think so. My hat? My hat is gone. My hair's a fright. We will be late for our appointment. We mustn't. *Monsieur* Worth will be angry." She went on into wild laments in French.

"Do not worry, *Madame,*" Lily comforted her while Marianne still had not found her wits. Nor had the *comtesse.* Instead the woman appeared dazed.

Marianne snapped to attention, discreetly lifting the *comtesse's* skirts above her ankles. She had to see if one of the lady's legs or ankles were injured.

"Your pulse is rapid," Lily said to Chaumont, holding her

wrist. "We should take you inside Worth's. We'll get a chair. A brandy."

The giant's dark-haired companion approached, leading the runaway horse.

"Can you stand?" Marianne asked their female companion.

The *comtesse* shook her head. Clemence Bernier, the widow Countess of Chaumont, moaned and ran a shaking hand through her chestnut hair, her hat askew, her white glove torn and dirty. She favored one foot over the other.

The dark-haired man frowned at Chaumont, then turned to his friend, "She should not walk, Remy."

The Frenchman nodded at Lily and her. "My friend is right. *Madame le Comtesse* is weak."

"But we must go inside for our appointment," Chaumont complained.

"Worth can wait," the dark gentleman said, his accent most definitely English. "*Monsieur* Worth has a sitting room, chairs, brandy and tea. *Madame* needs every one."

Lily absorbed his words as if she were mesmerized. But she shook her head and tore her attention from the dark-haired man to focus on the countess. "Can you point your toes, *Madame*?"

"*Oui*, you see?"

"Wonderful," Lily said with a smile. "Nothing's broken. But I'm not certain if she's injured her ankle."

Marianne turned to the blond man called Remy. "Can you carry her, *Monsieur*?"

He peered down at her with an intense regard that sent shivers of delight up her spine. "Of course," he said but turned to the *comtesse*. "Shall we adjourn, *Madame*? Hmm?"

"*Oui*," said the *comtesse* with a coquette's smile. "I welcome that."

*I bet you do.* Marianne bristled at Chaumont's joy and her own unreasonable jealousy.

"I'll see to the driver," Remy's friend announced to the assembly.

Lily stepped forward to thank him for his help.

Marianne could not tear her gaze from Remy as he caught the countess up in his arms and turned to the entrance to Worth's.

In his same formal clothes of black tails and gold waist-coat, disheveled as they were from his evening revels and from this daring rescue, he devastated her senses. Marianne could not get her fill of looking at this towering man. In the shadows of the cabaret, he'd been a phantom of her girlish dreams. In gay sunshine, he was a gilded god.

What's more, he moved like the wind. Swiftly. With precision. Without an iota of exertion, he held the delicate countess Chaumont in his massive arms and carried her to shelter beneath the awning of the House of Worth. Indeed, he cooed to her with all the comfort of a field doctor soothing a wounded man. His kindnesses sparked Marianne's praise, but Chaumont's simpering dependence on him inspired her ire.

Stunned by that rare emotion, Marianne stood rooted to the pavement. Ridiculous to feel that. She did not know the man. Only his looks. Only his strength...and charm. A dangerous combination for a widow who'd known few dynamic men with debonair manners or the compelling might of a Titan.

His incomparable blue eyes met hers once more.

And she could not tear away.

"*Mademoiselle*, the doorman has left his duties. Might you do me the favor of opening the door?"

"*Pardon.* Of course," she said with a polite bow of her head and scurried to pull open the heavy door.

At Number 7 in the glamorous Rue de la Paix, the English designer's offices and showrooms were the epitome of elegance. Brass fittings on the walls and doors plus the spotless glass gave a patina of wealth. But the commotion in the boulevard had distracted the attention of Worth's doorman. Suddenly, he stepped to them now with apologies and sprang to his duties. Inside, the receptionist welcomed them and indicated they should follow her up the winding marble staircase.

Marianne led the way, nervously aware of Remy on her heels with Chaumont in his arms.

In a private room Marianne took a chair as Remy placed Chaumont in another, then stood by the window. Lily, looking dazed for some odd reason, soon joined them and took her own seat. A stiff silence reigned while the four of them awaited their personal *vendeuse*.

"*Madame le Comtesse*," Remy said to Chaumont in that melodious bass voice made for candlelit boudoirs, "will you do the honors of the introductions, *s'il vous plaît?*"

"Ah! *Pardon e moi.* Of course." She fanned herself, touching his forearm, but extending one hand to Lily and Marianne. "Mrs. Roland and Miss Hanniford, may I present *Monsieur le Duc de Remy*, Andre Claude Marceau, *petit fil, prince du sang.*"

"Really, *Madame*," he said with a wince, "you need not add all the details."

"Remy is modest," the woman said with a titter as if she confided a secret. "He is that rare beast, a prince of the Bourbons and Bonapartes. Unique, *nez pas?*"

*A duke and prince of two royal bloods?* Marianne was in special company. But why was she surprised? She'd felt the appeal of him in so many indescribable ways long before she learned his name or rank.

He gave them a genteel bow. "My pleasure to meet you."

The countess continued her duty. "*Monsieur,* Mrs. Marianne Roland and Miss Lily Hanniford, both from Baltimore and Texas."

"I am delighted to make your acquaintance," he said with a smile curving those lips that formed words with sensuous allure. "Please call me Remy. My friends do. And I hope we will become so."

*Friends?* Marianne struggled for a breath. The last thing in the world she wanted from this man was his friendship. If she saw him again, too soon, too near, she'd want to touch him. Learn if he were real or a phantom of her lost childish daydreams.

Lily inclined her head. "I am charmed to make your acquaintance, *Monsieur le duc.*"

Marianne followed with the same sentiments.

"Remy, I insist," he said with a smile at her.

"Remy," Marianne murmured.

He took his clear blue eyes from hers and focused on Lily. "You have recently come to Paris?"

They talked about small things while Marianne tried to calm her racing heart.

A sales girl entered making apologies for the accident outside their establishment and for the failure of their assigned *vendeuse* to appear. She would make do, she promised, in the meantime. So she rushed to accommodate the ailing Chaumont with a stool for her feet and asked if they might wish refreshment. Only Chaumont requested a large brandy.

And to Marianne's irritation, the countess played up her disability, if there was such, to the very hilt. She simpered and smiled at Remy as if he were her gallant knight or her *fondant*, a confection to lick.

Marianne set her teeth. Uncle Killian had hired the widowed countess to instruct Lily and her on the intricacies of Parisian society. Accompanying them to modistes and museums, Clemence Bernier was charged with introducing them to French food, French manners and, if the occasion arose, French men. Here was one that the opportunistic countess had an interest in herself. *Damn her eyes.*

*When would this end?* She had to go home, retire, reassess her girlish infatuation with a man she'd seen twice. In the dark. In the light. In command of all he surveyed.

At last, their own *vendeuse* appeared and so did Remy's companion, the dark-haired gentlemen who'd calmed the horse in the street. This man with wavy brown hair and chocolate eyes was not only English but by his speech and manners, a gentleman. To all of them, he bowed politely and could not seem to take his gaze from Lily.

Marianne smiled to herself. It was a day for sudden fascinations.

Aside from Lily, the man was most interested in the accident of the public coach in the street and how it had come about. He related the details he'd learned in the street.

"One wagon wheel is precariously balanced," he reported to them. "One side of his cab is caved in. He'll need quite a bit of repair on that hack, I'm sorry to say."

"Oh, what damage! Will he charge me for it?" Chaumont ran a hand through her brown hair, now totally loose of its pins. "I don't know if I can afford to pay such a bill."

"The driver claims a pet dog ran into the street. Tangled up in the horse's legs. The person who should pay for the repairs of that hack should be the lady who owns that dog. Don't you think?"

"I agree," Remy said.

"We need to find that person here in the house," he said and asked the sales woman to do just that. He wished to confront her with the details of the accident her dog had caused.

The *vendeuse* was not happy to inquire of the other customers.

"But, Mademoiselle," he said with purpose, "I insist."

With a frown, she left to do so.

Marianne focused her attention on Chaumont. The woman was lagging in not introducing this Englishman. But at Marianne's nod, she took her cue and promptly announced him as Julian Ash, Lord Chelton. Marianne checked Lily's expression. But at the man's name, her cousin did not so much as blink. The dashing marquess of Chelton was a man known to them because Killian Hanniford had business dealings with his family. In fact, her uncle wished to buy property from him, but cool and calm, Chelton gave no hint of that in his demeanor. Nor did Lily. Marianne breathed more easily at that, not wishing to color any negotiations her uncle had with Chelton's family. Besides, the only man she really wished to know was Remy.

Chelton turned to Marianne and Lily. "Tell us if you will stay for your fitting."

"Please do," Remy said. "I offer my carriage to escort you home."

"Thank you, *Monsieur le Duc*," Lily said, "but no. We must remain. My father expects it. No accident of rain, sleet or frightened dog amid the carriage wheels should prevent it."

Marianne agreed. "Uncle Killian is a taskmaster."

Remy was not dissuaded. "I have my carriage close by, farther down the street and I'm sure my coachman is attempting to pull forward amid the crowd. I'd be quite happy to offer to take you home. All of you."

"*Merci beaucoup*, Remy," Chaumont was quick to accept. She leaned back, regarding him with hazel eyes misty from her consumption of alcohol. "I must not desert my duties. I am charged with escorting Miss Hanniford and Mrs. Roland through the rigors of Paris."

"No, *Madame*." Lily had other ideas. "Thank you, for your kindness. If you wish to return home, certainly, do go with the kind man."

"*Et vous?*" she asked Lily. "You also need assistance."

"Not at all."

"I'm uncertain." Chaumont demurred with a coy look up at Remy.

Marianne silently fumed.

"*Madame*, please." Lily was quick to continue. "We can proceed with our selection of fabrics and styles. Our carriage is scheduled to return for us in two hours. In the meantime, we would be reassured that you are recovering if you were in your own home resting."

Marianne sniffed. Chaumont wished to enjoy her recovery in the arms of this impressive French prince. Torn, hating her envy, she patted Chaumont's hand. "We can finish ourselves."

"If you think it possible," Chaumont postured prettily.

"I do," Marianne said, so conflicted that she was not able to discern if she wished the woman to go or stay.

"I insist," said Lily.

The *vendeuse* reappeared. "*Pardon*. The lady in question with the naughty dog is the Grand Duchess of Volenska."

Remy frowned at his friend. "Anna Drobova."

"Trouble?" Chelton asked him.

Remy rolled his eyes. "No angel."

"It matters not." Chelton inclined his head to Chaumont, Lily and her. "I will leave you and discuss certain financial matters with the grand duchess. It was my pleasure to see you again, *Madame le Comtesse*. And a pleasure to meet both of you, Mrs. Roland and Miss Hanniford. Remy, I leave you to assist *Madame*. When your carriage arrives, I'll have the doorman summon you both. Good day."

"I cannot leave you." Chaumont did protest too much. "My duty is here."

"No, *Madame*," Marianne said to her with finality. "You should return home. You've had a fright."

"Quite right," Remy took up the cause, polite but firm. "You shall come with Chelton and me, *Comtesse*. It's best that we leave these ladies to their dressmaker."

Marianne and Lily bid them *adieu*, standing as Remy carried the countess out of the room.

"Oh, my," said Lily after they'd gone. She was pale, her voice soft, a hand to her throat. "That was exciting. Papa knows him, you realize."

Lily meant Chelton. Clearly, by her dreamy expression, she was taken by him. "I do. He is quite handsome."

Lily blinked and looked askance at her. "Come now. You much prefer the duke."

"He is...arresting."

"Arresting?" she blurted.

*Why prevaricate?* "The height, the hair, the power of him. Yes."

"Ah, ah. I know that tone. You saw him as a subject to draw."

"I did," she admitted. Lily had often watched her discover a passion to draw a flower, a scampering squirrel or a baby.

"It's a wonder you haven't sketched him yet."

*But I did. Last night. With three good portraits as my prize. But seeing him today, I realize none of them does justice to him.* "He does have one imperfection."

Lily hooted. "Really? Pray tell, what could that be?"

Marianne tapped the tip of her nose. "He is very Gallic. The nose is out of proportion. Too long."

Lily rolled her eyes. "And I must eat my hat."

The Parisian *vendeuse* reappeared, narrowed her eyes and attempted a smile. She pointed toward the hall. "*Madame e Mademoiselle*, we are ready for the fitting, *oui*?"

"*Oui*." Marianne was quick to nod and sailed past Lily to the hall and the dressing rooms. "We are so very ready."

She must put the honorable Andre Claude Marceau, the Duc de Remy, from her mind. He was beyond her reach. Last night he had appeared to her as a handsome creature who frequented cabarets, drank wine and sketched lewd dancers. Today, he became a savior of ladies in distress. Even in his rumpled evening clothes, he was larger than her memory of him, a giant of might and manners, to say nothing of the fact that he was also a royal. All of which implied he was most likely a rogue of the first water. He probably had a wife and a mistress or two. Remy was no man who wished for a dalliance with the penniless thirty-year-old widow of a Virginia farmer, living off the good graces of her very rich and very generous maternal uncle.

❧

Chaumont clung to him like moss on a rock. Remy might have laughed, but he'd not insult her. The woman was indeed injured, her left ankle swelling even as it lay propped on the opposite seat of his carriage.

Chelton caught his gaze and wrinkled a rueful brow. "I do hope you will take care of that ankle, *Madame*. The quicker you ice it, the sooner you will have full use of your limb."

"I will, *Monsieur le Marquis*, I will." She squeezed Remy's upper arm.

"We did well to aid them, Julian. You did wonders with the horse." Remy arched both brows at his friend whom he usually addressed by his given name. He'd noted Julian's interest in Lily Hanniford and wondered if it was only her beauty that drew him or if it was that Julian had business dealings with her father. As for himself, he was dejected that the delicate blonde with the mysterious emerald eyes was married. Remy envied the man who had her to hand. He hoped to heaven that man was wise and reveled in the arch of her cheek and the fullness of those lips.

He shifted amid the leather cushions, his stab of desire for her sharp.

He prayed to god she was wed to a man who relished her. For if she were his, he'd lay her out as if she were a horde of platinum gold. His fingers twitched. He winced. He'd have to try to recreate her. She was too exquisite to forget, nearly too perfect for most mortals to contemplate. But was it not his duty to show others the perfections of this world along with the distortions?

Julian stirred, focusing on Chaumont. "How do you know Miss Hanniford and Mrs. Roland?"

Remy caught his breath and snapped to his senses.

Chaumont tipped up her head and put on her public face. "I have agreed to show them Paris. They are Americans, you realize, and so—" She waved a hand to denote they could be dismissed as déclassé. "They need a guide to ease their social path."

Remy winked at Julian. What Chaumont meant was that fees earned escorting *nouveau riche* Americans around Paris would fatten her pitifully thin purse. With such purpose, she could once more grace salons and ballrooms in finer attire than she'd been able to since her elderly husband had gone suddenly last year toes up into his family crypt in the *Montmartre Cimetière*.

"Good of you to aid them, *Madame*," Remy said.

"It is nothing," she said with a lift of one shoulder.

Julian ran a finger across his lips. "You've met Killian Hanniford, the young lady's father?"

"I have," she said with pride. "He is *formidable*."

"To say the least," Julian agreed.

"You know the man?" she asked, surprise in her tone.

Julian nodded. "I do. Quite well."

"*Mademoiselle* Hanniford is lovely," Remy said, attempting to lead her to more revelations. "Suits her name. How old is she?"

"Twenty. Untouched. A beauty with all that black hair and those large blue eyes."

Julian said nothing but Remy knew his friend well and the intent look on his face told a tale of curiosity about the American girl with such striking features.

"They are here for a few months and then we are all on to London."

"For the Season?" Remy asked because Julian had directed his attention out the window, lost in some thoughts that made him frown.

"*Oui.* I am to do what I can for introductions. You are my first, *Monsieur le Marquis*. And you, *Monsieur le duc*. If you see them in the future, you must do your duty, aid me, introduce them as they should be. Say you will."

"Of course," Julian said, casting the duty off absent-mindedly.

"I will," Remy agreed.

"Is your Mama up to a dinner party?"

His mother, at the grand age of seventy-five, held on to her position with an iron glove. As a *primiere* Bourbon *princesse* and also a descendant of a minor Bonaparte, she was welcome everywhere. Refined and discerning, a fixture of the Second Empire circles, she was a scion who had become more valued and more fragile these past few years. Yet once a week, she exerted herself and took her weekly champagne luncheons at her favorite restaurant with her friends. Afterward, as she did every other day of the week, she'd retire straightaway to her wing of their house in the Rue de Rivoli at four in the afternoon. She'd last hosted a party during the uprising of the Commune in 1870 and that, so fumed the *haute ton* in astonishment, was to feed the starving little orphans in St. Bartolome's parish school. Now a dinner party seemed out of the question for her. But Remy would play the gentleman here. "I will ask her."

"Oh, do!" Chaumont put a hand to his chest. "At your house in Rue de Rivoli."

"There, *oui.*"

"Not your chateau in Tours," she added. "Too big. Too far away. And the one in Montmartre would not be appropriate, either. All that dust and plaster, Remy." Chaumont forgot herself, slipping into the more familiar name of his title. He'd never invited her to use it and she immediately blushed. "Forgive me, *Monsieur.* The moment, you realize. My ankle."

"I do. Please do address me as Remy. We are friends, *oui*? Of many years." He'd lead her on, needing her friendship... and her knowledge of the fabulous blonde beauty whose essence struck him to the quick.

"Oh, indeed, we are," she eagerly agreed, her hazel eyes dancing at the new intimacy. "You must call me Clemence."

"Thank you. Overdue, eh? To be more friendly."

Julian fixed his gaze on him and when the woman chuckled, Julian widened his eyes at him, aware she wished to seduce him.

Remy bit his lip to hold back his laughter. But he was out of patience to learn about the appealing *Madame* Roland. "So then we have the delightful Lily Hanniford husband-hunting. Are there more at home in America or is she the only princess in this line?"

"She is the oldest daughter. There is a son, who is older than she. He goes by the name of Pierce. There is a younger daughter, Ada, who is still in finishing school in America. They both arrive next spring by boat to London. And then too, of course, Mister Hanniford himself is a widower."

"Dear god," said Julian. "He's old! You don't mean to say *he* is looking for a bride?"

"*Peut être, maybe, Monsieur, he* is not. But he is rich and very attractive. A wise woman would find herself in a happy state to marry such a man."

"And what of *Madame Roland?*" Remy was out of patience to inquire.

"Oh, I have heard *Madame* declare she is happy as she is."

*What does that mean? Are she and her husband estranged? Was the man in America awaiting her return?*

"I don't understand her at all," Chaumont sighed. "I have been alone since my sweet Gerard passed to heaven. And I long for a man in my home."

Remy blinked. Aside from her indelicate hint that she'd accept his advances, what did that imply about Mrs. Roland?

Julian caught his confusion, grinned, then beamed at Chaumont. "You mean to say, *Madame*, that Mrs. Roland is a widow?"

"*Certainement.* For more than ten years. A tragedy, *non?* Such loveliness and no man has celebrated her for so very long."

Remy frowned. *A widow. For more than a decade?* Why did a woman with so much vitality remain alone? Surely men had come to call upon the lady with the wealth of white gold hair and the dark green eyes of a jungle cat. Why had she not accepted them?

Was she one of those American puritans? A firebrand? Or a recluse?

None seemed probable. She'd gone to the *cabaret* last night. She dressed with style and verve. She moved like a willow in the breeze. If she was not a prude, was she the opposite? A lady of social decorum who had a taste for the lascivious?

He could not believe it. His instinct for human nature

told him her essence was neither puritan nor risqué. The way she looked at him had not been with indifference. On the contrary, the way her eyes devoured him had told him of her hunger. The way her lips parted when she considered him had told him of her fantasies. And who was he to her, but a man she'd only recently met, a cipher at least, an acquaintance at best?

She was a lady to be admired, petted and taught to love her own passions. She was a woman to treasure and to teach the joys of her own sensuality. She'd been in hiding from herself and her potential as a woman, as a loving creature. He could awaken her.

But how?

# CHAPTER 2

"Marianne?" Lily knocked at Marianne's bedroom door. "Are you ready to go down to dinner?"

"In a moment!" She clapped her hands together, standing back to admire her work, a thrill of success rippling through her. She'd done it. She'd created him. *Him.* Exactly as he should be. Big and bold and handsome as sin. "Give me a chance to wash my hands."

She closed her sketchbook and placed her stick of light grey graphite carefully in its little tray in her boudoir drawer, then shut it tightly. *As if that seals away my attraction.* She shook her head, suppressing her smile and chastising herself for her naïveté. Even Lily knew how she admired the man. Her cousin had detected her interest in the huge Frenchman within seconds. How could she hide it? *Why should she?*

The answer to that had her pausing.

But it was time for dinner not for dreaming.

She rushed to her washstand, poured water into the pretty china bowl and submerged her tired fingers in the cooling water. Traces of the black substance floated away. She rubbed soap over her hands, picked up a towel, rubbed her skin dry and hung the cloth on the rack. With a check of her mirror, she secured the pins in her coil and examined her pink day gown.

"Oh!" She mustn't forget to remove her apron. Untying the protective leather covering, she tossed it to the back of her chair and headed for the door.

"What are you doing?" Lily asked, mischief in her blue eyes.

"I'd say you know." She closed her bedroom door and headed for the marble staircase beside her cousin.

"Drawing him, I would bet." Lily speculated, gathering up her skirts and grinning.

"It's alarming that you know me so well."

Lily chuckled. "As if you can't say the same of me."

"So true." Marianne shrugged. "Lord Chelton is a dashing creature."

"And Papa knows him. What will I say?"

"Say you liked him." They had given Uncle Killian a short summary of the accident in the Rue de la Paix. He'd been intrigued but they had escaped his questions about meeting his business rival Lord Chelton and a mysterious Frenchman who was the Englishman's friend.

Lily nodded. "That is no crime."

"Not at all," Marianne confirmed.

"The same can be said about your interest in *Monsieur le duc*."

"He is a charming specimen. I will not deny. But you well know, he is not for me."

"No? Why ever not?"

"We know why."

"Money is no object. Papa says so."

"For you, my dear." Marianne readily defended herself against any hint of marriage for herself. "Not for me."

"Ah. Here you are. Finally." Uncle Killian greeted them in

the hall and extended a hand toward the dining room. As they filed in, the footmen advanced to pull out their chairs for them. "I despaired we would ever dine tonight."

"Fiddle-faddle, Papa," Lily said to him with a coy smile, and sat down.

As the servants poured the wine and offered the first courses, Lily began a discussion of the gowns they ordered from Worth.

Marianne hid her smile. Lily was adept at diverting her father from discussing topics she didn't wish to touch. But her talents lasted only so long and Marianne could bet that today's chance meeting of Lord Chelton was on her uncle's mind. Chelton was his quarry, and once sited, he never lost track of his mark.

He looked at ease, drinking his brandy and smiling at them both.

Marianne was not deceived, but bit her lip, waiting for his pursuit of topics that gratified him.

"What will you wear this evening?" Uncle Killian asked them both as the footmen removed the last of the dishes.

"I have the pale blue gown and the sapphire cape, Papa."

"Appropriate. And you, Marianne?"

"I haven't thought about it," she told him. That was true. This afternoon, to her dismay, she'd thought of little other than Remy.

Her blue eyes twinkling, Lily sent her a disparaging look. "We're delighted to go to the opera. Especially Marianne."

"I wouldn't miss it," she confessed. "Going to the Opera Garnier has been one of my fondest ambitions."

"A good one, too."

"I wish we could arrive at the beginning. Waiting until the ballet is so silly."

"Parisians are funny." Her uncle shook his dark head, his expression rueful. "They conduct business with leisure and if they wish to drink champagne while they do it, all the merrier."

"Not everything is an amorous adventure," Marianne said.

Her uncle and cousin barked in laughter.

She pressed her argument. "Why not use time to your advantage, hmm?"

Uncle Killian snorted. "Tell them that, would you, please, my dear?"

"I will." She laughed but didn't feel gay. Not yet. But she would tonight. She'd yearned to see the glories of the building ever since she had first read about it two years ago in the Baltimore *Sun*. The glorious architecture of the new civic opera building, the shining marble, the glittering chandeliers, the *creme de la creme* of society in their silks and tails. She knew of Garnier's extravagances of decor. She'd heard of Parisians who had rendezvous in the private boxes, even upon the divans in the cloakrooms. She'd hoped to hear strains of Bach and Brahms and Offenbach drift up from the orchestra pit. She'd wished to taste the champagne served in the refreshment room. The *Glacier*, they called it. "Why arrive late simply to prove that your social calendar is full?"

"It's expected to be late," her uncle said. "This is not Knicker-bocker Manhattan. Besides, shouldn't I take these moments to hear more about this meeting of Chelton and you, Lily?"

"No, sir. You should not." Lily gave him a blithe look and put her napkin to the table. She was ready to escape her father.

"And what of the Frenchman, Marianne? Was he so hand-some you must flee without explanation, too?"

"Yes, sir. He was. But you mustn't worry, Uncle Killian."

"No? Why not?"

"He is too—" She paused, unusually stumped for words, one hand dancing in the air.

"Well? What?"

"Overwhelming. He is huge. A giant of a man."

"And? So?" her uncle urged.

She blinked, her gaze suddenly dreamy. "His blond hair hangs to his shoulders and his hands are callused and scarred."

"Chelton has a friend who's a laborer? Yet he offered you his own carriage?" He arched his brows high. "Damned intriguing."

"No, sir." Marianne objected.

Lily caught her eye and shook her head in warning.

But Marianne, brave in many ways, said anyway, "He's a duke."

Hanniford laughed.

Lily rolled her eyes at Marianne.

Marianne shot from her chair, came round the table and hooked her arm in Lily's. "Escape with me."

"Tell him no more," Lily pleaded as the two of them hurried from the dining room.

"I heard that!" he called out, but they raced up the circular staircase up to their suites. "I need details."

"We've no time, Uncle."

"We don't want to be late, Papa," Lily called down.

"We don't want to change the fashion." He came to the foot of the stairs.

Lily took hold of the hall banister and peered over the side. "Not on your life. It's a small soirée and then the opera, dear Father. And you've paid good money for it."

"I have not paid a penny. We're guests!"

"All the more reason. Get dressed yourself," Lily told him, whirling into Marianne's sitting room and shutting the door behind her.

"Oh, Marianne, you realize that now he knows Remy is a

duke, Papa will investigate his family all the way back to the dark ages."

"He can do what he wants," Marianne said, feigning indifference. Her uncle wanted her settled. Married. *Safe,* he called it. He'd said so, a thousand times. And she had refused him a thousand times. *Married* and *settled* and *safe* were not synonyms. She had experience to prove it. "I'll not have another husband, ever."

Her vehemence about the subject of taking a husband was not new. And she wished she might appear less adamant about such a thing. But she couldn't.

Yet Lily had seen her interest in the French nobleman and she knew she'd never before displayed any attraction to a man. But taking a lover was a different story. And this Remy was so enticing that she might consider him a candidate.

In that, the risks were high. Social censure. Her family's disgrace. Even if she had the courage to be so risqué, she was not made from such cloth. She could not chance it.

She turned away from Lily and strode to her dressing room. "Besides, I most likely won't see him again."

"And if you do?" Lily was quick to ask.

"It won't matter. Your father cannot persuade me to receive him."

"Or buy him for you?"

Marianne whirled to face her. "No. Not at any price."

☙❧

Remy checked his watch, tucked it back inside his waistcoat and cursed.

He was so late. His mother's latest attack of breathlessness was his excuse. Julian would understand that. But his friend expected him to assist him tonight socially. Julian was to escort his mother and younger sister, Elanna, to the opera and he'd planned not to arrive until the third act or later. Remy had estimated the time to be approximately eleven, perhaps later. But his mother's delicate heart had palpitated too quickly tonight and he would not leave her until she assured him she felt calmer. That, thankfully, had occurred an hour ago and he'd donned his evening attire as quickly as his valet Pierre could assemble him into a presentable picture.

Climbing out of his town coach, he strode to the doors and through the lower rotunda. He swept off his top hat and undid the leather clasps of his opera cape. The ticket master bowed to him, recognizing him immediately. Good thing. He'd held season's tickets to the Opera Garner since its opening two years ago. His mama had often come with him, but last season, she'd refrained. He'd agreed that it was best she keep her strength for her frequent afternoon champagne luncheons with her friends. Amalie Sabine Marceau, *Princesse d'Aumale et Duchesse de Remy* was a pillar of Parisian society and she would not fail to appear, unless she were lying in her coffin.

"And that, *mon cher*," she'd said earlier, shooing him off, "I will not permit until I have no breath left. Do go now. I will live. You must enjoy the music for me and come with tales of the horrors of the tenor's cracking voice. I live for that. Go, go!"

He chuckled as he took the flight of the rose marble steps to the grand circle. Julian, his sister Elanna and his mother, the Duchess of Seton, would be eager to take their places in their seats. As he rounded the assembly area, he saw them in a group not far from him. He smiled in greeting, but no one saw him.

Then he halted in his tracks.

Julian was there. His mother, too. His sister Elanna a young beauty of verve in frothy pink, was overly polite to an older hawkish-looking creature who was quite obviously interested in her. Beside that man stood another. Tall, dark with angular features that implied brute strength, this man was impeccable in black formal tails and white cravat. With him stood two young women. The dark-haired beauty of this morning's accident in the Rue de la Paix, Lily Hanniford, was beside him, a vision in a sapphire and silver fox cape. Next to her stood Remy's own compelling fascination, the ethereal willow in royal purple sateen trimmed in white mink. The glorious widow. His unforgettable blonde.

The sentiment warmed him, head to toe.

Julian spied him and welcomed him to the gathering. "We're delighted you're here."

"*Bon soir.* Forgive me my tardiness." He decided not to discuss his mother's health. The subject was delicate, alarming perhaps, and not a note he wished to strike here in the presence of Madame Roland. He chose the less personal subject. "There was another accident in the Rue de la Paix. I fear we have a contagion on our hands. "

The Duchess of Seton picked up her lorgnette on its gold chain, peered about and introduced him to the rest of the party. The Setons he knew. The gentleman who was so attentive to Elanna was the Earl of Carbury, whom he'd never met before. He bowed to Lily Hanniford and her cousin, then tore his gaze away to meet Killian Hanniford, the famed rebel blockade runner whose inglorious reputation proceeded him in polite society.

His duties accomplished, Remy gave a slight bow to the lady whose image had teased him all day. The jewel-like purple of her gown contrasted with the faint pink in her skin and highlighted the beauty of her large green eyes. "*Madame* Roland, I am delighted to see you again."

"*Monsieur le duc, merci beaucoup.*" She dipped in a small curtsey, much too formal for his taste. "I too am pleased to see you."

"I hope you have recovered from this morning's troubling incident." *Now that I see you again, I fill with exuberance.*

"We were but by-standers. Of course it is Madame Chaumont who suffered more than I. She was noble throughout. But it is to you and Lord Chelton whom we owe all our thanks."

He suppressed a naughty grin. She was being so polite, so proper. But the very way her lush lips formed words heated his blood. Her mouth was quite exquisite and much more sensual, erotic really, than his poor memory had allowed. What she could do with that mouth would be worth a thousand days of his life. She was precise in her language, even if she had that odd drawl that denoted she came from one of her southern states. But she was also soft spoken. Was that a trick perhaps to lure him closer? Ha. He did not mind. He gladly drew nigh. She smelled of some flower. Not roses. Peonies? Sweet but not cloying.

He longed to inhale her fragrance more closely, capture it as it wafted up from her bare skin.

He grinned at her.

"What did I say?" she asked him, her remarkable eyes wide with humor. "You smile at me. Did I commit a *faux pas?*"

"Oh, no, *Madame.* I enjoy your words." He had to keep her talking and yet ameliorate any fears she might have that he was laughing at her. On the contrary, he wanted to impress her, seduce her, claim her before his enchantment with her evaporated. Such addictions to women did happen to him. Rarely. But when they did, he knew enough to seize the moment and attempt to imbibe them before sharp reality splintered the image and broke the fantasy in a thousand shards. "You have that accent that denotes you are from the South. I find it soothing."

"Do you?" she asked with a skeptical glance. "Most don't."

"They lose then."

"Lose?"

"The chance to hear the melody in your heart."

Her cheeks flushed. "You are poetic."

"Your reaction tells me that few have been poetic for you."

"None, *Monsieur*."

"Then you have not yet met the right people."

She lifted her perfect chin and took him in fully with those incomparable emerald eyes. "Do the right ones speak as eloquently as you?"

"They try." *But I hope to keep them at bay.* He offered his arm. "May I take you in to the theater, *Madame*?"

With a twist of her head, she noted that the others in the party were indeed headed for the Earl of Carbury's box. She looped her gloved hand through his. Her fingers loose upon his forearm, he welcomed their warmth. And to keep them there, he pressed his hand atop them. The gesture was improper, but he'd done it out of need to secure her to him.

She caught her breath.

"The threshold, *Madame*," he said, indicating the carpet as they stepped into their box with the others.

"Oh, my," she said, halting as she gazed at the cavernous theatre decorated in ruby and gold fittings. Everywhere the rich velvets and damasks, the heavy fringes around them, the box adornments seized the imagination. Even the red velvet expanse of the cloak room with its *chaise longue*, and the tapestry upholstered chairs in Carbury's box assaulted the senses with sumptuous display. "This is quite overwhelming."

The others were removing their cloaks. He gestured to help her with hers and she presented her back. His fingers touched her skin, a spark racing up his arm as he hung her cloak and his on the large hooks.

"It's astonishing, isn't it?" The innocent delight of her

appreciation for the decor reached out to him like a hand to his heart.

Her gaze ran once more over the opulence. "Sublime."

What was sublime was the angelic fascination on her face. "The loveliest thing I've ever seen."

Was this the expression she wore when she gazed at a man she adored? *"Certainement."*

"So much of it," she whispered. "All this red. Like passion."

"The stuff of life."

She spun to face him, her gaze searching his, afire with enthusiasm that mesmerized him. "Are they wonderful?"

"Who?" He was lost in her. How could she be this mature and find the beauties of this place so fresh? She was a child discovering sugared fantasies.

"The singers? The dancers?"

"*Mais oui.* As divine as the music. You will enjoy them."

"I never thought I would have the opportunity."

"No?" He tipped his head. "Why would you not?"

His question broke her enchantment. She frowned, turning away, seemingly embarrassed. "A trifle."

"I don't think so." He put a hand to her elbow. "What did I say?"

She glanced up, her polite demeanor firmly back in place. "Nothing, *Monsieur.*"

"But I did. It made you sad and I do not wish that." He pressed his fingers into her flesh. "Tell me please so I do not make the same mistake again."

"It's difficult to behold this and realize so many will never see it. So many starve or suffer illnesses and I—" She put up a hand. "I'm sorry. I'm maudlin. Very poor manners on my part." She swept aside her skirts and sat down.

He took the chair beside her. "I apologize."

She nodded. "Please do not, *Monsieur le duc.* I am the one who is not used to the grandeur of this."

"That is refreshing, M*adame.*"

"Oh, sir. You need not humor me."

"Ah, but I am used to those who would never exclaim over such richness. Never find delight in draperies or chandeliers."

She cocked her head. "I could shock you more and say I enjoy full meals and blazing hearths."

"As we all do and yet few who have such each day boast of them." He leaned closer to her, wishing she'd share details of her past to draw them nearer to each other. A widow, she had lost her husband. Had she loved him? How deeply? Had he died in their war? And how had she fared in that conflict? "What is your reason for such admiration of the ordinary pleasures of life?"

She went quite still, her focus on the stage. "I lived without them for years during our civil war. When your stomach growls, when your enemy sets fire to your barns and eats your pig and your chickens, when you have no wood to burn in your own hearth, you value food and shelter for the rest of your life."

He took her gloved hand and she did not pull away. "You may always share with me anything you appreciate, *Madame.*"

Her sweet green eyes met his and he watched her give in to a laugh. "Might you like old Flemish tapestries?"

"From the reign of Louis the Fifteenth, I do."

"Hmm. Why?"

He lifted a shoulder. "He's an ancestor."

She gaped. "Am I to assume you own a few?"

He demurred. "Three."

"A group. Oh, my."

"Scenes of a stag hunt at Rouen. They hang in one of my homes."

She clapped her hands together, eager. "Rouen. My grandfather fled Rouen to go to America. May I see your tapestries, perhaps?"

"Name the day."

She giggled and stopped herself short like a child at play. "Do you like art?"

He warmed even more to her test. "Sculpture. Painting. And you?"

She narrowed her eyes on him. "Caravaggio?"

"Dark and dangerous," he said. Sensing she disliked the painter's work, he refrained from sharing that he owned two of that man's works too.

"Agreed. Exactly like Goya. Do you own any of his paintings?"

"No. And I'm glad I don't."

"Too realistic?"

He acknowledged that with a wince. "One of my ancestors died in Spain with Napoleon. His passing was not pleasant."

"I'm sorry."

"No need. I know only of his trauma. Tell me instead if you like the works of any French artists?"

"Delacroix?" she asked brightly.

"My father bought one of his landscapes."

That took her aback, her thick blonde lashes fluttering in confusion. "My uncle wishes to buy his portrait of Frédéric Chopin."

"Does he? Well. He'll pay an outrageous price for that."

"Money is no object to my uncle when he wants something badly."

Remy wondered what might stand between him and this fascinating widow. If anything, it was not money. He had enough for the next century. And unlike Julian, he need not marry to acquire anything he wanted. Except the woman herself. "It's for sale. He should buy it."

Her plump lips parted and in her expression, he saw excitement. "Tell me about the singers. The dancers. The music."

"The orchestra is accomplished. The singers are expert. You will enjoy them." He watched her as she imbibed that. God, she was lovely. "Have you been to the opera in New York?"

"No. We live in Baltimore and often we're at my uncle's ranch in south Texas. Our entertainment consists of our own piano and neither Lily nor I am very good at that."

"Have you lived with your uncle Killian and his children a long time?" He was being intrusive, but he had to take this chance to understand her. How else to draw her? Sculpt her?

"Almost thirteen years."

"A very long time."

"A very happy one."

He did not understand why such a lovely woman remained cloistered and unmarried. "And your parents?"

"They died soon after I was married. During our war."

He ached for her. "And your husband?"

She stiffened her spine. "He died in a battle in a small town in Pennsylvania."

"My condolences, *Madame*."

"I was fifteen." She tried to smile and failed. "Half a lifetime ago."

"*Mon dieu.* You were too young to endure such loss."

She stared down into her lap. "My parents wished me to wed him despite my age. They were ill and had lost their land early in the war. My husband was a friend of my parents', so it was natural that we wed."

Remy reached out to take both her hands in his. "You have suffered greatly."

"It was long ago, *Monsieur*. I made my way north eventually and my uncle took me into his home and his care. My aunt, his wife, was still alive and she was kind to me. When she died, I welcomed the chance to help my uncle. I'm grateful to him."

"And so you helped your uncle with his small children."

"I did."

He wished to cup her fragile cheek, kiss her nose, her eyelids and wrap her close. "What have you done for yourself?"

That stumped her. She stared at him.

"You must have cultivated a part of yourself for yourself."

"I have." She pulled away once more.

Now was time to challenge her. "What is it?"

"I have nursed the ill and dying."

"*Pardon?*" That was not what he expected.

She licked her lips, chanced a glance at the stage and turned back to him. "I worked as a nurse in a makeshift hospital during the war in Virginia. It was necessary. There were so very many who were wounded. I was whole and healthy and able."

The orchestra took up their instruments, the rattle of bows and sheet music sending a ripple through the audience.

"They begin," she said and dismissed their topic as she shifted around in her chair.

He could not take his eyes from her. To look upon her was to behold a beautiful creature. To speak with her, to learn her of her interest in tapestries and painters was to become intrigued with her turn of mind. But then to hear of her hardships and her reactions to them was to become astonished by her uniqueness.

He chastised himself for his inability to act the gentleman and look away. Crossing his arms, he forced himself to survey the audience, the stage, the painting on the domed ceiling.

Women of his own class whom he knew were well educated. Many cared for others, the downtrodden, the poor, the rabble. Most did it with contributions to charities. He understood compassion. He thought he had it for those less fortunate than he. And he thought he used it in his work. Emotion was the stuff of his art, carved from marble, poured into the bronze or baked into the porcelains. Yet he had never known poverty or hunger, fear or depravity. Not from others. Not from the state, not even during the horrors of the uprising of the Paris Commune six years ago. Even when the Prussians had been so beastly to so many during their occupation of France after they booted out his cousin, the second little Napoleon, Remy and his mother had not wanted for food or enjoyment or frivolity. His mother, gracious and giving had shared her staples from her cellars and clothes from her trunks. No one, especially children of the parish, had starved. Yet here in this pristine beauty was a lady who had labored in the catastrophe of war to aid others.

He was horrified that she'd seen bodies broken, bleeding, dying. He was smitten that she had done it and lived to tell of it.

He was proud of her.

He'd never felt his heart swell with so much pride. For his mother, in her largesse, for her grace and generosity, yes, he'd applauded it. So too, his applause for the peasant women who labored daily in his vineyards and farms was justified.

But this woman had walked in a living nightmare and worked to ameliorate its worst horrors.

The orchestra played on and Mrs. Roland was rapt. If he could sketch her now, even in the half view of her profile, he would draw her and call it Rapture. But to mold her in clay....

The arch of her brow, pale and long. The curve of her cheek, sharp, feline, distinctive. The straight line of her nose, small, delicate, her nostrils flaring as she flowed with the music. She was quite perfect.

The music died. The conductor turned from his musicians and strode off to the wings.

Intermission had arrived and he must steal more minutes with her alone before she dissolved in the night.

Mrs. Roland slid her program from her tiny purse and examined it.

He leaned toward her and whispered, "Allow me to show you the promenade and take you to the *glacier*."

She checked her uncle and Lily, both of whom were engaged in conversations with others. "I wonder if I should."

"You can. It is acceptable. A glass of champagne and a view of the gold in the gallery are both necessary to truly say you've been to the Garnier." He stood and extended his hand. "Come with me, *Madame*."

A hint of humor passed her features as she put her hand in his, then got to her feet. "I'd like that."

He wrapped her forearm against his and led her out of the box. They passed along the marbled circle and toward a long hall glowing with bright light from gold and crystal chandeliers.

"Oh, this is so lovely. We have grand buildings in New York, but nothing to compare to this."

They strolled along the full length of the mirrored gallery into a circular room where waiters poured champagne. She peeled back one glove from her fingers and tucked the fabric inside near her wrist so that she might hold the glass.

Remy handed her a flute and took one for himself. "To you, *Madame*."

She drank, blushing. "You're kind."

*Am I? No. I am calculating how can I get you alone and hold you in my arms.*

"Do you know *Monsieur Garnier*?"

"I met him years ago." He told her about the architect Garnier and the interior designs. "This took more than a

47

decade to build. Disputes over the funding and the decor delayed construction."

"And the final price?"

"A mystery!" He laughed as he told her about the never-ending invoices from tradesmen and stone masons and carpenters. "Many claim they will never receive their full wages. But according to the bankers, we Parisians will pay for it until the next century."

She took a long drink of her champagne and grinned. "Ah, but some items should bear no price."

*Like your smile.* "Indeed."

She finished her drink and placed her glass on a nearby tray. He disposed of his own.

He offered his arm and they walked toward the far end of the gallery where they'd begun.

She peaked out toward the street. "May we go to the terrace?"

That she would risk censure for being alone with him in the dark surprised him. He could face criticism himself for taking her there, but he would protect her good name. He would not advance his suit too much and shame her or kill his own chances of gaining her friendship.

"If you do not wish it," she said with a hint of humor and staunchness in her spine, "I'll protect you from my Uncle Killian."

He barked in laughter. "Not what I fear most."

She threw him a winsome smile. "I won't ask what that is. As for me, I want the air. The champagne was far too wonderful."

The heat in her eyes as she absorbed his features fanned his hopes of kissing her. "You drank it too quickly?"

"I like it too much," she said with a gay air of confession. "So many things here draw me."

He hoped to be one of those. "I understand."

"Paris inspires me to—" She glanced away, her throat working at words. Then she stopped and faced him. "I am a creature used to ordinary means but here, I am...transported. I like the gaiety, the music and—"

*Me?*

"I like the Parisian night. The air, the melodies of people singing in the cafes. I love the smell of bread baking in the morning and the apple trees in blossom. My grandfather Duquesne came from Rouen but he had a house here. I think I must have Paris in my blood."

"I would say so. When did he go to America?"

"During your Revolution."

"He was an aristocrat?" he asked.

"Papa said he was a count. But he gave up his title and his land to leave here."

"Many did. Even my own great-grandfather and his wife emigrated to England during the Terror. Wise of them to go."

"We should be happy because otherwise we would not be here."

He opened the first door to the upper terrace to lead her to overlook the confluence of three wide boulevards. By now, it must be midnight. Stars twinkled like diamonds in a black velvet sky and he prayed they conspired with him so that he might enchant her.

She shivered.

He unbuttoned his coat. "Are you cold? Here."

"Thank you."

"Your uncle would never forgive me if you became ill because of my carelessness." He draped the garment over her shoulders and forced himself to remove his hands from the delicate line of her body.

She strode forward, out of his reach, toward the huge concrete balustrade and leaned over it. The carriages in the streets below made muffled sounds. The wheels rolling over cobbles, the horses' hooves clopping and the shouts of the drivers combined to give sweet cadence to the night.

"Have you always lived in Paris?" she asked him, wistful.

"I have an estate south of the city. It's a day's coach ride. Near a town called Tours." He would not tell her how big the chateau was, for fear he'd seem pompous. "I spent my childhood there until I was twelve when my parents sent me to school here. I love the city. She is a curious creature, a blend of ancient and modern. Growing, improving. Raucous, dear and full of amusements."

A few feet away, another couple—man and woman both in formal attire—appeared on the terrace. The man, murmuring husky phrases of desire to his companion, backed the lady up to the rail and, circling his arms around her, drew her close and kissed her.

Remy longed to do the same to lovely Mrs. Roland.

She saw the couple, her lips parting as she savored what she watched. Quickly she turned back to him. "The freedoms here are many."

"We are more open about our affairs than, say, those in London or America."

"Is there as much censure afterward for those who commit transgressions?"

He pursed his lips. Intriguing she should ask. "For Englishmen, there is much condemnation for those who are too liberal. I rely on you to tell me of Americans. But here, we understand certain human emotions more than others."

"Why is that, do you think?"

"Perhaps we Frenchmen have condemned others too quickly, too easily and much more harshly than others. Perhaps our revolutions have been so many—or so violent—that our inhibitions are gone. Who's to say?"

She turned around to face him, her large eyes luminous in

the light from the street gas lamps. "I could spend my whole life here."

*Could you?* "And what would you do with your days?"

She smiled at her own thoughts. "I'd take an apartment where I could walk out on the roof at night and chart the stars. I'd smell the air. The garlic and the shallots."

He loved her like this, carefree and eager for pleasure. "The bread in the morning."

"The flowers from the market," she continued with a little giggle. "And I'd buy a ticket to come here every night to listen to the creations of others."

She was so charmingly impetuous.

He placed a hand on the balustrade, drawing nearer to her. "Do you play the piano? Or sing?"

She threw her head back to laugh. "I don't play a thing. But I do sing. Last night, I did. We were in a cabaret in the Rue des Abbesses."

*Last night, she sang and I missed it?* "I would have loved to have heard you."

"No. You wouldn't. I was horrible with my poor French but no one shouted at me. So I was satisfactory. But I saw the dancers in a cafe in the Rue des Abbesses, doing their *cancan*. They were risqué but wonderful in their red skirts and black stockings and garters and— What?"

Had she seen him? Had she admired him as he had her? "What did you sing?"

She cast him a rueful glance. "A ditty about a milkmaid from Lyon. It was quite naughty."

"Do you know where you were?" His voice was a rasp. His hope was absurd.

She held her breath. "A small cabaret. The Arabesque? The Ardennes?"

He nodded, winding one of his hands around her waist. She was small, delicate. His hand spanned her back. She was finely muscled, well proportioned and strong. "The Ardennes."

"Yes, that's it." She breathed heavily. "I saw you there last night."

*Did you? And what did you think of me?* He stepped forward and cupped her cheek. Her skin was warm silk.

She swallowed and flexed. Through his fingers, he could feel her confusion and her fascination with him. "You are a man women notice."

*This is a mutual magnetism then.* "*You* saw me and I am content."

"Oh, *Monsieur*," she shook her head, from her tone ready to dismiss her enchantment with him. "This is not proper."

He touched the tip of his finger to her luscious lower lip. "But very right."

"This is too soon." She would have left him.

He put his leg between her own. Her gown swirled around them in a swish. His senses vibrated to touch her lips with his own. "Time is as immaterial as money when you see what you want and decide to have it."

Arching backward over the balustrade, she panted as she grabbed for air. "We are to be friends, *Monsieur.* Friends."

"Yes, friends, Marianne." He withdrew slightly, not wishing to frighten her. "It is 'Marianne' is it not? And you must give me leave to call you that. Just as to you, I am Andre."

She shook her head. "No, sir. That is too much."

*Or too good? That we should find each other time and again among throngs?* "How then do you explain the coincidence?"

"What coincidence?"

"That I saw you when you entered the cabaret, Marianne."

Her mouth fell open.

He slid his other arm around her and pulled her against

him. She fit him, her long legs against his own, her breasts and hips against his torso, making him hungry to press her naked skin to his.

She squeezed shut her eyes and pressed her face to his cravat. The feather in her little evening hat tickled his nose.

He sank his fingers into her coif. Her hair was satin. Her scalp perfectly formed. Like every other part of her, she was sublime. Christ, he'd never wanted a woman so urgently.

"Forgive me," she said and raised her head to peer at him with trepidation and a smack of bravado. "I've been very forward."

Fearful she'd fly from him, he held her gently. A tendril of her hair had escaped her pins and he curled it back over her ear. "You have?"

"You as well." She tipped her head toward the door. "Now we must go inside. I'm cold."

Beside them, the other couple moaned as they continued their love play.

"Marianne—" he beseeched her.

"Please, sir." She stepped aside, her chin up, valiant and yet vanquished. "I saw you too last night. I couldn't believe my eyes today when I saw you again in the street."

*I felt the same.* He could tell her of his own surprise, but then he might not learn why she recounted it with breathless unease. "And so?"

She flowed against him. "I thought you magnificent."

He'd been described in many ways. Huge. Rough. Inelegant. But her word infused him with incredulous joy. If he were a woman, he'd have said his knees went weak. His mind certainly did. But his hope to have her bloomed like an arbor long denied rain.

She put one hand to his jaw, her thumb outlining the edge of his lower lip. "All this might deserves..."

"What?" he asked in a whisper of his desire.

"Applause. An audience. Beauty is rare in this world."

He bent and dropped a kiss into her bare palm. "Marianne, the beauty is in you."

She opened her mouth, her gaze rapt on his mouth. "*Monsieur*—"

"Andre."

She clamped her eyes shut, but when she opened them, she was adamant. "Andre, you are too complimentary."

"No, *ma petite*, the compliment you gave me is a treasure." He drew her closer still. "I am quite honored."

"Oh, don't be. After all, who am I? No equal to you."

He urged her nearer.

"No, please, *Mons*—. Andre, let us go in." She stepped backward.

And he would not compel her.

"We are of two different worlds. We would not—must not ever suit."

He noted sorrow and despair in her countenance. And he pitied her that. Why she should think them so ill matched, appalled him. Certainly, he did not. But then, she had her reasons and he wagered they were sound to her. Whatever the particulars of her past, she had suffered. Perhaps from the brutalities of war, perhaps from loneliness or feelings of inferiority to her uncle's household. But he could not cure such challenges with a kiss.

He would be patient. Kind. Draw out her reasonings. He perceived she'd had no one who really listened to her. And he would be that person. That confidant. That friend.

Perhaps, then he might merit becoming her lover.

That particular joy he would not do without. Not in this life nor the next.

"Come. We'll speak of this another day."

"No. We won't."

"I may call upon you, surely, if—"

"No. We will not speak and you will not call upon me."

❦

How Marianne endured the rest of the performance without screaming in frustration, she could not say. Stupidly, she'd foiled herself, robbed herself of a joy—an escapade—she'd dearly desired.

Gentleman that he was, Andre had not argued, but escorted her back to Carbury's box. Like two statues, they had sat beside each other until the bitter end.

Minutes later when the lights came up, the two of them rose and conversed, mingled and laughed with the rest of their party. Nothing seemed amiss. Andre was a good actor and she pretended so easily. Chastising herself for lying to them all, she wished she could sprout wings to fly away.

Andre rose, his expression hopeful as his blue eyes met hers and held. "Shall we adjourn to a café for refreshments?"

Marianne almost applauded him. Charming man, he was not deterred by a woman's rejection.

"Forgive me." Lily was first to respond. "I've enjoyed this tremendously, but I fear I must return home. It's been a very long day. Excuse me, please. But Papa, if you wish to continue the evening, do."

Marianne breathed more easily when Uncle Killian made his own excuses. They would leave, thank heavens.

The party reclaimed their coats and made their way down the massive staircase, into the rotunda and on to the portiere where the carriages lined up.

Andre and his friend, Lord Chelton, were perfect gentlemen, seeing them into their carriage and bidding them a polite good evening.

From her vantage point in Uncle Killian's town coach as they drove off, Marianne had a long view of Andre Claude

Marceau. It must be the last time she saw him. For a very long time, at least.

Because if they met again, she must be stronger. More careful. Less irrepressible. She must have learned to school her interest in him. How to do that, she was not aware. But she would. Must.

For when they met again, she must not fall once more under his spell. She would not permit it. He was so much man. Too much for her. And though she yearned for a lover, she never would take one who would seek to control her.

Never.

# CHAPTER 3

**February 20, 1878**
**Ile de la Cite, Paris**

"Enjoy yourself," Marianne told Lily. They stood at the entrance to Lily's favorite book store near the Conciergerie. "The other day when we were out, I spied a milliner's shoppe whose hats I rather liked."

"But don't you want to come inside and browse?" Lily pushed up her fur collar against the chill wind along the Seine. "You've finished your latest Trollope. You said so last night."

"I didn't care for it as much as his last few." Marianne made a face, then patted her green plaid toque. "And I do need a new *chapeau*."

"All right. But you shouldn't go alone." They'd both come out today without their personal ladies' maids because both servants were ill with coughs and sneezing. Not even the Comtesse de Chaumont was out with them today because she was busy closing up her house in Paris to travel with them soon to London.

This was the perfect time for Marianne to accomplish her objective. "The day is young and the *gendarmerie* can save me from any person of ill repute."

"If you're sure...?" Lily asked, eagerness in her tone.

"I am." Lily could spend the entire afternoon in the book shop, spending a fortune on novels. Since well before Christmas, Marianne had been hoping for an opportunity to walk in Paris alone. "Take as much time as you wish. Stay and I will come back for you when I finish."

"Very well." Lily bid her goodbye and pulled opened the bright blue door to the cozy shop along the river.

Marianne whirled around and made for the Place Dauphine. She'd memorized the address of the exhibit and though she'd never traveled there before, she knew where it was and that it was a fine neighborhood. She could walk there safely, a woman alone in the middle of the afternoon on a crisp winter's day.

She was grateful for the whip of the wind and the way she had to keep her little wool hat from flying away. Fighting the weather kept her mind from fighting her skepticism—and from giving in to the voices in her head that asked the same alarming questions over and over again.

*What if this Remy, the sculptor, is not the same man as the duke she'd met?*

Ridiculous. There could not be two dukes of Remy. Plus, the article she'd read in an edition of last week's *Paris Monde* had spoken of the "*prince du sang*" who was "becoming recognized for his *nouveau* style." Her subsequent conversation with Chaumont about him revealed that he did work in bronze and marble and worse, that he was renowned in society for keeping one mistress at a time for a very long time.

He had told her nothing of either. Not that he should. Nor even that such were proper topics for polite conversation between acquaintances. But the first omission saddened just as it intrigued her. The latter sparked jealousy. It also infuriated her.

"As if I have the right to be angry with him," she murmured and walked on.

Still she'd seen the billboard for "*Une Exposition pour duc de Remy!*" and her curiosity would not die.

She paused. *What if I dislike his sculpture?*

*What if I see someone there whom I've met?*

*What if they require my name and tell Andre I was there?*

No matter. Really. Was she a ninny?

She marched onward.

But she fretted. *What if Andre is there?*

Indeed.

*What if he is?*

The answers did not kill the hunger that had plagued her since last she'd seen him in September at the opera. To feed her memory, she'd drawn him. Over and over again, she created him. She had sketchbooks full of him. His face, his cheek, his hands, his eyes. His remarkable eyes. In graphite or ink, he lived in her hands, in her mind, in her foolish fantasies. There, he appeared without threat to her equilibrium. There, he became more human than myth. There, he was flesh beneath her fingers and wild emotion for her soul to feed on. Her conclusion was that she could not continue as she had without knowing him better. Because he had taken her order not to call upon her, she was left no other recourse to satisfy herself about him than to view what he loved, what he had created.

She hurried along the boulevard, proud of herself for this necessity to attend his exhibit of his latest works. During the past few months, she'd sometimes thought she might go mad with not being able to admire the symmetry of his form or the drama of emotion in his face. Summoning courage, she'd committed herself to feeding her hunger by drawing him.

Now there was this visit. Pure whimsy. To do it easily. Anonymously. Many weeks ago, she'd seen the billboard near the Louvre advertising the display of his works and she'd lost her breath with the hope it aroused. She'd view his artistry and—she assured herself—feel nothing. She'd recognize no chord in his work that spoke to her. Nothing of the man who had bewitched her. Then, and only then, would she force herself to accept that he was not what she had imagined.

He was not kind or sweet. He was assertive, self-centered, driven. Even arrogant. What artist could become accomplished without such characteristics?

No. He was not for her.

Not her kind of man. Her type of friend. Not at all one whom she could take to her arms and her bed and her care.

Not.

She stood in front of Number 10, her destination. A three-story stone structure with grape leaves carved in relief into the frame, the building had two abnormally large doorways. They appeared to be proportioned to receive a sculptor's works. The one with a large cut glass window seemed to be the entrance. Inside, the concierge in a somber black suit spied her, hurried out and opened the door for her.

The address was the same as on the billboard. The plaque on the door proclaimed it as the "*Gallerie de la Cite.*"

"The Duc de Remy's exhibit is here?"

"*Oui, Madame.* Through the foyer and up the grand staircase."

"*Merci beaucoup.*" She sailed through the lobby and up the steps. Four other patrons casually climbed the broad steps.

At the top, she halted her in her tracks. A man and

woman passed around her. But she stared at the sculpture before her. It robbed her of breath.

Here upon a black granite plinth stood a man of white Carrara marble, eight or nine feet tall. All muscle and bone, honed by battle and hewn by strife, massively masculine and robust, he was of such proportions that any other human would fall down in honor of him. He stood in the center of the oval entry to the rest of the exhibit, sunlight from a semi-circle of windows shining on him, shadowing the arc of a bicep here and emphasizing the indentation of a deltoid there.

Yet he did not stand tall, but was hunched. His back was curled, bowed in new defeat. His hair long and ragged, etched in the pristine marble to invoke its filth, shrouded him to the waist. Ropes circled his torso and hung from his wrists. His noble head hung lax from his corded neck as he stared at the nothingness before him.

The beauty of this body was nothing to the grand agony of his face. She gasped at the sight and could not look away.

She walked around him and bent to face him. He looked at her, but beyond her. He was blind, in torment. She drew back, aghast once more at the brutal honesty of what she saw.

This was a strong man brought low. By loss. By self-destruction.

She ached with him. Once proud, dynamic. A man others had once envied and emulated. A man so capable, so honored and now, abandoned by others and most tragically, by himself.

She stood for how long she did not know. The power of him infusing her. And the power that he'd lost draining her of envy and inspiring pride at Andre's talent to portray him so precisely.

Across the room, beyond the giant, a young man in an apprentice's smock tipped his head in question. Not at her.

But someone who stood behind her. He tipped his head and, as if on signal, he departed.

Her skin tingled.

The hunger she'd felt for months dissipated. She'd be sated now.

"*Bonjour, ma petite*," Andre said in that bass voice she heard in the bleak hours of her lonely nights. "I dared not hope you would come."

She closed her eyes, wishing to hang on to this moment when he was happy to see her and she was as delighted to be with him. In this slice of time, there was none of her inner conflict, no yearning to find him, see him, laugh with him. There was just satisfaction. But it could not last.

*Why not tell him the truth?* He had asked for honesty and he did not deserve duplicity. He had only told her how he admired her and she had rebuffed him out of...what? Not convention, no. But her own fear to allow such a strong man near her heart or body. Perhaps even her own fear of her outrageous ambitions to enjoy him physically? She faced him, and oh, the delight to see him again ran through her like cool water after a drought. He was as tall, as incomparable as she remembered him. Perhaps more so, since she had pined for him so badly.

"*Bonjour, Andre.*" She gave him that, his given name as he had allowed her use of it. During these past months, she'd thought of him that way, the sound of his name slipping through her lips at night as she attempted to draw him. *Andre.* "I saw a billboard and I could not stay away."

He stood against the white marble wall, the gold veins of the stone highlighting the gilded mien of his own long waving hair. He had folded his arms and one leg was casually crossed before the other. He wore a loosely cut black wool suit, a bright vermilion vest, a white linen shirt open to his strong throat and a purple kerchief tied at his neck. Every inch of him denoted the artist at his leisure.

"I'm glad I've come. This—" she said and lifted a hand toward the statue, "—this is glorious. I heard others speak of him but they did him no justice."

He gazed at her with hollow eyes.

"No words can," she went on, wanting to give him more praise and unequal to the task. "Will you tell me about him?"

"Him?" he asked, as if she had insulted him with the question.

She knew why. He wanted her to ask about himself. And she would. She would.

He stared at her. "You know who he is."

She did. "Who could not? To view him was to know. No pamphlet or placard need declare it."

A light glimmered in Andre's blue eyes. "What do you see?"

"A man torn by his own desires and ruined by his own misjudgments."

His marvelous mouth firmed. Pride lit his face. "And?"

"He will never see himself again."

"He did not truly see himself before he was blinded."

"A punishment," she acknowledged, "to fit his crime."

Andre shifted, peering at her with narrowed eyes. "There is another he will not see."

*Oh, yes.* "He will never see her again."

"The one who betrayed him."

She nodded. "The one whose beauty he believed was soul deep."

Andre pushed away from the wall and approached the statue. "He must pay for his own failure to perceive her true nature."

"She was not equal to him."

He whirled to face her. "That's not what he believed. He thought she was the most beautiful creature he'd ever seen."

"The beauty was outside. Her core was hollow."

"He pays for his miscalculation," he said.

She dropped her gaze to the floor, anxiety eating her that they spoke of more than the statue or the Biblical story of the blind man and the woman he had loved so unwisely.

"Do you think she pays?" he asked, his deep voice wistful.

She raised her face to consider the statue's tortured expression. "Delilah?"

He waited.

"Oh, yes. She forevermore will hate herself for her own failures and unworthiness."

Andre took her by the wrist. "Come with me."

Her pulse jumped.

He led her down a hallway toward a room where he shut the heavy wooden door and drew her into an *atelier* crowded with bronzes and plasters, scattered about on tables and shelves. Two ivory overstuffed chairs stood in one sunlit corner near a sumptuous black velvet *chaise longue*.

She had not expected a private audience. Whatever he wished to discuss in private summoned her defenses. To examine his works would help soothe her. "May I...may I see these?"

Hands on his hips, he glared at her. Silent, he tipped his head as if to give her permission.

Before her was a glazed multi-colored china bowl, large as a Virginia farmer's whiskey vat. The huge green and blue base was balanced by the figures of four muscular men who held it on their shoulders. Their strength reminded her of the Samson in the entry, but she knew these were Titans holding up the world. On another table stood three plasters in various stages of completion. All were of the same figure, a lithe woman rising from a frigid white foaming sea. The model's facial features reminded her of herself. Alarmed, she shrank backward and wondered why the model was incomplete. "Why is she unfinished?"

"I thought I knew her, but I was wrong."

She inhaled sharply. His words reminiscent of their conversation about Samson and Delilah seared her—and compelled her to look again at the woman. Indeed, it was an attempt to recreate her. "This is not Delilah."

"Perceptive of you," he said and strode away from her toward the window. "She was to be Diana. I miscalculated."

Unable to stare into her own face again, Marianne moved on to the far table where a model of a child stood. Done in bronze, he was a chubby baby holding his toes and giggling. Yet he was not complete for his face was half obscured by one foot. She turned to Andre. "You have not seen him fully yet?"

"No." Glancing at her over his shoulder, he shook his head. "I allowed the casting and should not have. Next time when I have a half-formed vision, I will know better than to rush to form him before he is truly whole."

She continued onward to view other pieces in wet clay, all of a woman, nude, arching upward as if in ecstasy or pain.

"How long have you been sculpting?" she asked, facing him. So far across the room, she felt safe from his allure.

"Since I was young. Our chateau in Tours is old and filled with friezes and sculptures. The house needed new plaster on the walls and I amused myself to watch the peasants work. Then I joined with them. When they finished the walls and the painters came to do the murals, I wanted to draw as they did. My mother gave me graphite, pen and ink and parchment. I drew until my fingers ached, filing sketchbooks that I keep in the chateau as a reminder of how I began."

"I should like to see them."

His stern demeanor drained to compassion. "*Ma petite*, to see them you would have to be with me for days."

She seemed to soar, light as air in her ripe desire to do just that.

"But only just now are you capable of bringing yourself to be with me for minutes."

She lifted a shoulder in apology. "I go slowly."

"A creature of your society?" he suggested with a small crooked smile.

"I admit it, yes."

"Nonetheless," he said now with the first sign of warm welcome, "I'm glad you've come."

"So am I." She let her gaze travel the array of his creations. There were dozens here. She yearned to touch each one, learn their contours, their secrets. "You are prolific."

He grinned. "One must work every day to improve one's skill. Not every object is superb."

She knew that herself. How many times had she witnessed her own inadequacies in her sketches and paintings? "I have proof of that."

"How so?"

Well, she had led him to this juncture. She would confess her actions. "I draw you."

Humor fled his features. Raw desire supplanted it. "Since when?"

"The night I first saw you in the Rue des Abbesses."

He stared at her and seemed to fail to breathe. "Are your sketches any good?"

She gave a small laugh. "I get better. The more I see you, the more I draw you—"

His blue eyes flamed.

She gathered her courage. "The more I try, the better the portrait."

"Are your drawings substitute for the man?" he asked, a note of ruefulness in his tone.

*Safer, but not as fulfilling.* She shook her head, less afraid now that she saw him in the flesh. Pulled by his charm, she took a step forward. "I didn't expect to see you here. In fact, I hoped not."

"Well, then," he said with dark impatience, "why are you here?"

She moved about in a circle, extending a gloved hand to his works. "I thought I could interpret who you are, what you admire, what you yearn for if I could see what you create. Then perhaps I could draw you more accurately."

"Why is that important?"

She frowned at him.

He strolled toward her casually but his face held harsh intent. "Why must you draw me repeatedly? Why must you assure yourself you know me? Is it artistry? Do you not recall the exact arch of my nose?"

A hard question, but here with him she suddenly knew the answer. "I don't want to be wrong about what I perceive in you. Who I think you are."

"Which is what?"

"Sweet. Lovable. Unapologetic for your raw ambition. Even aggressive."

He grimaced. "Ah, well."

She smiled at him, his modesty surprising and refreshing.

"You like me?" His question was as whimsical as the light in his eyes.

"I do," she said with relief at speaking the truth.

"I'm pleased."

Relief flooded her. "Oh, so am I. I want to sleep more easily."

His face fell. "You do not sleep?"

She wanted to shake her head but she could not take her eyes from his. "I walk the floor."

"Is that normal for you?"

"Only since I first saw you."

"What must you have to sleep?" he asked, his voice hoarse.

"Peace," she told him with certainty. "I draw you to...to draw you near to me."

He inhaled. "Is my visage so scary that I keep you awake?"

"So elusive that I yearn to see you more," she admitted, pleased at her own veracity. She would have him for her lover if he agreed.

His hands flexing, he strolled away. When he faced her again he said, "You've asked others who I am, what I am?"

"I have." Uncle Killian, Lily and she had been invited to soirees and dinner parties in Paris. She'd met a few French aristocrats who'd casually mentioned Andre and his ancestry. He was thirty-six, immensely wealthy, a blue blood. He was indeed descended from the dethroned Bourbon kings and the rascally Bonapartes. He was a welcome guest, a superb horseman, an expert at cards and a leader of Parisian society as was his mother. To top it off, she recently confirmed among her acquaintances that he was a burgeoning sculptor and painter whose works gained critics' praise. He was a friend of the *impressionist* painters DeGas and Renoir who lived up on the Butte in Montmartre. For his ancient name, his money, especially for his male magnetism, he was a prime catch for any young woman. Dozens—young, virginal, widowed and jaded —had him in their sites. She was no competition to any of them. Nor did she wish to be. "You've become increasingly popular."

"Fame is not my intent."

"I never assumed it. But fame comes with artistic acceptance."

"I've always had friends. Money, land. My work allows me unbridled private indulgence. An exploration of the mind."

Exactly the exuberance she felt when she drew women, children, babies. *Him.*

"You understand that?" he asked her.

"I'd like to think so."

He arched a brow, appearing nonchalant. "Meanwhile, you are a mystery to me."

"I'm no one you would notice."

"Oh, but I have *Madame* Roland. I have." He took a step nearer.

She could not move, did not wish to. Part of her mourned that he had not called her by her given name. Was she to him once more the removed, the polite, *Madame* Roland?

He peered down at her. "Your hair, your brows, your chin, your very person. I see you and I am enchanted by the *ensemble* and the *façade*. Tell me about the woman beneath."

His praise had her rushing to answer him. "There is not much more to my story than what I told you the night we were at the opera. I am ordinary, *Monsieur*. Born on a farm near a small town in Virginia. Married to a neighbor I'd known since I was a child. Appalled by how shells and bullets destroy a man. Compelled to nurse the wounded. And widowed now for many years."

Beyond the walls, the sounds of patrons in the halls swelled. If they intruded, they'd ruin her one chance to talk privately with him. She yearned to remain, talk with him until she emptied herself.

"That is a very long time to be alone," he said as he examined her closely.

"I wasn't." Twirling her Grandfather Duquesne's gold signet ring on her finger, she set her jaw. She hated talking about the war. "I avoided Confederate renegades and Yankee barricades to cross to the north to get to my uncle and his wife in Baltimore."

"You are valiant. More than any woman I know."

"Not valiant at all. I had to leave. The hospital I worked

in was bombed by the Yankees. There was no food and I was hungry. Tired. And I wanted family."

"And they took you in."

"Yes. Yes, they did. And they were kind to me."

"I understand," he said with compassion. "And all these years, you've been alone?"

She frowned. "No. With my uncle and my cousins."

"Forgive me." He seemed ill at ease.

*Why?* "Did you want to ask me something else?"

"You are an extraordinarily lovely woman, charming and..."

"And?"

"Have you truly been alone all these years?"

"Ah. You meant to ask if I took lovers?" When he nodded, she said, "No. Never."

"Why not?"

She lifted her face and examined the ceiling. "Oh, any number of reasons. Perhaps I don't know how. Or I'm not adventurous. Or that I haven't found anyone I'd like to take to my bed."

He was so close now, she noted how the sky blue shards of his eyes darkened to azure. "Would you find peace if I were in your bed?"

Her lips parted. How had he known her temperament so well that he could ask that of her. "I wonder myself. Often."

"And your answer?"

Truth would help her maintain her freedom. "I'm not certain if you would bring me peace. But I do know one thing. You would remake my life."

"Ah, Marie, I would not change you."

She laughed tremulously at his use of her shortened name that her father had preferred. "Not perhaps intentionally."

"I like you, *ma cherie*, as you are. Quietly stalwart."

*And I like you. Too much.* "You see me as fierce. I'm not so much that. But you would not like my independence."

"How do you know?"

"Men don't care for that in any woman." *My husband did not.*

Andre chuckled. Crossed his arms. "But I am not any man."

The truth of that roared through her like a siren call to decadence. "Definitely not."

He reached out to run a fingertip over the outline of her lips. Where he touched burned. She yearned to bite him, keep him, show him she could be as bold as he. Memories of them on the balcony at the Opera Garnier swamped her. "Are you afraid that you would want your independence less than you would want me inside you?"

She grabbed a breath. "I doubt that."

He stiffened. "Why?"

"Because our interlude would be short."

He scowled at her. "How short?"

"I'd want you only for one night."

Astonishment brought him up short. He blinked. "One?"

"I'd not risk more."

"Gratifying to learn I am not worthy of more."

"That's not the reason," she blurted.

"No?" He smiled, fiend that he was. "Why not?"

"You'd be difficult."

"*Would I?* How so?"

"You'd demand things of me."

"Such as?"

She frowned at him, but a smile lurked inside her. "Rendezvous."

His mouth tipped up in a lop-sided grin. "So many."

"Precisely," she agreed.

"In secret places, too." He feigned a grimace. "The challenge would unnerve you."

"Frankly, that I'd welcome."

He shot her a look of disbelief. "I shall remember that."

"No need," she told him, happy to have the upper hand at the moment. "We'd be discovered."

"Half the fun...for some." He ran his gaze over her in appreciation.

*How he could melt her with those ravenous looks.*

He bent to her as if to share a secret. "I'd want to lock you away with me."

She threw out a hand. "There you are. You'd want me—"

"As long as I could keep you," he said.

She swallowed hard. This kind of possession was dangerous. "That's scandalous. I could never do it."

He hooted in laughter. "Nonetheless, you'd test my resolve and chance to come to my bed for one night."

She stood her ground. "Yes."

He tilted his head to one side. All humor fled his visage. "Very well. I accept. One night. Beginning at what time?"

"What? Well...um.... Six."

"Six o'clock, I see. Until when?"

"Six the next morning."

"You'd rise early, I suppose?" he asked with measured reason.

"I would."

"Before the shops are open?"

"Correct. And so that—"

He smirked. "You could arrive home before your Uncle Killian knew you were gone."

"Exactly."

"And before he took one of his pistols and came to my home to kill me."

"No, of course not. He'd never do that. I'd tell him of my plan."

"Would you? Oh, *mon dieu*, I must definitely put final touches to my last will."

"Uncle Killian understands passion," she said, not believing but hoping that the rebel blockade runner knew how to temper his emotions.

Andre lowered his chin and stared at her. "My darling, you understand nothing about men. Your uncle would challenge me on the matter of honor."

"Not if I told him we were intimate just once."

Andre winced. "Once, *mon dieu*."

"What's wrong with once?"

"It sounds as if we were blasé about our affections. I assure you, my pet, with you, nothing about our affair would be light or easy."

"It could be," she pressed him.

He chuckled. "You stand before me, breathing heavily, your cheeks pink, your lips parted. If you come to me for an affair, it is for days or weeks or months."

She shook her head. "I wouldn't. I promised my uncle one year."

"One year of what?" He froze, anger slashing his features in harsh lines.

"One year to aid Lily. The rest to launch her sister, Ada."

"You are their guardian? Their governess?"

"No. Their older cousin. A chaperone of sorts."

"Your gratitude to him demands that you do as he wishes?"

She wrung her hands. "That I help his daughters enter society easily and marry well, if they like. And that I behave responsibly."

His brows rose. "Are you prone not to?"

"No! But he has set aside a dowry for me. And I want it."

"Do you? A dowry." He crossed his arms, anger staining his cheeks red. "Do you plan to buy a husband then?"

"Oh, no." *There'll be no husbands for me.* "Listen to me."

He spread his arms. "I am."

"I've never had money. Not a lot. Not any to speak of. I was a child, and then I was a child bride. And then I was..."

He focused on her, his blue eyes hot. "You were what, *ma cherie?*"

"I was a wife." *And I hated it. Him.*

Andre waited.

"And I—was obedient. Quiet and hard-working in the house and attentive to the slaves."

"Slaves?" This shocked him.

"We had them. Four in the house. Forty-two for the fields."

Andre cursed roundly in French.

"They left, all of them, during the war. Thank god they did. And I—I'm old enough that I do want my own home, my own life, my own—"

"Your own what?"

"Affair. If I wanted it."

"Do you?"

"I've never considered it...until lately. Until you."

"You want a man in your bed simply for the fun of it?" His eyes danced in merriment.

"Well, yes! You make it sound awful. I'm not. You're not and you've had mistresses! For the fun of it, I would guess."

"Fun, *oui.* There is much to say for fun."

"Oh!" He infuriated her. "It doesn't matter. I came to see your work. I have. So I'll go." She whirled for the door.

He caught her by the wrist. "Stay."

She wanted to. His arms came around her waist and his big warm body pressed against her back.

"Marianne, stay and talk to me." His words were whispers on her skin. "Stay."

She turned to face him.

He gave her a small smile and pushed hair from her cheek. "I thought you said you valued your independence."

"I do." *What was he talking about now?* He befuddled her.

"An independent woman makes her own rules."

"I did. I do. I've wanted that since I was young and..."

"And now?"

"I still need to, but frankly—"

He arched an inquisitive brow.

"At the moment, it pales. And the only thing I want is you."

He crushed her against his strong hot body. Deliciously hard in all the right places, his body enflamed her. "Oh, *ma cherie.*"

She pushed away. "But it cannot easily happen. Not even for one night."

"What? Why not?"

"For a lot of reasons. The most important is that it may take awhile, even years for Lily and Ada to find men they'd marry. I cannot act in such a way that damages their prospects. That's no way to pay back my uncle for his generosity to me."

"That's a lot of work and a long time to wait for only one night of bliss." In his eyes, hope and humor mingled.

She had to make him smile. "Ah, but then you may not like me once you've seen me for hours on end."

He arched his brows. "I could say the same."

"We could prepare so that neither of us is disillusioned." Horrid thought that he might take her, she might adore him and afterward, he might not care a bit about her.

He lifted her chin with two fingers. "Ah. You have an idea how that is done?"

She gave in to the joy of possibility, the daydream he might desire her. "First?"

"Yes?"

"I thought we'd see if we truly liked each other."

"How?"

She filled her sight with his magnificence. "We'd start with a kiss."

He smirked. "Prudent. When?"

"No time like the present, don't you think?"

He grinned at her.

With a smile, she rose on her toes and put her lips to his. His flesh was cool, firm. He tasted of mint. She wanted more of him and brushed her mouth on his.

He did not move.

Bracing herself by cupping his shoulders, she leaned into him and kissed him once and then again.

He wrapped his arms around her, a cocoon of rapture, and he kissed her in one long dive into deep enchantment. His lips claimed hers in a hot river. His tongue explored the caverns of her mouth and she gave the same ardor back to him. Moaning, he pulled away and skimmed his lips over her cheek to her temple. "That was too many kisses."

"Are we rationing them?"

He set her away from him. "We are. Too dangerous to continue until you are fully ready."

"Are you?"

"You, my darling, may be thirty but you are naive about men."

"About you, *oui, certainement*," she corrected him.

Both his brows arched high as he considered every inch of her before him. "Then hear this. I've been mad to hear each sigh of yours since first I saw you in the Rue des Abbesses. With us? Speed is not wise."

Disappointment rang through her.

"You must come to Montmartre. To my studio. There you will see more of me. More you need. Now you must go. I'll send an invitation to my studio. Bring your cousin if you must." He strode to the door and put one hand to the knob.

She did not follow. "I cannot. There is another problem."

He stared at her. "Tell me."

"My uncle, Lily and I close up the house in the Rue Haussmann and leave for London in a few weeks for the start of the Season."

"How long do you remain?"

"Perhaps only during the spring for my cousin Lily to begin her introduction to English society."

"After that where do you go?"

"My younger cousins, Lily's sister Ada and her older brother Pierce arrive in London in June, but we're to come here for Ada to go to Worth's to have her wardrobe designed for next year." She smiled at him and the opportunity that might give her to see him again. "That may mean we arrive here in July."

"And if I came to London, would you receive me?"

That she hadn't expected of him. He had a life of his own long before he'd met her. He was a prince, a man of means and, by the crowds here and stories about him in the newspapers, he was becoming a sought-after artist. "I would."

Frowning, he thought for a minute. "I will follow you when I can."

She'd never had a man take extraordinary measures to please her. Hope blossomed like a rose.

"But I have one matter that may deter me."

She held her breath.

"My mother is frail."

Marianne was taken aback. "I'm sorry. I did not know."

"Nor would you. She gives the cut direct to anyone who sends tales of her to gossip sheets. But you must know that she is the light of my life. If I am to visit in London, away from her, I must arrange that someone is with her every hour. I'll write to my cousin who lives in Tours and who, I hope, can come to Paris to stay with her. She herself needs companionship in her older age."

"Andre," she said as she approached him, "I do not mean to change your life—"

"Not if our affair is to last for only one night?" He was teasing her.

"Yes, it must be." She lifted her chin, valiant and sad that she'd ever stipulated such restriction.

He eyed her critically. "My darling, one night, be damned." He looped an arm around her waist and brought her with one mighty pull up against his massive chest. He took her mouth in a searing kiss that branded her and left her light-headed with soaring satisfaction. Then with a sigh, he put her to her feet.

"We will drink from each other all there is to give, *ma cherie*. Now, go, please, before I take you to the *chaise longue* and your visit here becomes the one night you wish for."

# CHAPTER 4

**March 1878**
**No. 110 Piccadilly**
**London**

Marianne sailed into the dining room early their first morning in their London house. In the rush to prepare to leave Paris, she'd found no opportunity to talk with her uncle privately. Usually she'd find every reason to confide in Lily about her desire to ultimately return to Paris, but she was reluctant to reveal her scandalous intentions to her cousin. Lily was not naive about the nature of intimacies between men and women because she'd lived on a ranch observing animals. Yet Lily thought Marianne's references to taking a lover were witty by-plays. Nothing she'd seriously consider. And in fact, she never had until she met Andre, the duc de Remy. Lily would learn soon enough her intentions, if her hope ever became a probability. In the meantime, Marianne wasn't confident that her Uncle Killian would easily accept her wishes, let alone condone them. Still she owed it to him to notify him.

As she hoped, he was already in his chair finishing his breakfast. His two newspapers to hand, he furrowed his black brows as he read the page before him.

"Good morning, Uncle Killian." She took her chair and the footman backed away. "Something disturbing in the papers?"

"News about a company whose shares I'm interested in buying." He picked up his coffee cup and drained it. "You're up early."

"I hoped I might have an opportunity to talk with you. I wonder if you can spare me a few minutes."

"I can. Always. What's on your mind? A problem?"

"Not at the moment, no."

"Will you have something from the sideboard first?" her uncle asked.

"I'll eat after we talk. Thank you, Foster," she said and smiled at the butler who draped her napkin in her lap and poured her coffee.

"Chaumont should appear here today or tomorrow. She sent a note around this morning that her house in Hanover Square is almost ready. She brought with her more of your wardrobes for the Season." His humor lit his large silver eyes, as she remembered her mother's had once done. At forty-six, Black Killian Hanniford was a handsome devil. Marianne had watched many women cast their eyes on the American robber baron. He was a desirable catch for his looks and his outrageous wealth, if his nefarious reputation as a civil war blockade runner did not recommend him. "Are you and Lily perhaps suddenly out of clothes?"

She feigned a withering look. "Not for the next century. Chaumont sent over one of the trunks from Worth yesterday afternoon. I'm awash in silk and satin, Uncle."

"Wonderful. I want you all to feel like queens when we start the Season."

"Oh, we do," she assured him.

"I think we here are ready to receive callers. The furnishings are in place. What do you say?"

"Even Delacroix's portrait of Chopin is spectacular," she added with a little lift to her shoulders. Her uncle wanted the original painting by the French artist to give a special touch of integrity to his rented house on London's grand thoroughfare. "I cannot get over his talent. It's really spectacular."

"Even if it is only half the original painting?" he said, laughing and putting his napkin on the table.

"I know." She sipped her coffee. "What idiot cut the damn...darn thing in half!"

With a grin, he sent her a scolding look then reached to take his watch from his vest pocket. "Time marches on. What worries you?"

She folded her hands in her lap while her well-rehearsed speech fled her brain. "I was sorry to leave Paris. I enjoyed the city very much."

"I know." He rolled his eyes. "The cabaret especially."

She grinned. "That was only once."

"I think more visits are in your future."

His words showed her, as he often did in other ways, that he not only knew her nature well, but he tolerated her foibles. "I'd like to go."

"You've had too little fun in your life. The war stole your youth and even your husband."

She tried never to speak of Frederick. Discussing the war was slightly more bearable. "I made the best of the loss of the plantation and our slaves."

"You set them free."

"Most ran."

"You did not call the sheriff or the dogs on them. That in itself was noble."

"Noble? Frederick called it stupid. He wrote me from camp and scolded me for it." *Called me an idiot. Said he'd beat me black and blue for it.* "Most of them fled when Lincoln declared them free after the battle at Antietam. I couldn't work four hundred acres with only seven Africans. Even my cook and two housemaids ran away." *No wonder. They high-tailed it when they had the chance to get away from Frederick.*

Her uncle reached over and squeezed her hand. "We're a long way from you telling me why you'd like to return to Paris."

She checked his expression. If he knew the true nature of Frederick Roland, her uncle never indicated. But he was sensitive to her reluctance to speak about him and so he had changed the subject.

"I'd never hurt you or Lily. Not Ada or Pierce either."

His silver eyes twinkled in mischief. "I know you like to sing, but are you telling me you plan to become a regular *chanteuse* in a cabaret?"

"Never that. But perhaps worse."

"So then, what?"

"I would hope that in time here you might not need me as much to chaperone Lily and Ada."

"Until they're married, they'll require an older woman to watch over them."

She winced at that last. Her life was passing her by and nothing had brought that home to her as quickly as living in Paris—and meeting Andre. Her visit to his exhibit in the Place Dauphine had overwhelmed her with joy and expectation that she might revel in a man, a decadent escapade, a period in her life when she was her own person, free of all in her past that saddened her.

Her uncle caught her eye. "You're day dreaming, my dear."

"So I am. Oh, Uncle Killian you've been good to me—"

"Marianne, just tell me what it is you want and I will get it for you."

"You cannot buy this for me, Uncle."

"Ah." He inhaled and sat back. "But I can bless this for you, is that right?"

She grinned. "You could allow it to happen without censure."

"Oh, I don't like the sound of that. You could get hurt, badly."

She lifted her chin. "At some point, you see, I want to live in Paris by myself."

"Not in Rue Haussmann?"

She nodded. "Not there. I'd like a taste of freedom. Not that I don't experience it here and—"

He lifted his hand to indicate she need not continue. "I understand. You see Madame Chaumont and you want that independence."

"I do."

He cocked a brow. "She is French and they have different expectations of their widows than we do in America."

"I'm aware. But I don't want to return to America."

"You've thought a lot about this obviously."

"I have. I want the cafes and the Louvre, the exhibits and the—"

"Place Dauphine?"

She stared at him. "How did you learn that I—?"

"Went to Number 10 one wintry afternoon alone?" He gazed at her with kind regard. "My dear, one of my associates spied you in the street. He was concerned when he saw you walked alone and he followed you to ensure your safety."

"I had to go before we left the city."

"I understand. I went to see his exhibit myself the next day. Remy was there. We talked."

She had a new appreciation for her uncle. He'd known she'd visited but never raised the subject which must mean—"You like him?"

"My dear, I even liked Remy's friend, Lord Chelton, and trust me when I say, I have little reason to care for him. His father foils me at every turn to buy the shares in his shipping company. But the Duke of Remy? I have no conflicts with him. A fine man. A very talented one. And ethical."

She frowned. "How do you know? What did you discuss?"

"Don't worry. I did not challenge him to a duel."

"No but—"

"Marianne, he was honest with me about your visit."

"Andre was a gentleman throughout and never took advantage of me."

"So he is 'Andre' to you? Well, I am not surprised."

She sagged in her chair. "I like him."

"And he has a fond regard for you, my dear. Fond enough that he made me a few promises."

She sat straighter. "What do you mean?"

Her uncle glanced up and with the arch of his brow, Foster the butler and the footman backed out of the dining room. The butler shut the doors.

He pushed away from the table and crossed one leg over the other. "After we met him that night at the Opera Garnier and I saw then how you were attracted to him, I had my man in Paris collect a dossier on the Duke of Remy."

"Oh, Uncle Killian." She was aghast. "Why? How could you? Does he know?"

"Not that I investigated him, no."

"Oh," she said, a hand to her chest. "Thank goodness."

"But I had to learn more about him. *Why?* Because despite how independent you are, my dear, despite what you want, you are tender. Frederick, god rest his miserable soul, was not a proper husband."

She was horrified her uncle knew anything about Frederick. "He was no man you would befriend."

"You are too kind to him, Marianne." Killian shot up a hand to deter her from speaking. "Over the years, your reluctance to talk about your departed husband has implied much. But then, long before you came to our house to live, I had friends among General Lee's officers who told me tales about Frederick. Stories I will not repeat for anyone's ears, most of all yours."

He rose and walked to the sideboard where he brought the pot of coffee to the table and poured for her and him. "You endured starvation, enemy soldiers eating your crops and sleeping in your barns, desertion by your house slaves, and still, you nursed Yankee wounded in your parlor and then in town. That took gumption, Marianne. And courage few other women—may it please God—will ever have to summon. When you escaped across the Potomac River to come running to us in Baltimore, I was damn glad to give you a safe home. So was my Aileen. She loved your mother as I did and she feared for you for years."

"I was happy to see her before she died."

A gloom fell over Killian. He'd treasured his late wife with a fierce devotion. Marianne had seen love like that between her own mother and father.

"I once hoped I might find a husband who cared for me like my father loved my mother or as you cared for Aunt Aileen," she said with sorrow. "I grow older and my hope dwindles."

Killian took his chair and faced her. "And this man is one you could care for?"

"I am attracted to him. Surely you've been attracted to a woman who is not..." She groped for polite words. "Not one you'd marry?"

"You're right. But a man can do that with some impunity."

Anger flashed through her. "A woman can. She just needs courage and a pinch of discretion. I have those."

"I do agree." He gave her a sad smile. "Have you thought how you'd do it?"

"I've laid out my terms with him already."

Killian's eyes went wide. "Bold of you. Did he agree?"

She feigned confusion. "I think so."

"You could leave him to many of the details."

"Details? There shouldn't be many."

"My dear young woman, he is prominent in society. You are too. People will notice a dalliance and talk to the scandal mongers."

She laughed. "Oh, no, Uncle Killian, you have this wrong."

"What do I have wrong?"

"I don't want Andre for an affair."

His cup half way to his mouth, her uncle paused to stare at her. "Now I am really confused."

"I want him only for one night."

Her uncle dropped his cup to the saucer with a clack. "Marianne." He put his napkin to his lips.

"You think I want a grand affair. To be in his house for nights? For days?" She shook her head, recalling Andre's expression when she told him she wanted the diversion of a brief liaison. "You're right that I want some fun. I want to laugh and sing and learn how to really make lo—"

She cleared her throat.

He turned serious. "You deserve all of that."

Her gaze locked on his. "I could have it. In a year or two, after Lily and Ada are married. Pierce too. I wouldn't hurt anyone's chances of marrying well. Not for the world."

"You'd wait until the girls are married?"

"Of course."

"Marianne, I know your heart is in the right place for all of us. But my dear, you are forgetting a few things here."

Frazzled, she sat quietly and folded her hands. "I'm listening."

"The Duke of Remy is a charming man. Thirty-six, educated, landed, rich and prominent at the height of Parisian society. His mother is a princess of the blood of the Bourbons and a descendent of the Bonapartes. They are a revered family, respected in politics and foreign affairs with extended family in Germany and Russia. They are wealthier than I am by three times. And more to the point of his relationship with you, he is experienced in affairs of the heart. My dear, he has had many women in his bed. Just recently he divested himself of a woman he'd supported for more than six months. Furthermore, he has taken no new woman to his care."

Marianne knew all of this except for two things. Andre must be worth at least twenty-nine million dollars. An unbelievable fortune. And he had rid himself of all entanglement. Money, as much as he possessed, did not matter a fig to her. Money was immaterial after the normal needs it bought. But she bubbled with delight that Andre had ended his relationship with another woman to take up with her.

Or was she foolishly thinking he'd done that to be with her?

"Marianne, are you listening to me?"

"Yes, absolutely, Uncle."

"Remy might be wealthy and respected socially, he might be a leader in his own circles, but he is an artist with all those intemperate tendencies those men seem to cultivate, Marianne. He's a man of great talent."

That was apparent in Andre's Samson. Even the unfinished Diana showed the frontiers of his vision.

"But when I spoke with him, Marianne, he seemed balanced. Not prone to anger or boasting like those artists up on the Butte are known to be. And he mentioned you with reverence."

Reverence was not the emotion she wished to evoke in the breast of the dashing French duc de Remy. "He is impatient."

"I agree."

"He is charming."

"Without a doubt. He understands your sensibilities. Furthermore, he can seduce you when and where he pleases."

"I trust him not to do that."

Her uncle pursed his lips, thoughtful, pensive. "I hope you're right."

"I am," she said with confidence.

"You say you want him for one night?"

"I do."

"Because you cannot cope with the challenges of a long term affair?"

She shifted in her chair. "So I thought." *Even though I'm terribly tempted to take all that's offered to me.*

"But did you consider, he might not wish to end the affair quickly?"

*So Andre had said.* "To him, I am a novelty. An American. I wouldn't amuse him for long."

"You think he regards you so nonchalantly?"

"I don't know him. I don't know what he thinks. Except that he likes me. My looks. My odd background. My—"

"Innocence."

She blinked.

"He likes you as you are, Marianne, because he does not know anyone like you. Wise about war, bold in the ways to survive, but artless, without guile. A lamb when it comes to navigating the rigors of a love affair. He wants you. And he may be ruthless in his pursuit."

"The very reason I have not succumbed yet to his allure."

Killian sighed. "But you will do this."

She bit her lip. "I will."

"If he ever hurts you—"

"He will be blameless. I do not go to him blind to the consequences."

"We are always your family, here to give comfort and respite from the storm." Killian reached over to squeeze her hand.

"I know. Thank you." Inside her, every nerve sparked with delight. She shocked herself to be so giddy about losing all her inhibitions and acting on impulse with a scintillating man. "I will be careful."

Killian nodded. "I believe you."

She got to her feet. "I think I'll take a walk along Piccadilly."

"Of course."

She went toward the door. But she paused, remembering what he'd said earlier. "A question for you."

"Yes. What?"

"You said he made you promises. What were they?"

"To treat you with respect and gentleness."

The last word made her panic. "You told him? About Frederick?"

"I leave that to you, my dear. It's your story to tell, if you ever wish to. A man you love might wish to hear it. Might need to."

She looked down at the pink and rose Aubusson carpet, the colors swimming in her vision, her eyes stung by grateful tears. She quickly brushed them away, raised her face and smiled in great thanks to this man whom others thought was nothing but ruthless. "Anything else?"

"Yes. One more promise."

"What?"

"Not to get you with child unless he wanted the babe as much as you."

Her hand went to her throat. She hadn't considered that possibility. Her times in bed with Frederick, frequent and painful as they'd been, had never led to any indication she might be pregnant. Still, with another man she might conceive, though she thought the chances very small. She must consider how she would act if she were to carry Andre's child. Must come to her own terms with that. Was she capable of raising a child alone allowing him or her bear a burden of ridicule? She had to decide that quickly and abandon her plan for an affair if she was not brave enough or wise enough. "I will act responsibly. Thank you for your thoughts, Uncle Killian."

"You're welcome, Marianne. For all the good you've done in the world, you deserve to be happy. I wish you well of it."

Tears sprang to her eyes. She spun for the hall and a welcome walk in the crisp London air.

⚜

"*Monsieur le duc, pardon,* you have a visitor."

Wincing, Andre pushed his *pince nez* up his long nose and caught a glimpse of the dying rays of sun streaming through his studio skylight. He hated intrusions when he was at work. This piece, like four other previous attempts, eluded him in its final form. He dropped his clay onto the granite table and wiped his brow with a swipe of his forearm.

The young man stepped back. Carré was his newest apprentice, skittish enough without Andre barking at him for allowing someone into the parlor. "Most know not to disturb me. You hung the sign outside the door?"

"*Oui, Monsieur, oui,* but this lady demands you receive her."

A woman?

He'd parted with Collette Nemours back in February. She wouldn't call on him. After coming to his bed for many months, she knew him well and had more sense than to question his decision to end their arrangement. Besides, he'd given her enough francs to buy that house she'd wanted in Compiegne. Nor was his visitor delicious Marianne Roland. She was in London going to teas and house parties, chaperoning her cousin Lily and awaiting her other relatives' arrival from America. Julian Ash had written to him that he had seen Marianne at the Hannifords' home in Piccadilly.

"She looks well, as if she enjoys her duties with the Hannifords," his friend had noted. When Julian had added that she is well regarded by English gentlemen, Andre fought the urge to run to London himself and declare himself her suitor. But he had promised her time and when her uncle had appeared before him, Andre had promised him restraint. Then too, between the lines of Julian's letter, Andre had sensed that his friend was more than smitten with the dark-haired beauty who was the daughter of his adversary, the millionaire Killian Hanniford. If Julian was beginning a courtship of the American heiress, Andre hoped to heaven he got on with it quickly. The sooner Lily Hanniford married anyone, the sooner he himself could appear in London and begin his own pursuit of the widow whose image he could not seem to duplicate in any medium, save his own lusty imagination.

He pushed up from his workbench, hope dwindling Marianne could be in his parlor. "Who calls, Carré?"

"*Oh, Monsieur.* She says she is your mother."

"My—?" *What was she doing out of bed? And here? She never came to see his works in progress. She wished for only the finished product to coo over.* He marched to his basin, poured water from the pitcher and scrubbed his hands free of the sticky clay. Peeling bits of it from his nails, he wiped his hands dry with rough paper. "What is she doing here?"

Carré had only a shrug for answer.

Andre strode for the door. "Get the maid to make tea. Run down to the patisserie and buy two apple tarts, chocolate cakes, something else, anything. And bring the bottle of brandy from the kitchen. Two cups. On a tray. Quickly!"

Taking the three stone steps at a clip, he crossed the foyer to thrust open the door to the parlor. The house was only four years old, three-stories tall, built by him after the Commune and the Prussians abandoned the city in eighteen seventy-one. Compared to his family homes, this house was small, with a coal and wine cellar in the basement, three servants' bedrooms in the attic, a front hall, a parlor, dining room and large kitchen. But he'd purchased two plots when he'd bought the land and extended the house toward the back where the ceiling soared for two stories over his workshop. Chunks of stone, vats of clay, tubs of elements for plaster lined the bare ivory walls. In the center stood a raw six-foot tall gold-veined marble slab that he contemplated from all angles each morning and night since he'd left his mother's house in the Rue de Rivoli two weeks ago. All were illuminated by the spectrum of sun streaming through a thick, clear glass sky light. At one end was a set of French doors opening to his bedroom where he slept when he in was 'in mode' and creating.

He loved this section of Paris. Montmartre was thriving, full of artists who strived and starved, but it was a rowdy, welcome place to talk about image and beauty, art and the future of expression. It was Andre's favorite place to sketch, to plan, to create. And not a place the illustrious *Princesse d'Aumale* frequented.

"*Maman!*" He went to her as she turned slowly away from the tall windows that faced the street bustling with shoppers and merchants. Taking her elegant hands, he kissed her downy cheeks. "A wonderful surprise. Come and sit. Why did you not send word you were coming?"

She tipped her head and teased him with affection in her azure eyes. "*Mon cher*, if I told you I would come, you would rush home to bid me stay where I am."

He led her to the overstuffed Louis Quinze sofa and sat beside her. "You know me better than I do you."

She slid her hand from his. "Ah-ah. You scoundrel, you need not attempt to take my pulse. I am well."

He examined her with a critical eye. She wore a walking ensemble of malachite wool that complemented her flawless skin and contrasted with the pure snow white of her hair and brows. This morning, her cheeks were a subtle pink which he happily concluded was not the total result of the application of rouge. Her eyes, the color of an Italian lagoon, were bright, even through her tiny glasses.

The past two years had been difficult for her. She'd suffered and recovered from three weaknesses of the heart, robbing her of breath and energy. Her last episode in January had sapped more of her stamina than the previous ones and her doctor had ordered her to bed for four weeks. In the following two months, she'd regained strength and some weight so that in sunny spring weather, she took a daily carriage ride.

"You came in the landau?" he asked, unable to glimpse which conveyance stood outside his doorstep.

"*Oui,* our Valmont has the reins. We do not pay him enough."

Andre laughed. "If you pay him any more, he will revolt and move to Tours just to show you he is his own man."

She let her eyebrows dance. She was in her mid-seventies, but despite her illnesses, she had the vivacity of a coquette of twenty. "He uses all his wages to pay for school for that precocious daughter of his. She finishes with the hatters' soon and he wants to send her to Monsieur Worth's to apprentice with the drapers. To audition for Worth, she must produce three chapeaus in different materials. That costs money."

"I don't begrudge any of our staff more pay. You and I have enough for ten people. Increase Valmont's wages. Increase them all."

She pursed her lips. "I think it useful."

He heard the pause in her voice. "What are you getting at, *Maman*?"

A rap came at the parlor door.

"Come in! Ah, yes, Nanette. *Merci, beaucoup*. Please place the tray here." His maid-of-all-work scurried in, curtsied and backed out. But she lingered in the shadows in the hall, craning her neck to catch another glimpse of the *princesse* whom Louis Napoleon had tried to seduce away from her devoted husband, the *Prince d'Aumale*. "Shall I add a bit of fuel to your tea, *Maman*?"

'Fuel' had always implied aged brandy and his mother enjoyed it. Even her doctor encouraged her to drink it by the cup full.

"*Mais oui*. I am dry and this conversation requires sustenance."

"I see," he said as he poured tea into a Sèvres cup he kept here just for special visitors. He knew she'd come for a specific purpose. She'd never disturb him to have a meaningless tete-a-tete. For whatever her intent, he was happy to lace her tea with the spirits that would relax her. "I would hope you are here to view my latest work."

"Why else?" she said as waggled fingers at him to be more liberal with the dose of brandy. Satisfied, she put her finger in the air and took the china cup and saucer from his hand. She drank, her eyes closing as she swallowed. "One thing Louvan does is make fine liquor. His politics are a shambles, assuming women can be shut out of his factory and the vote. But we must educate the weak minded, eh?"

He poured straight brandy into his own cup and took a sip.

Another knock came at the door.

"*Entrez*," he called and the maid came with a tray of patisseries. "*Merci*, Nanette."

He indicated the tray of sweets to his mother. "Shall you have the chocolate *mille-feuille*?"

She nodded and fixed her gaze on him. "After you've taken me back to the studio."

"You cannot wait to hear me describe my latest, then?"

She waved a hand in dismissal. "You dally. Walk me back."

"There's nothing to see," he told her with a sigh. "I wish there were."

"You have not been here for two straight weeks and produced nothing. I know you. You are incessant, compulsive, especially when here. You itched to leave Rivoli. You must produce here. So. Tell me no lies. Why is there nothing to see?"

He inhaled. "I have trouble envisioning the final figure."

"Show me." She put down her cup and made to rise. She had difficulty.

He offered his arm. "You did not bring your cane today. Why not?"

"Is your arm not strong enough to support me?" she challenged him.

He tsked at her as he led her from the room toward the hall to his studio. "Do you leave it in your bedroom every day?"

Frowning, she pursed her lips. "I did not feel the need. I foresaw no tumbles or missteps. Now, tell me what you've been doing here since you left the house two weeks ago."

He led her along the corridor, up two steps and opened

the massive wooden door to his *atelier*. The sunlight hit him with warmth.

In the brilliance, his mother grinned. "I adore this place. You did well to sweep this high and wide. Reminds me of Delacroix's studio near Saint Germain. But your's has more of what God intends."

He led her to a bench, wooden but comfortably curved for just such visits by those who wished to linger with him. "I wish God would tell me what He intends because I am, at the moment, bereft."

Facing the six-foot block of marble, she studied it. "Well at least I see that you know how tall the piece will be."

"I thought I knew when I bought it months ago. Now, I'm not certain."

"Is it for your new commission for the city of Paris?"

He walked toward the monolith, his arms crossed. "No. I see another shape for that. The city fathers' want a heroic piece to symbolize the survival of the city after the Prussians won the war."

"Tell me please not another winged victory?"

"We have enough of those, don't we?" He placed his hand on the cool white surface.

"*Certainement.* Europe is full of them."

"I see a woman free of her chains." No sooner had he said it, than he narrowed his gaze on the stone and perceived an outline he'd not envisioned before.

"I grow tired of waiting for you to tell me, Andre." He sensed that his mother rose from her seat and moved toward the table where his clay figures sat in clusters. "Andre? Andre, look at me."

"*Oui, Maman.*" He turned to see her holding up the figure he'd been sculpting before Carré came to tell him she'd arrived. "What is it you said?"

She held the figure up to him in her palm. "This. Who is she?"

"A woman I met months ago."

His mother arched her elegant white brows.

"She is American. Delicate in form but hardy in spirit, like a willow bending to the wind." He hesitated to tell his mother more. She grew eager to see him wed begetting an heir to take the titles that graced her life with riches and obligations. Encouraging him to go out in society often to find a woman equal to his erudition, his mother had expressed her disappointment with his progression of mistresses. Andre had learned not to exaggerate the depths of any of his affairs. "She fascinates me. Has done, since I first spied her in a cabaret last autumn."

"This gives me no idea of her. Yet—" she said as she turned in a complete circle, her hand out to denote the dozens of other clay figures on the tables and shelves, "—I see no facial features. Only the lift of a delicate jaw. Why is that, Andre?"

"I recall her essence. I sculpt that." He pulled off his glasses and pinched the bridge of his nose. "I should stop trying. The compulsion destroys me."

"How well do you know her?"

"You are too perceptive, *Madame*. In practicality, I know her hardly at all. I go by instinct and so I imagine who she is. What she was as a girl, a young woman, a wife."

His mother's face fell. "She is married?"

"A widow."

"*Bon.*" His mother caught a long breath. "Well, we will be grateful for that. Take me to the bench, *mon cher*. Good. Good." She settled onto the wood. "What else must I know?"

"There is not much to tell."

"Of course, there is, Andre. You have not been yourself. You do not sleep well. You walk the floors and the gardens. I thought when you left the house in Rue de Rivoli and came here, you might find solace in the work. Do you?"

He was not sleeping well here either. Every night, he dreamt of one incarnation or another of Marianne Roland. He'd startle, rush to a sketch pad but her vision evaporated into air.

"I take that for 'no.' You released Collette Namours. You have no other woman to your bed, or so I hear. You do not eat well. You've lost weight."

"*Maman*—"

"Let me speak. For months, I have watched you, Andre, and it is my penchant not to interfere. You were always one who knew his mind. As a child, impetuous but with desire. Stubborn but with cause. I have not seen you want for a woman you did not win. Is this American widow more than a model for your work?"

"I have more hope than substance, *Maman*."

"Why are you not pursuing her then? Erasing the mystery? Filing the void? This is not like you to wait and ponder if a woman is worth your attention."

"I promised her I would wait until a proper time to court her."

"Court her? So, it is as I presumed. She could be more than a *petite chou*."

"She will not come to me for more than one night."

His mother laughed heartily, a trilling sound.

He grinned, shaking his head. "I'm serious, *Maman*. These Americans are intriguing creatures."

"Stubborn?"

He snorted. "As if they invented it."

"More's the pity," she said.

"Or my advantage. If...*if* I can ever gain her company for long enough to press my advantage."

"And do you have one? Does she like you?"

"Oh, never doubt. She does. Surprising as it is to her and shocking as it was to me that first night and the second, even the third, the very sight of her sets me to flame."

"You have seen her only three times?"

He nodded. "Too few."

"And your work suffers for the lack of her." His mother smiled. "What must she suffer for the lack of you?"

He hadn't considered that. But as he pondered it, he wondered if Marianne did feel the lack of him. If she did even in some small way, it might connote that there was more for them than one hasty affair. More than that was what his heart had hoped for for months.

His mother put her hand atop his and squeezed. "The days grow long, *mon bonheur.* Summer will be upon us and the nights will be made for soft whispers. Why do you not find reason to go to her? Take your life and your opportunity in your hands? What can it cost you to learn?"


Ten days later he had no cause to speculate on costs. Julian had written to him with news that he and Lily Hanniford were to be married within the week. Andre was to come for the festivities.

That afternoon, Andre hired a public hack to drive him down to the house on the Rue de Rivoli. When the butler opened the door to him, the old man grinned. "*Bonjour, Monsieur le duc.* We are delighted to have you with us."

"My mother? Where is she?" he asked as he handed over his hat and cape.

"In the music room, *Monsieur.*"

"She is well?"

"Very well indeed. She has told us you will soon be very well too. A new commission. A new reason to create."

Andre laughed. His mother had a way with words. "*Oui*, she is correct."

"Tea, *Monsieur*?"

"*Oui*, but of course. Brandy, too. And please tell Pierre I wish to see him after I talk with my mother." Up in Montmartre, Andre never dressed formally and did not require his valet's services, but Pierre would be vital to dressing him well in London as he tried to impress Marianne Roland.

"Certainly, sir."

Following the strains of one of Chopin's piano concertos, Andre took the stairs up to the main floor in quick strides. The old hall smelled of polish and beeswax. The green and white checkered marble floor sparkled juxtaposed to the ruby papered walls. He pushed open the door.

His mother inclined her head in recognition of his arrival, but as was her wont, she continued to play. An expert pianist, his mother could perform miracles with her long fingers hitting all the trills and impossible chords. Seizing the chance to absorb her talents, he sat in one of her overstuffed chairs smiling while she finished.

And then she spun to examine him with a mother's knowing look. "You've brought me good news?"

He rose to walk to her and kiss her on both cheeks, his exuberance spilling out of him as if he were six. "What you longed to hear."

"You go to London?"

He leaned an arm on the grand old Pleyel. "I leave Monday."

"You'll bring her back?"

"As soon as I can."

She rose from her piano stool. "I expect to be introduced."

"You shall."

"She will be a joy to you."

"You cannot know, *Maman*."

"I see the way you look when you speak of her. I note upon your face the thrill of meeting her again. This is no infatuation, Andre."

Wrestling with that truth no longer, Andre knew it was impossible to live rationally or even productively without seeing Marianne Roland once more. In London, he would woo her and win her or give her up completely.

# CHAPTER 5

**June 7, 1878**
**No. 110 Piccadilly**
**London**

Marianne winked at Lily and grinned. "Take one more look. Then we absolutely must go down. We don't want your father to call us on the carpet before the ceremony."

Nora, Lily's maid, fluttered about, looking for Lily's white gloves and chattering about losing them.

Lily widened her eyes at the bottle Marianne had tucked into her skirts. They'd both had a few good nips this morning and Nora, busy as she always was, had spied them at it. Marianne was certain that the servant would try to turn it to her advantage.

Lily rolled her eyes. "Nora, I wonder if I accidentally put the gloves in my trousseau case? Check there, would you?"

"Right you are, miss." The maid paused to stare, then sniffed, but lumbered off toward Lily's dressing room.

In two short steps, Marianne tucked the bottle of brandy into Lily's wardrobe and shut the door with a click of the latch.

Lily bit her lip and swallowed a chuckle, then gazed once more in the cheval glass. Her soft blue eyes clouded with doubt.

Lily's wedding to Julian Ash, the marquess of Chelton, required a bit of Dutch courage. After all, Lily had not planned to marry him. Not soon. Not ever. But she and he had been caught alone in his country house by his parents and Uncle Killian. The scene, Lily had recounted later, was ugly. Uncle Killian had demanded Julian wed her and quickly. Chelton, fortunately, was ready to do the right thing. Lily, unfortunately, had no say in the matter.

Avoiding a scandal was everyone's primary concern. Still, two gossip sheets had gotten whiff of the story and speculated "if the American Girl L—H— had urgent reasons to accept the proposal of a certain Marquess of C—. She skips her presentation at Court to marry. What can compel her?"

*What indeed.*

Marianne sought to cheer up Lily. "You are stunning, my dear. He's going to swoon at the sight of you."

"If he does, Papa will scoop him up and make him say the words." Lily leaned close. "Our Texas friends would call it a shotgun wedding."

"But it isn't. Because you didn't..." Marianne flashed a consoling look at her cousin.

Lily rolled her eyes. "Almost."

"Almost does not qualify. Now let me see that you are perfect." She circled her cousin and admired her in her elegant ensemble.

Fitted to Lily's curvaceous figure by the seamstresses at the House of Worth, her gown of white satin and tulle trailed a four-foot train. On her head was a little crown with a three-foot French Chantilly lace veil. In her hands, Lily held a nosegay of baby's breath and small white trumpet lilies.

"Shall we?" Lily nodded toward her door.

Marianne hurried behind her.

"That bit with the brandy was close," Lily whispered.

Marianne pulled open the door for her. "We'll know for sure if I find the bottle empty."

Lily caught back a chuckle. "Oh, you don't think she'd dare a drink, would you?"

"Why not?" She fussed with the folds of Lily's skirts. "Part of me does not trust her."

"Neither do I. And I've no cause to wonder why."

"Nora has other things to think about than swiping our brandy! As do you."

*And so do I.*

One look at suave duc de Remy in his formal black suit last night and she'd needed more than the wine at supper to soothe her nerves. Invited along with Julian, his parents and his sister Elanna to the dinner party, Andre had arrived in London yesterday and taken rooms at The Ritz across the street from the Hannifords' house.

Last night, he'd been placed far down the table and she'd had only a few polite exchanges with him before they'd gone in to dine. This morning, at the breakfast reception, she hoped for more. To merely look at his commanding figure sent ripples of excitement up her spine.

"Ready, finally, Lily?" Lily's eighteen-year-old sister sailed toward them in a rustle of Corinthian green chiffon that complemented her rich cinnamon hair and crystal blue eyes. Ada had arrived only yesterday in London with their older brother Pierce. This was her first time abroad and she was giddy with the opportunity to meet dukes and princes.

"Now or never," Lily said with a shiver of excitement.

"You look fabulous and I am pea green." She swept a hand

across her bodice and giggled. "I hope I can do as well. Just think. For you a marquess, one day to be the duke of Seton."

Lily knit her brows at her younger sister and Marianne understood Lily's reaction to Ada's belief she'd trapped the man. "I never set my sights on him."

"I didn't mean to anger you. Don't be cross with me, please." Ada squeezed Lily's hand.

"I'm not. I just want you to understand how I feel about this wedding."

"I do, honestly, Lily." Ada flashed apologetic eyes. "Still it's wonderful. A duchess in the family. And last night, Marianne, I saw the Prince d'Aumale focused on no one but you. How can a man be a duke and prince at the same time?"

"A discussion for later, Ada," Marianne said, hoping she could explain Andre's complicated ancestry with some accuracy—or better yet, not discuss it at all. "We must get our Lily married before Uncle Killian marches up and carries us down."

◌◌◌

"Come walk with me through the garden?" Andre had finally managed to sequester his lovely quarry from the crowd at Julian's and Lily's wedding. The ceremony had been short, but Marianne's social duties had kept her busy mingling with the guests. To some degree, he hadn't minded. The interim had allowed him to watch her, imbibe how she glided as she walked, how she laughed when amused, how she caught glimpses of him and spoke to him with longing her gorgeous green eyes. She filled his starving senses with her beauty. He had occupied himself well. How could he not when she looked so delicious in her wedding finery that he thought her a raspberry confection?

She looked up at him with those luminous eyes and he

calmed, more at peace than he'd been in weeks. She was here within his grasp and looking at him as if he were a pastry she could sink her teeth into. He yearned to find a place to let her do just that—and schooled his desires to caution.

"It's daylight and I've inspected the maze." His hope to lead her there flooded his mind. "I assure you, *ma cherie,* there are no benches on which I may seduce you."

She checked those milling about in the ballroom.

To him, everyone of the guests seemed well-occupied with champagne and *hors d'oeuvres*. Ada and Killian Hanniford conversed with Julian's parents, the duke and duchess of Seton. Most importantly, Lily and Julian talked quietly with each other, lost to those who swirled around them.

"I'm safe then?" Marianne tossed her head of bright curls and teased him with a saucy grin. "Very well. Yes, let's go."

He walked a step behind her as she led them from the party down the hall and out toward the rear gardens. A six-foot tall maze of yews wove through the green grass. Here and there rose bushes wafted in the gentle June breezes and lifted a subtle fragrance to the wind.

Pausing at two entrances to the maze, she chose the one with a long corridor of evergreens. She and he strolled side-by-side for a few minutes in silence. The peace of that mingled with his excitement to have her all to himself for a few moments.

"You look well," he ventured, the sight of her in the sunlight electric to his senses.

She reached out to brush the petals of one ripe rose. "I am, thank you. And you?"

"I slept better once I knew I would come here soon."

"*Et moi ouci,*" she whispered with sweet affection in her glance. "But I still do not have you to rights in my sketches."

His heart swelled at that news. In that alone lay reason to magnify their relationship. "Nor I you in my models."

She stopped and bent to inhale the fragrance of a red bud. Even turned in profile to him, she could not hide her nervousness. "How is your mother?"

"Quite well. Recovered from her recent malaise. In fact, she has retired to the country for the summer months."

"And did your cousin arrive to keep her company?"

"She did. And she was happy not to go to Paris. My cousin was born and raised in the Loire valley, where her family always grew fat goats and made mounds of fragrant cheese. She was never more happy than when she could cook all day and drink Sancerre from her own cellars every night. To remain there and be companion to my mother is Lucienne's fondest existence."

Marianne focused on his lips, her concentration stealing his own.

He had to stop to admire a clutch of red roses, their aroma swirling about him in a dance that spurred his desire for her.

She moved away from him, walking on. "When do you return to Paris?"

"I haven't decided." *First I wanted to gauge how well you received me. If you still think of me or wish to be in my arms.*

"I see." She shook back her hair, the wealth of the curls heavy and drooping from her elaborate coiffure down around her slim neck. She appeared valiant...and hesitant. "Have you business here in London?"

"One matter." *Only you.* "I remain as long as I see fit. And you? Will your family come to Paris soon?"

"All of us go to Paris the day after tomorrow, yes. Now that Lily is married and Ada and Pierce are here too, we have much to do there."

That surprised and pleased him. Julian had written to him about his sister marrying Carbury and Andre had wondered how that would affect the Hanniford clan's travel plans. "Will you not attend Elanna's wedding in a few weeks?"

"We do and we'll return here for that. But Pierce and Ada have only arrived from America yesterday and just in time for today's wedding. Still Ada has no proper wardrobe and needs to brush up on her manners and her French."

"With Comtesse Chaumont, I imagine," he added with a grin.

"Who else?" she joked. And then she fell silent, her eyes darting here and there, looking self-conscious and at a loss for words.

Elated, he had no such problems. "I will go home to Paris tomorrow."

The smile she sent him could have warmed him for the next year.

He wanted to crush her to him then but steeled himself. Over the next few months, he must cultivate Herculean powers of restraint not to seduce her. "I will call upon you in the Rue Haussmann and you shall come to tea to my home."

She beamed at him. "You must invite Ada and Pierce. Even Uncle Killian."

"If you wish."

"I do, but you must know that I may not have much time to receive you or to call," she said, her blonde brows knitting as she fretted about that. "Ada has attended finishing school, but she's not as fond of being 'polished' as some girls. Uncle Killian insists she work harder and so I cannot promise you that I'll be readily available to you."

He clasped his hands behind his back. "I will invite you often. All of you. Come with them or come alone and bring your maid. I care not. But do come."

"I want to," she said with hope emanating from her.

"I wish you to visit me in Tours. At our chateau. All of you, of course."

"Oh!" The compliment swept across her features, quickly followed by the terror it inspired. "Uncle Killian will be honored."

"I want you to be honored."

She swallowed.

Andre could not help himself. He picked up her hand and kissed her smooth skin. Beneath his lips, she was warm, fragile and quaking like a baby bird. He hoped it was joy that rippled through her. "I want you to meet my mother."

She frowned, snatched her hand away and looked at every rose, every leaf, everywhere but into his eyes. "That is kind of you, but we need not be so formal."

He would not answer until she looked at him once more. And when she no longer eluded him, he said very definitely, "We do need to be. My mother requests I introduce you."

"But—" She shook her head, confused and yet a small light in her eyes said she was also complimented. "You told her about me?"

"I did."

"That was kind but you and I are mere acquaintances."

He snorted in laughter. "We are more than that, *ma belle*, and you know it. Give over and enjoy this, will you, darling? We're to have fun. And I suspect that you have had precious little of that in your life. Am I right?"

She gave a nod. "You are."

"There you have it. So." He began to walk once more around a tall green corner to another little cove of greenery and leaving her to scamper after him. When she was beside him, he said, "In Paris, I will come around and take you to luncheon along the Seine. I'll feed you snails and razor clams."

She made a face.

"I'll have my chef pack a hamper and we will nibble Roquefort and baguettes in the Tuileries gardens. The next day, I'll bring round my landau and we'll ride in the Bois de Boulogne. I'll bring champagne. You like it, as I recall, very much."

"Ohh, yes."

He clamped his jaw, so tempted to kiss her until she begged for his bed. "I'll arrange for a night at the opera. We'll go late."

She clapped her hands. "As one must."

He inclined his head. "We'll have Ada and Pierce."

"Chaumont, too."

"Naturally. And afterward, I will persuade Pierce to help me escort all of you to take in a certain cabaret in Montmartre."

She giggled.

He grinned. "I promise to make you laugh like that often, *ma chou*."

"*Chou*? What is that?"

He chucked her under the chin. "My cabbage."

"Grim. I'd hope you could call me something more elegant."

She was joking, but he was nodding and arching a brow. "I can think of a few terms of endearment I might employ."

She pretended a look of dark green reproof. "Nothing scandalous."

He feigned innocence and crossed his arms. "Not at all."

"Good. Because I like cabarets."

"Do you? How delightful." He offered her his arm to continue their stroll. "Tell me more."

"I like to sing."

"On key?" he asked with severity.

She pinched his arm. "One always hopes so. But I sing only in the lower middle C octaves. I am no coloratura soprano."

"With that voice of yours like good brandy, *ma cherie*, you could never sing an aria. So enlighten me, what do you like to sing?"

"German drinking songs."

He choked on laughter. "What? How could you?"

"In Texas, we have many Germans. They like their beer and they like to clink glasses as they do. I tended a few soldiers during the war who would try to sing to pass the time or ease their pain. Do you sing, *Monsieur le duc?*"

"Quite well, in fact."

She wiggled her brows. "I long to hear you."

"And you shall in the Rue des Abbesess."

"We shall be a scandal," she said on a whisper as she leaned on his arm and nestled to him. "And Uncle Killian will find out—"

"He'll never learn."

She scoffed. "You dream, *Monsieur le duc*, if you think—"

"I will bribe Pierce if I must. But I doubt it. After all, would your uncle not demand his son maintain some kind of decorum while in the city of sin?"

Despite the fact that she laughed, she shook her head. "My uncle has friends. He'll hear of it."

Andre touched his fingertip to her nose. "Never worry. He'll read nothing because soon after we will all return here for Lady Elanna's wedding to the earl of Carbury."

"Hmm. You've done a lot of planning."

"I have." Pivoting away, he led her onward. It was that or kiss her until he raised her skirts here and took her like a half-starved boy. "You and I will be together for those festivities as well. I understand there is to be a ball the night before and I plan to waltz with you."

"Waltz?" Her heart was in her eyes. "Oh, you waltz?"

He paused, his body so hard he could not take another step. This need of his to be a gentleman, he realized ruefully, might ensure he was permanently aroused until the hour he could sink inside her. He had to make light of this and arched a wicked brow. "*You* do waltz, I presume?"

Sunlight washed her in a brilliant palette of yellows and she sparkled so his eyes hurt to gaze at her. "I do. That is, I haven't in years and years."

"Then when you come to my house in Paris, we will practice in my ballroom."

"I used to be quite agile at waltzing," she said, breathless as he'd never seen her.

He shoved his hands in his trouser pockets lest he use them to grab her and kiss her senseless. "You shall dance on air with me, *Madame*. As will I."

She stepped toward him, her palm to his heart. "Andre—"

The warmth of her hand, the need in her eyes killed his noble intentions. He tipped up her chin and—

Within the maze, they heard muffled voices. Angry ones.

Andre froze, then pulled her into his arms and lead her into a small nook in the shrubbery. Like a cat, she snuggled against him and he was, for this minute, content to hold her.

"You cannot do that!" a man said.

"Yes, I can," a woman replied. "If only you had the nerve to allow me."

"You're mad."

"That's Pierce," Marianne raised her face to whisper to Andre's ear.

"Give it to me," the woman insisted. "You don't think I have the nerve."

"Elanna," Marianne told him.

"*Oui*, Andre recognized Julian's sister's voice.

"They'll know you smoked, my lady," Pierce pointed out. "The fumes will remain in your clothes."

"You said you'd give me anything if I smiled. You didn't like my sad face. Well, then, Mr. Hanniford, can you live up to your own promises or not?"

"I didn't promise, my lady."

"Men," Elanna fumed. All the same. You shouldn't tease women with temptations to assist them, sir, if you won't follow through."

Pierce scoffed. "I wouldn't be praised for it by your fiancé."

"Ah, but he's not here, is he?"

"Just where is he today?" Pierce demanded.

"He had a problem with some tenants on his estate and he had to go down to Kent. I do not miss him."

Sucking in air, Marianne curled closer into Andre's arms. He put his lips to her temple. She was so soft, so lush. He wanted more of her like this, willing in his embrace.

"Well, another time, another place, my lady," Pierce said, "but I will not surrender my pipe to you here. The rest of the party would know you'd been out here with me and ridicule—"

"What do you care?" Elanna shot back.

Marianne stiffened in Andre's arms.

"I must care, my lady, for your reputation."

"You Americans don't care a fig for that."

"But we do. We don't go about ruining young ladies for no reason. Simply to allow her to smoke a pipe."

"Really? What would you ruin a lady's reputation for?"

"Far more than smoking a pipe," Pierce said, laughing. "Let's go in."

Fearing what came next and hating eavesdropping on the two of them, Andre tugged at Marianne's hand. He'd lead her inside away from this.

But Marianne did not budge.

"No," Elanna shot back. "You won't let me smoke so give me something else I want."

"Fine. What would that be?"

"A kiss."

"Ha! No."

"Why not?"

"Because I—"

The rest was lost in the sounds of rustling skirts and sighing kisses.

"No more," Pierce said at last, his deep voice gruff with desire. "I'm leaving."

"Oh," Elanna declared with anger, "do *please* let me chase you off!"

"Don't be foolish. Wait a few minutes," Pierce barked at her. "Then follow."

Elanna cursed at him. "Wretched man." And she stalked off, the sounds of her feet along the gravel punctuating her outrage.

"Oh, Christ," Pierce moaned and moved off more deeply into the maze.

A minute passed as Marianne rested her cheek on Andre's frock coat. She was quiet, still.

He ran his fingers along the fine line of her spine.

Presently, she sighed and pressed closer to him, her arms tight around his waist. "Elanna does not want to marry. Not the man she's engaged to."

Andre drove his lips into her fragrant hair. "That's very sad, but it does happen. Occasionally, between husband and wife relationships improve."

"I doubt it can between those two, although I can't tell you why I feel that way."

"Carbury. I didn't care for him when we met the night in the Opera Garnier."

"The same. I've been in company with him since then and I find him oppressive."

"He seemed intent on her from the start," Andre said, recalling how the older man poured over the young sister of his friend, Julian.

"Lily says she must marry him because there are financial needs. The Setons are not able to support her with more Seasons or much else."

"As if she'd need such formal exposure. She is lovely and charming when she's not hunted."

"Or run to ground like an animal," Marianne said with a shiver.

"Come inside. We'll have more champagne, *oui*?" He gave her a tiny hug, then stepped away from her. "We will talk and laugh and plan our walk in Paris. In three days' time, don't you think?"

Marianne halted, impish and tugging him around to face her. "*Monsieur le duc*, you mean to tell me you didn't bring me out here to kiss me?"

He shook his head once. "No, *ma belle*. I did not."

She was crestfallen. "Why not?"

He smiled faintly and pushed a silken blonde tendril of hair over her ear. "I intend to kiss you, darling, but not here. Not in England."

Her heartbroken expression gutted him and pleased him. "What are you doing to me?"

He put a finger to her lower lip and rolled it down. The lush beauty of it spurred his body to painful need. "When next I kiss you, my Marianne, I pray we have hours to explore every part of each other. Lips and hands, breasts and hips. More. Much more."

She caught a breath and hope spread like golden sunshine into her green eyes. She put two fingers to his lips and he kissed them away.

"Holding you here for these minutes has proven to me what I suspected. I cannot touch you and be content with only a small part of you. Your lips, lovely as they are, are the icing on a beautiful creation. I yearn for all of you."

"Andre, that is—"

"Madness?" That's what he expected her to say. To demure, to postpone, to deny if she dared, the inevitable.

"Not that. No."

"What then?" he asked her tenderly, not expecting any affirmation of their attraction. Women did not do that. Not women of Marianne's status. Statements of desire were not ones taught in any etiquette class.

"I yearn for every part of you, as well."

His heart exploded in his chest, hopes of her surrendering to him blending with her agreement that indeed they would make love. Stunned that her statement could assuage his impatience, he pulled at her hand and wound it around his arm. "Come inside. We begin our journey toward friendship. Good friends, who understand the other. Who come to each other for all the benefits that friends share."

*So that soon, you can come to me for all the passions that lovers share.*

# CHAPTER 6

**June 27, 1878**
**Seton House**
**London**

"Would you like another champagne?" Andre bent near to ask Marianne. The Setons' London ballroom was a crush of society, every lady in their finest satins and each man in the stark black beauty of their formal suits and white cravats. None, however, seemed as arresting as the Duc de Remy, her Andre.

"*Merci beaucoup* but we are waltzing soon and I've a care not to step on your toes."

He drained his own glass, put it aside and chided her with an arced brow. "*Ma chou*, you've never stepped on my toes."

"No. As I recall, I tripped over them."

"You're finished with that," he assured her. "As we should soon be finished with the formalities here."

Stepping to one side, he indicated the approach of the

Duke of Seton and his wife, the Duchess. The couple took to the center of the marbled expanse of their ballroom and offered a nod toward their daughter Elanna and her bridegroom, soon to be her husband, the earl of Carbury.

A more mis-matched pair Marianne had not seen in years. *Not since my own wedding, in fact.* Carbury, since she'd last seen him at the Opera, was suddenly running to fat, jowly and paunched. His predatory nature surfaced with his eagle-eyed vigilance, stalking his intended wife minute by minute. Elanna, twenty and impossibly lovely with her slim form and excellent carriage and pile of rosewood hair, once warm and sweet, had, since her engagement, become a shrew.

The duke introduced the two to polite applause. Carbury, taking his due, gave a slight incline of his head in thanks, while Elanna offered only a lowering of her long lashes and a stiff lip.

Marianne might have once thought that Elanna's demeanor was the norm for well-brought up daughters of the English aristocracy. Since she'd overheard Elanna's encounter with Pierce in the Piccadilly garden, however, she tended toward the belief that this future bride had little to smile about. She smarted at her station in life and hated the horrendous bargain she was about to make tomorrow morning at ten o'clock.

The duke glanced at the orchestra and the maestro struck up a Viennese melody. The two couples took their partners and led off the dancing, round the chalked floor. Of the four, the Setons appeared to be relishing their turn more than Carbury who took small steps and huffed, while Elanna placed her lifeless hand on his shoulder and gazed off as if she saw hell in the distance.

"I fear for her," Andre whispered as he turned away from the sight of them.

"As do I. I wish I could reassure myself there's some saving grace for the two of them but I doubt it."

"Julian is furious that she accepted him. He wanted her to wait. He wished to give her at least another Season to find someone she might care for, but he was too late. She had already committed herself."

"I know the Setons have financial issues." Marianne hated talking of such sensitive matters, but she and Andre had passed the point of politesse. They were friends. Over the past two weeks in Paris, they had passed each afternoon and many evenings in each other's company.

The day they'd arrived in Paris, he had come to call and brought an armful of white roses, the color of new butter. Though he said they were for all the ladies in the house, he'd told her the next day when he called for tea that they reminded him of the color of her hair. "Pale and silken," he'd murmured when Ada had left the salon for a few minutes.

Nor was that his only gift or his only compliment. He came the next day, and as promised, he'd arrived in his own landau, his coachman at the reins. Pierce and Killian had claimed a business meeting but Ada had come along with them to the gardens of the Tuileries. Andre's chef had packed a basket with charcuterie, cheeses and breads, white wine and for dessert, macarons from Ladurée.

Seducing Marianne with flowers and food and picnics in the gardens were preludes to his arrival the next day and the next, this time in a sleek red lacquer barouche. Off they went, his coachman at the reins, two matched grey geldings trotting onward, Ada next to her and Andre opposite them. The day was sunny without a cloud in the perfect blue sky as they made their way to the Bois de Boulogne, a glorious expanse of greenery and water, rocks and fauna in the middle of Paris. Ada by now was tuned to the attraction between Andre and her. Throwing all her social training to the winds, Ada remarked that she thought them both charming in their restraint.

But the drives, the picnics, the scenery, the food, the wine were nothing to compare to the glory of going to Andre's Paris home in the Rue de Rivoli and waltzing in his own ballroom.

Ada, impressionable and gushing over the opulence of his house, had clapped her hands and sighed at the sight of the vermeil-covered ballroom walls and the profusion of crystal chandeliers.

"How do you dust all that?" she'd asked him, her gaze turned up to admire the glittering lights dangling from the ceiling. "Forgive me. I would guess *you* don't dust it."

He'd laughed. "I know the three downstairs maids take two days each month to accomplish it."

"Worth it," Ada concluded, hands on her hips, gazing at the lights.

"I wonder, Remy," Pierce said as he bent to examine the wainscotting. "How old is this house?"

Andre looked pained. "Would you like the long or short version?"

"Long, definitely."

"Oh, Pierce," Ada complained and extended a hand toward the four musicians Andre had hired for the afternoon. "You will pre-occupy the Duc de Remy with that for hours. Can you not come another day or at least wait until after we waltz?"

Pierce flapped his arms. "I bow to necessity. I'll ask you for the detailed version soon. I think city planning such as your Baron Haussmann did depends on saving gems of private dwellings, too. Wouldn't you say?"

"I do, Pierce," Andre said with a smile, "I am at your disposal for another day. Choose it."

"Thank you, Remy. Tomorrow, perhaps?"

"At ten o'clock?"

"Agreed." Pierce stepped toward Ada. "When you are ready, I am."

"Finally." Ada rolled her eyes at him. "Do know, *Monsieur,* that my brother has never favored dancing."

Pierce shook his head. "Not with you, my pet. But I am improved. I'll show you."

Marianne struggled to quell her laughter. "These two, Remy, have bated each other since childhood. She loves to dance. He loves to torment her and usually challenges her to make up for his intended clumsiness."

"Today we shall all be superb." Andre lifted his chin and spoke to the musicians upon the dais. "We can begin, eh?"

She licked her lips, put one hand to his shoulder and another in his own and when the musicians began their tune, off she and Andre went round the long pink marbled floor. Outside, the day was grey. Clouds were heavy and the air thick. Inside, the room was cool, brightly lit and sparkling from the refracted rays of crystals in the chandeliers.

Most delightful of all were the lights in Andre's eyes as his gaze caressed her and told her tales of charms to come. In his arms, she was weightless. In his care, she was a creature of the air. He was graceful and decisive. She was flexible, agile, well-tutored by his instructions. Enchanted by his devotion to improving her skills on the floor. Rediscovering that she could be gay, frivolous and dance in a man's embrace and be proud of her conquest, eager to hold him.

They'd practiced for an hour or more that day. And twice more, they'd gone to his home. Once solely to feed Pierce's desire to learn more about the house. The day before they'd all left Paris to travel to London for Elanna's wedding, they'd practiced again with Andre's musicians in attendance.

Ada marched up to them as they waited for Lily and Julian to take the floor with the rest of his family.

"Honestly, will you two show them how well you practiced or stand here all night?"

Andre gazed down at her. The two of them had become fast friends, Andre treating her almost as irreverently as Pierce did. "We must find you a beau, Ada."

She waved her fan and sighed. "Please don't bother. I haven't seen anyone here who in the least appeals."

"I see someone who might," he said as he raised his chin to acknowledge someone across the Seton's ballroom. "At least try to talk to him. Then Marianne and I can leave you here."

"Fine. Introduce me and then shoo."

The tall, blond elegant man who joined them resembled da Vinci's David. His jaw was square. His eyes liquid gold. His shoulders broad. His hands massive. His attire impeccable. His demeanor, attention, polite. His burnished hair perfectly combed back from his high forehead. Yet when he spoke, Marianne was shocked. The man stammered.

"He virtually quakes when he talks to her," she whispered to Andre as they left the Ada to muddle on with him.

"Lord Henry Drake is noteworthy." Andre led her out to the edge of the circle. "He's the second son of the Duke of Stratton."

"That earns him favor," Marianne chuckled as she placed her hand in Andre's. "But only with Uncle Killian. Ada is bored to tears."

Andre slid his hand around her waist, his long fingers strong and insistent on her back. "Perhaps she can teach him a thing or two about spontaneity."

"You know her." Marianne laughed. "She won't take the time."

"He wants to enter politics."

She blinked. "He's devilishly good looking. An arc angel, really. But to win votes, he'll need a social reformation."

"She could inspire him."

"Or shock him and leave him where he stands."

Andre frowned. "Harry's loss. Shall we dance, *ma cherie?*"

He led her off and the world opened up for her. They'd danced in his ballroom and he'd held her like this before. But this in front of others was so different from ever other time she'd danced with him. She was his partner, a natural element of him, and he of her. He took her into the turns gracefully, lithe as a feather and she floated, as enchanted with him in the middle of a dance floor as in private beside him on a blanket on the lawn near the cascading waterfall in the Bois.

The others in the room fell from view. Only he existed for her. Only the music lifted them up and sent them on their way. Even in the faster movement of the chase, she was his, mesmerized by his command of her body. Thrilled by his desire for her.

All too soon the orchestra stopped and the two of them stood facing each other, breathless, smiling like clowns at each other.

"Come for a ride with me now alone."

She opened her mouth, wishing she might. "They'll notice we've gone."

"Please." He held her hand, his fingers urgent on her palm.

She nodded. "We must tell my uncle."

"Darling, you are old enough—"

"And wise enough to tell him so that he's prepared for the gossip."

Andre sighed and nodded. "We'll go now."

Marianne glanced around to find Uncle Killian in deep conversation with Ada and a young man whom Ada had met before and dismissed as a bore.

"Yes, let's."

But the gentleman asked Ada to dance and led her away.

"I'm stunned she accepted him," Killian said to Andre and her.

"Can she bear him for five minutes?" Marianne asked, as Ada went into Lord Gerald Winton's embrace looking like a sleep walker.

"When I came upon them," Killian said, "she was giving him what-for about whatever he'd said about Apache Indians."

"What does he know about our Indians?" Marianne asked her uncle.

"Not much." Killian shrugged. "I gather he must've said something about indigenous people needing an understanding of economics. She was setting him straight about how some tribes of Apaches did raise their own crops and traded farm goods."

Andre and she chuckled.

The three of them watched, glued to the sight of handsome Lord Winton sweeping Ada into the line of those on the floor.

"One good thing, the man can dance," Killian said, shock on his face.

"Ada looks like she's as surprised as we are," Andre offered.

"If he can't converse, it won't save him," Marianne said.

"He'd better not damage her reputation," Killian said. "She'd not tolerate the wallflower chairs."

"I doubt she'll have problems, sir," Andre said.

Killian snorted. "There must be a few Englishmen who can dance *and* talk. Maybe even a man who can joke. Ada needs a man with wit."

Andre turned around to face her uncle. "Sir, this evening I take Marianne home in my carriage."

Killian's silver eyes shot to hers. "You know what you're doing."

"We've come to know each other well, Uncle."

He stared into Andre's eyes. "Remy, I ask that you honor the commitment you made to me."

Marianne blushed.

"I will, Mr. Hanniford."

◌⑅◌

Andre glanced at Marianne as she left him to join Lily and Ada. The guests for Elanna Ash and the earl of Carbury's wedding milled about the duke and duchess of Seton's drawing room. Andre had eyes only for Marianne who looked particularly luscious this morning in a gown of yellow and ivory. Last night, alone with him in his hired carriage, she'd been more appealing, her lips ripe strawberry temptations. Though he had kissed her only once, that was all he would permit himself. Playful and yearning, she tried for more and placed her mouth on his even as she begged for more kisses.

"I cannot do it, *ma cherie*." He'd pushed her away but nestled her against his chest, safely in his arms. "You return to Paris in a few days and then we shall see."

She'd jerked away, frustrated and peeved. "Maybe you should go back to your mistress."

He barked in laughter. "She is gone for good."

"I would fight for you if I were sophisticated enough."

"Come here." He'd pulled her back into his embrace, settled her securely there and kissed her fragrant hair. "No more talk of other women, *s'il vous plait*. They are not your equal. You are the only one I wish to hold."

*The only one I wish to keep.* Gazing at her in her wedding finery, he thought he saw contentment in her demeanor. Her cheeks were pink. Her green eyes danced. She radiated happiness. That warmed him, inspired him to thoughts of what he would propose to her once they were both in Paris again.

"I say, you look chipper." Julian approached him.

Andre noted the weariness in his friend's eyes. "Better than you, I dare say. What's wrong?"

Julian inhaled sharply and indicated with a tip of his head his sister who spoke with her groom. The newly married couple stood nose-to-nose hotly whispering. "An hour into this arrangement and we have challenges."

"We could intervene. But to what end?" Andre put a hand to Julian's arm. "She's smart. She'll find a way to deal with him."

"Not if he won't compromise."

"The mark of any sound relationship," Andre offered.

"What I don't understand is that we've known Carbury for years. I saw him with his first wife and I never suspected he could be such a bully."

Andre considered the woman who had changed his own thinking about women...and marriage. The very thought of waking up each morning to see her, touch her, laugh with her filled his body with adolescent expectation and his heart with comfort. "Some people change us."

Julian's gaze turned to consider his own bride of three weeks. "Very true. And for the better."

"You're happy. You wear it like a glove." Andre lifted his glass to toast his friend.

"Delightfully shocked too." Julian arched his dark brows. "But I'm here to discuss your relationship."

"Ah. Sent by your father-in-law, I assume."

"He's worried about Marianne's reputation."

*Was the millionaire worried about his niece's image or his own?* "I have reassured him twice. What more can I do?"

"I understand you have sent your mistress packing."

"You hear correctly. Is there a question in your statement?"

Julian smiled at him. "You know there is."

Andre's mood fell. "I court her. She is reluctant. I move slowly because I must, not because I wish it."

"I would venture that I know what that challenge is."

"Oh?" Andre considered the sparkling wine in his goblet.

"Lily tells me Marianne never speaks of her husband."

"And there you have it. My challenge is to chase him from her mind. I see before me a woman who wishes to emerge from her old life. But that is as strong as marble, and I see her as she is meant to be free in her fullness. Effervescent. Gay. I wish her to emerge and she wants it too. She chips away at her prison and I help her remove her facade. I show her how to trust me. And come to me. One day soon, please God." He drained his glass of wine.

Julian marveled at him. "I never thought to see you fall in love."

"Nor I." *And I'm impatient to enjoy her.* "Not to worry. After tomorrow, we go to Paris. The Hannifords and I. Next week, Marianne and I—"

"I will not, I tell you!" a woman yelled.

All in the room froze. The silence turned everyone to ice.

"You cannot force me."

Julian and Andre pivoted toward the sound of Elanna addressing Carbury, each word a bomb.

"But I will, my dear." Carbury tried to cover his sneer and took his bride by the wrist.

Hatred on her lips, she yanked free. She clenched her fists, triumph in the tilt of her head as she marched away.

Pierce came abreast of Lily. "Bastard. I could kill him."

"Stop!" Lily caught his arm. "Dear god," she whispered to her brother, "don't move."

Carbury's eyes bulged from his head as he whirled on Pierce.

Julian stepped between the earl and Pierce. "Come now."

"Nerves, nerves." The duchess of Seton fluttered among

them, her lips quivering with restrained anger and chagrin. "Nothing more. Do play on," she encouraged the cellist who had been giving forth some Bach or Beethoven.

Carbury glared at Julian. Straightening his waistcoat, he reddened. "I'll see to my bride."

Julian turned aside.

The duke hastened behind Carbury, muttering to himself.

"Forgive me, Andre," Julian said and followed his sister, parents and Carbury out the far door.

Andre stepped to join Marianne and her three cousins. Pierce fumed but the three women appeared stunned.

Marianne took his arm. "This marriage was never going to work."

Ada glanced from Marianne to Lily. "They never liked each other?"

"Like?" Pierce gave a joyless laugh. "She loathes him."

With a flick of her eyes, Lily warned her brother and sister to say no more.

"Should you go?" Marianne asked Lily as they watched the duchess scurry from the ballroom.

"Do not." Remy stood beside them, his attention riveted on the vacant doorway. The duchess would cringe at the interference, jealous of her reputation as she was.

Down the marbled corridor from some far room, voices rose and rushed toward the reception in echoes of hate. Male, female, high-pitched, accusatory.

"I'll get the butler," murmured Remy to the assembled group. "I know him well. He must close all the doors. Excuse me."

Out in the hall, the butler and two footmen stood gazing down the hall where the others had disappeared. Paralyzed in horror, the servants swung their attention to Remy.

"Let's close the doors," he told them.

"*Monsieur le duc?*" The butler looked fevered. "Shall we offer more champagne?"

"The doors, please. The guests need not hear this row."

"No, *Monsieur*." The portly butler shooed the two footmen to the task. They went so quickly, they were slamming the doors as they passed them. Farther down the hall, the screaming of insults and crying rent the air. Closed doors would not diminish the din.

Remy turned on his heel for the drawing room. But as he entered, a crash of china and a woman's scream tore through the house.

With a wide-eyed look at Marianne, Remy pivoted toward the sounds.

Julian ran toward him. "Come, come quickly."

At a jog, he followed Julian down the corridor. At the entrance, he came to a halt. The duke of Seton lay upon the bright red Axminster carpet, shards of a Ming vase lying about him, his arms out, jaw slack.

"No, no." Julian knelt beside the body of his father. He pressed two fingers to his brow and picked up his wrist. "Oh, hell."

"You did this," the duchess seethed, rushing toward her daughter, hands out to grab her and shake her.

Elanna eluded her mother. Eyes blazing with fear and superiority, she barked. "Touch me and you will have the same from me."

"You killed him! You ungrateful twit."

"Stop it," Julian yelled at them. "Remy, get me Lily and Marianne."

He spun for the hall and the drawing room. He found them standing precisely where he'd left them. "Come quickly. They need you."

Pierce sprang forward too, but Remy grabbed his arms. "Don't move."

"What's happened?" Pierce demanded of him.

"The duke has had a stroke."

Minutes later, Marianne and Lily gazed at each other over the body of the Duke of Seton.

Marianne shook her head.

Lily gazed up at her husband, tears in her eyes. "Your father is dead."

# CHAPTER 7

**July 1878**
**Rue Laffitte**
**Paris**

"I'll go across the street to the cafe for a cup of tea while you finish your selections, Ada."

"Oh, do. Then I won't feel so badly that I take so long to decide," Ada urged Marianne. In her corset and petticoats, her cousin turned this way and that in the mirror as she held up a bolt of pale pink taffeta to her cheek. "I can stand for the measurements by myself. Francine and Ezzie can advise me on the new rage in negligees. Can't you?"

Marianne caught Ada's wink at Francine Lang. Francine was a flibberty-gibbet, a spoiled American debutante with an angel's face and a wizard's dark eyes, who focused on nothing but men and how to catch one quickly. Ezzie Moore—Esmerelda by birth—was another American in Paris, a debutante brought by her parents to buy a husband. Both girls had attended the same finishing school as Ada and had come abroad a few weeks ago with their families. But plain-faced Ezzie hadn't a clue about what color looked good on her let alone what fabric. While the other girl in the dressing room, Francine Lang, knew little that was good for her.

Ezzie was harmless.

Francine, however, was not to be trusted. She, more than Ada, had little interest in the finer points of decorum. Worse, she was often rude, cutting into others to speak over them. The girl, who was the daughter of a Manhattan department store owner, had arrived in Paris in June with her mother. That woman, once a salesgirl in her husband's Fifth Avenue store, had polished up her manners and pushed Francine at every eligible man between twenty and eighty.

"I'll wait for you there, Ada. Good afternoon, Ezzie. Francine. We'll see you at nine this evening."

They all bid her *adieu,* Francine practically frothing to get rid of her. Ada looked like she'd just swallowed laughing gas.

*They're planning something.*

Irritated that Ada would risk her future on a lark with her friends, Marianne made her way down the stairs to the foyer and out to the bustling boulevard. On the cobbled footpath, she snapped open her parasol and hurried across the boulevard. Her minutes alone were few. Her minutes with Andre these past three weeks even fewer. Plus, Madame Chaumont had been ill, out of reach, since they'd returned. As a result, Marianne was on duty, in charge, round the clock, seeing to Ada's fittings, her etiquette and language lessons and the tours of Paris meant to educate Ada in provisioning a noble household.

Each day, Ada objected to the rounds. She abhorred the cathedral at St. Denis. "Too many statues of dead kings."

She found the tour of the *Sèvres* china factory unnecessary.

"Why do I have to know how it's made? I'll just buy what I like."

She cancelled her French tutor three times last week, proclaiming he was a bore. "Forever talking about verbs."

In addition, she was becoming petulant and argumentative. Though she'd always been impetuous, she'd never been so whiny.

Three days ago, the morning after a supper party for twelve at Rue Haussmann with Ezzie and her mother plus the three Langs in attendance, Uncle Killian had summoned Ada and Marianne to his library.

"I don't approve of Francine Lang," he said from behind his massive desk. "Never have."

"Oh, Daddy, she's just fun."

"Ada, she's a disaster. She laughs like a loon. Hasn't learned a lick of French. Chatters of nothing but silks and diamonds. To say nothing of her blasted father's dry goods store. I won't have you associating with her in private. Marianne needs to be with you whenever she's about."

Marianne smarted at the task. They'd been in Paris three weeks and though Andre had been to supper twice and tea often, she hadn't had any opportunity to talk with him alone and didn't expect she would any time soon.

Ada gaped at her father. "But Francine expects it. Needs me. Her mother is so *gauche*."

"Exactly." Killian peered over his glasses at his youngest daughter. "I won't have you destroying your good name."

"You mean yours," Ada tossed back at him.

"Don't be impertinent."

Ada bristled. "We all know Lily had to marry her duke. I'll bet any day we hear her announcement that she's *enciente*—"

"Enough!" Killian slammed a hand to his desktop. "It's worked out well. She cares for him and he for her. If you continue with that Lang girl and get yourself in a pickle, I can't guarantee I be able to get you out."

"What if I don't want to get married?"

Marianne shut her eyes. The only thing Ada had ever spoken of was finding a beau who adored her. She'd declared herself "in love" so often, she might wind up with ten husbands.

"Don't want…?" His face turned red in anger. "And what would you do instead?"

"Perfect my poker."

Killian shook his head. "That'll take a few years."

"I'll go to Texas and—"

"Ride herd on cattle?"

"I can do that," she said, crossing her arms.

"Oh, my girl, as if that was ever your preference. Go to your fittings. Call upon Esmerelda Moore. Ask her to tea."

"Oh, Daddy, Ezzie is so dull."

He rose up from his chair, put two hands to his desk and leaned toward her. "Then help her become exciting."

Ada jutted out her chin. "And if I won't?"

"Then you will return to Texas. You'll herd cattle with the *vaqueros*."

"You wouldn't!"

"Try me."

"I'll run away."

"Not without any money, you won't."

That set her back in her chair. "I have to have some fun."

Her uncle turned to Marianne. "Find her some."

"Sir?" Marianne was surprised at this request. Since the family had returned from London and the funeral of Lily's father-in-law, the Duke of Seton, all the Hannifords had refrained from balls and *soirées* out of respect. As distant relatives, Uncle Killian had decreed they didn't have to observe a year of mourning. Not in Paris, certainly. Plus he had business to conduct that could not wait.

"How about an exhibition?" he asked Marianne.

"Oh, Daddy, I do hate the Louvre. That's what Marianne likes. All those paintings and sculptures. May I snore?"

Marianne set her jaw.

"Be kind." Killian gazed at his daughter with a hint of humor. "Besides, I bet you'll appreciate naked statues."

"Well," Ada said, tossing her head to and fro, "now that you mention it."

"Marianne, take her up to the Butte. Show her the view of the city and how the builders have progressed on Sacre Coeur."

"A church, Daddy?" Ada groaned.

"When the Duc de Remy comes to tea today, I'll ask him to take you both to Montmartre to one of those summer balls."

"Oh, Daddy." Ada glowed in expectation. "And Francine and Ezzie, too?"

"Very well. Maybe it'll wean the wildness out of all of you."

"I know the duke doesn't want to dance with me especially." Ada beamed at him with a sly look at Marianne. "But if he agrees, I'm ready now."

Andre had promptly decided that Ada, her two friends and Marianne needed their outing immediately. Tonight, he'd bring a friend and the two men would escort the four women to the *Bal du moulin de la Galette*.

"*Bonjour, Madame*," the waiter broke her reverie. She indicated she'd like a table outside on the terrace under the awning. From there, she could watch who came in and out of the front door to *Madame Rousseau's* lingerie house. Ada possessed some judgment, but she could be easily led by the likes of Francine. Ezzie was just an innocent, led to any escapade, by her own desires to keep the other girls' friendship. Marianne had to keep an eye on all of them.

"*Bonjour, Monsieur.*" She closed her little parasol and followed him to the table. At once, she returned the menu to the man without looking at it. "*Je voudrais commander du vin blanc, s'il vous plait.*"

"*Une moment, Garçon.*"

Marianne gazed up into the tanned face of Andre Claude Marceau. He was grinning at her, handsome and dashing in his casual day attire of white shirt, azure linen waistcoat and tailored navy suit.

"Bring us a bottle of Veuve Clicquot and an *hors d'oeuvre* of *crab en croûte*." He swept off his straw hat. "May I join you, *Madame?*"

Instead of the chair opposite her, she indicated the one beside her. She'd like him as near as propriety might allow. "I'd welcome the superb company. A diversion from my normal diet."

"Too much of one thing is bad for one's digestion."

"Or one's sanity." She laughed, aware two ladies at the next table stared at Andre and whispered behind their fans. With a new commission for the City of Paris and articles about him in newspapers, he was famous. Invited everywhere, he declined most invitations and told all he focused on his work. But he came almost daily to Rue Haussmann for tea. And with hot regard in his velvet blue eyes, he courted her with every word he uttered.

He took his seat, his hand briefly brushing hers as he sat. His generous mouth curved up in humor. "I happened to pay a call on my banker and saw you emerge from Madame Rousseau's. Is chiffon the fabric of the season?"

She rolled her eyes. "I haven't the foggiest clue. But I have learned that rose is not the best color for a girl with sallow skin."

He grimaced. "You're having a terrible day."

"Weeks, *Monsieur*. Weeks."

"*Je suis désolé.*"

"Ha, I'm sorry too." She examined his marvelous face, the contours so bold, so balanced. Every time she saw him, he became the embodiment of masculinity. "Suddenly I do feel better."

He leaned close and in the moment, she caught a whiff of his cologne. Fresh and subtle, the hint of lime and some other manly fragrance wafted through her senses. She relaxed in his company, her nerves unraveling.

"I called at Rue Haussmann earlier. Happily, Foster told me where you'd gone."

"Foster, good man. I'll speak to my uncle about giving the man an increase in his wages."

"I was right behind a messenger who delivered camellias."

"Oh, god. Another bunch."

"For you?" he asked with an edge to his voice.

"Heavens no. They're for Ada. From the *vicomte de Montresor*."

Andre knit his brows.

"You know him?"

"I do."

The waiter arrived with an ice bucket, the bottle of champagne and two flutes.

"Tell me about him."

"A few years younger than I. Educated. Of an *ancien regime* family." Andre paused to watch the waiter pop the cork on the wine, pour it for him to taste. "Wonderful," he said in approval to the *garçon*. "He's a distant cousin."

She gave a laugh. "You're related to half of Europe."

"A joy," he said and leaned back while their waiter served them both a generous pour. "Also a terrible burden when one feels responsible for their failures. But Montresor is a good man if a little…"

"What?"

"A little more attached to his former governess than he can be to a comely young wife."

Marianne snapped shut her mouth. "He has an *entendre* for his old governess?"

Andre took a hearty drink of his wine. "By all reports, a lovely blonde a decade older than he."

"And does he keep her?"

"He does." André nodded and put down his glass. "In fine comfort. In his house in the country. Or rather, I should say, she lives in the garden house."

Marianne took a long sip. "Marvelous to learn. So you are implying his pursuit of Ada could not be for love?"

"Only he can say that. But he's not destitute. Not yet. His mama lets every franc slip between her fingers. She speculates on every scheme that might immediately make her millions. But she chooses poorly. Hence, she's in debt to her plucked eyebrows. So he's intent upon a wife with a sizable dowry. The castle, you see, requires a new roof and the rookery is in disrepair. Has been since peasants burned it after Napoleon lost at Waterloo."

"Well! Good to know. Ada would love a castle but wouldn't begin to understand how to handle a man who kept a mistress. Or much about men at all. She simply adores each one who has a pretty face and an air of romance. Montresor is pretty. Too much so."

"Enough of him." Andre covered her hand with his upon the tiny table.

The women next to them saw, smiled and shared the naughtiness of it with a flash of widening eyes. Marianne decided not to care.

"I miss you." Andre whispered. " I look forward to tonight when I may waltz with you."

"I do too." She got lost in his gaze. "I wonder..."

His expression hardened. "You don't want to postpone, do you?"

"Not that. The girls would make me into mincemeat."

He squeezed her hand and let go. "What then?"

The waiter arrived with a tray of crudités and little pillows of pastry dough steaming with the aromas of crab and butter. He served them each a few, left the salver and departed with a bow.

She sat forward. She was tired of catering to Ada and her friends. It was high time she took her happiness into her own hands. "Would you mind if we didn't start at six o'clock?"

"Six? But—It's nine that the dancing—" He frowned and when she grinned at him, hope danced in his eyes. "Are you saying you wish to change the terms of your proposal to me?"

"I do. Might you reconsider for...say, midnight?"

"After I return you and Ada home to Rue Haussmann?"

"And I have a few minutes to allow Foster to summon a hackney cab, yes."

"You will ride in no public conveyance at that time of night, *ma cherie*."

"Andre, I need an unmarked carriage."

"I'll send my own brougham. No crests on the doors. You'll be safe."

"I must go inside with Ada. Briefly. She mustn't suspect me of shenanigans."

"I understand."

"Plus I'll need time to change and collect my valise."

"*Ma petite,*" he said with a pained look on his face, "you don't need clothes."

"I do. A gown. A robe. My hairbrush."

"I have all that," he said, his voice a rasp. "You'll use mine."

She grinned at him. "I need at least my own toothbrush, darling."

"Say that again."

"I need my own toothbrush...darling."

He let his gaze drift over her curls beneath her prim little toque. "I will brush your hair. I want it loose, flowing through my fingers and wound around wrists."

"Well, hello, there!" Ada stood before them, chipper as a bird, with her two friends. All three girls did a polite curtsy to Andre. "We've done with lingerie. Thankfully. Frightfully expensive there. I say, good to see you, *Monsieur le duc.*"

Andre rose and bowed as Ada reacquainted her friends with him.

For the next half hour, Marianne marveled at her cousin's sophisticated banter. Ada could rise to the occasion of social niceties. If her two friends achieved no such heights, but sat star-struck with the handsome prince and sculptor in their midst, Marianne could only smile to herself.

When he rose to leave them minutes later, Andre gave a small bow to each young lady. "Remember tonight to wear a day dress, very plain. No fancy hat, no gloves and no expensive jewelry. You must appear to be *bourgeois.*"

They happily agreed.

"*Merci, Monsieur.* We'll be good," Ada assured him.

"I count on it." He took Marianne's hand and kissed her on each cheek. "*Au revoir, ma cherie.* I'll arrive promptly at nine."

۝

"None of these ladies comes alone?" She arched her elegant neck to note the hundred or more dancers on the sawdust-laden dance floor. Ada waltzed with his friend, the *Comte du Maine*, who'd come along tonight as additional escort for them. Francine and Ezzie were going round with two other friends of Andre's, both painters who lived in Montmartre.

"A few, yes. They shouldn't." In the gaslight, Marianne looked made from starlight. Her heavy blonde hair in a care-free knot, fell about her temples and her cheeks. His body hardened, eager to touch her hair, the cords of her throat, the swell of her breasts. He'd spent his afternoon readying every inch of his Montmartre house to welcome her tonight. He, himself, had been prepared, starving to have her for months.

She glanced at him, whimsy in her gaze. "You're not thinking of them."

"No, I've done enough of that. I concentrate on you." He leaned closer to her, his hand curving around her opposite shoulder and drawing her back into the circle of his arms. Soon he'd explore the perfection of her naked, as God had made her. He set his jaw as his cock turned to stone. "I've done my best for them. But they're on their own. The rest of the night is meant for you and me."

A frisson shook her. Gratified that he could stir her, he bent to put his lips to her ear. "Did you bring your hairbrush?"

Staring straight ahead, she arched her brows. "One small one."

"You'll use my robe?" he whispered as he bit her earlobe.

"Your robe, your sheets, your bed."

He caught her back into the full embrace. She felt wonderful, completely his. "I have other delights for you."

She snorted. Eyes still straight ahead, she said, "I dare not ask."

"Mmm. I plan to give them to you one-by-one." He nuzzled her neck behind her ear.

She swayed against him and beneath her breath, murmured his name. "Is seduction allowed here?"

"Only for me." Their table nestled into a clutch of shrubs, secluded yet public enough to be proper.

"Ah. So you've seduced other women here before, have you?"

"Never." He pulled away slightly and took her other hand in his to raise it, examine the length of her fingers and kiss each tip. "These are my friends. Renoir, over there. Alain du Bois, at the next table. They know I have never brought a woman here."

She faced him, alarm in her darkened expression. "Why with me then?"

He cupped her hand in his and took it to his lap where she could feel the rigid outline of her effect on him. "You tell me why."

Removing her hand, she swallowed hard and focused on the dancers. "I'm still leaving before six tomorrow morning."

He nodded. "I assumed so."

"You won't stop me."

He heard her statement as a question. But he knew what his answer must be. "No."

"Thank you."

"You're welcome." *If you wish to stay with me, it will be because you want it, never that I ask for it.*

"I told my maid I would not need her in the morning."

His heart took wing. No servant to check on Marianne meant she could escape the rigid timetable of the house if she wished. "Wise. She need not worry about you."

"And your coachman?"

"Valmont has his instructions to wait for you across the street. When you emerge, he will draw up in front of your door." Andre gave her a tiny hug. "I ordered him to take out the unmarked brougham. No one will know whose coach you enter."

"I'll wear a veil."

"Of course."

"And exit the servants entrance in the back."

"So any observer would conclude a servant left the house?"

"Exactly."

He sensed her rapid pulse. "Look at me, please. If you wish to come to me and we only talk, we can do that."

She opened her mouth to speak but her lower lip quivered.

He caressed her jaw with a swirl of his fingers. There was his biggest challenge with her rearing its head again. "You have not been with a man for many years. Whether you realize it or not, I know you may be as tender as a virgin, *ma cherie*. And I believe that by now you instinctively know that I would never hurt you. Say you trust me in that. Say it. You must. Or we will not go on until you can."

"I do trust you. I'm just so..." She lowered her head and in the flickering gaslight, he saw her cheeks redden.

"So what?"

Her head came up and she was embarrassed. "Unschooled. Unsophisticated. And if you think that I am capable of—"

"Of what?"

"Effusive..."

He tipped his head in question.

"Erotic..." She waved a hand.

"Ah." He pinched the tip of her nose. "Acrobatics? The can-can?"

She burst out laughing. "Oh, that would be lovely in your bed."

He longed for the moment when he could haul her into

his embrace. "The can-can in my bed." He widened his eyes. "Revolutionary."

"You are quite terrible, you know."

"Where you are concerned, I am. Once an *enfant terrible*, I am a changed man. You make me patient. I have never been. You make me compassionate. I have never valued what I could not take. You make me happy. I have always been, but to make you happy has become the primary purpose of my life."

If he ever thought he could seduce her with the power of his words, he saw that he could dissolve her into a flowing reservoir of delight. The expression on her face, the part of her lips, the mellow adoration in her dark eyes, was one he would carve into his memory and remember until his last breath. This was love. If she knew it yet or not, this was rapture. All he had worked for, all he had waited for with her was about to be his. Theirs. Maybe not tonight but soon. And when she came to him, without the shackles of her past or the lonely existence she had endured, she would come with this look of love. And he would have her, treasure her, ensure that she would gaze upon him like this and that she would enjoy her life. With him. Always with him.

He took her hand to his lips. "Come dance with me, *mon amour*. It's time."

৩%৪

*Almost midnight.* Marianne dropped her pocket watch into her tiny evening purse.

"I'm ready to leave, too." Andre whispered into her ear as the two of them watched the three young women dance with partners on the wooden floor in the park.

She felt as if she were made of pins and needles, so alive so excited to make love to him soon. "They're having such a good time, you realize we've created ravenous creatures. They'll want to come every night."

"Only if they stay on good behavior."

He dragged his gaze from her toward Ada and her friends with his own. They'd danced for hours. "After this song, shall we leave?"

He slipped an arm around the back of her chair. The night she'd yearned for had come. "Let's."

"Stay here while I talk to Valmont over at the bar. He'll have the groom bring the coach around to the entrance for us, then drive the brougham himself to Rue Haussmann to wait for you."

At the notice that they were leaving, the three young women pouted and argued, but succumbed to the stern decrees of Andre and his friend, the *Comte du Maine*. They settled into the opposite seat of the coach, grim.

Ada perked up. "When might we come again? Do the same men go each night?"

"No." The *Comte du Maine*, tapped his fingers on the armrest, the look of him was one of restrained amusement. He was a handsome man with red blonde hair and dark brown eyes, even tempered. He seemed older than Andre by a decade, yet he'd told her they were the same age. "A cross-section of gay Paris."

"Wonderful." Ezzie piped up. "Might we go tomorrow night? Will you please take us, *Monsieur le duc*?"

Francine scowled at Ezzie. "We shouldn't. Remember that's the day after tomorrow we come to your house, Ezzie, for your special party."

"Oh, you're right. I'd forgotten."

"What party is that?" Marianne had no memory of any plans by Ezzie's family to host an event.

The girl checked the expressions of Ada and Francine. "I'm hostessing my own ladies' excursion."

"I'm sorry, Marianne." Ada did look apologetic. "I forgot to tell you."

"It's only for our friends who went to Miss Winston's," Ezzie added.

"Two more arrived last week from New York," Francine hurried on. "At ten o'clock, we're meeting at Gare de L'Est, boarding the train to Rheims to tour the cathedral."

"A church?" Marianne focused on Ada. "I thought you'd given them up?"

Ada flourished a hand. "Aren't you pleased, Marianne? Be pleased. All the kings of France were crowned there. A bit of history for us, you know."

"We'll stay the night in a fine hotel," Francine announced. "My mother chaperones and my maid comes along. Ezzie's too. They're very old, you know. And mine's French."

"I made all the arrangements myself," Ezzie announced with great pride.

*Did you?* "I'm certain," Marianne said, "your mother is very proud."

"Indeed she is. She wants me to become more assertive."

*And right she is to encourage that too. Especially with Francine hanging around.*

Andre sent Marianne a consoling look, then crossed one leg over the other. "I can arrange a luncheon for you at a friend's, if you like."

"Oh, no!" Ezzie shot a glance at Francine. "We can't. I mean...another time, perhaps?"

Francine quelled her friend's outburst with one firm shake of her head. "Any other day, we'd welcome it, *Monsieur. Merci beaucoup.* Is your friend young and unmarried?"

Marianne fought the urge to roll her eyes.

Andre had the good manners not to show any offense. "She is. And she owns vineyards. She makes champagne."

Ada and Ezzie, both sheepish, sat quiet.

Francine narrowed her big dark eyes at Andre and said, "I'd be delighted to learn. We all would, wouldn't we?"

Ezzie nodded like an eager three-year-old.

"But I think," said Francine, "another time would be best. My mother, you see, doesn't like to amend her schedule."

"I do understand," Andre acquiesced.

Alarm in her crystal blue eyes, Ada stared at Marianne then turned to Andre. "Thank you, *Monsieur le duc*. I look forward to the education."

Ada's gratitude pleased Marianne. But something disturbed her about her friends' behavior. Was the trio planning some escapade during their trip to Rheims? What could they slip by Francine's mother? Leave the woman? Go off on their own? No, surely, they'd not try that in a strange city.

Marianne would ask Ada later. She had greater delights to think of and she settled back between the two men, content for now to feel the warmth of Andre's thigh against her own.

The ride could not go quickly enough.

Valmont had his instructions to deliver the Moore girl and Lang to their home first. Next he drove round to the home of the *comte du Maine*.

That man did his duty bidding Ada good evening then focused upon Marianne. "I enjoyed meeting you, *Madame Roland*. I hope we see each other again soon. When we all return to town for the autumn, I will plan a dinner party and would like all of your family plus this devil, too. Of course."

"*Merci, Monsieur le Comte*. I know my family will be honored as I am."

"So would I," Andre added with a wicked eye at his friend.

"*Au revoir*," Maine dipped his head in homage and climbed down from the carriage.

The ride to Rue Haussmann was brief. So was the conversation.

"Thank you, *Monsieur le duc*," Ada said, a carefree toss of a smile as she gathered her skirts and her purse. "I hope we can go again."

"We will, Miss Hanniford."

"A promise?" She urged him a twinkle in her eyes.

"Certainly."

With a wink at Marianne, Ada murmured *au revoir* and out she got.

Marianne picked up her skirts. Her heart pounded so heavily she could have sworn Andre could hear it.

He seized her hand—and frowned.

"Don't worry," she told him. " I won't change my mind."

"Can you see Valmont on the opposite corner?"

"I do." She leaned across Andre to peer out at the black unmarked carriage parked beneath the golden gaslight. Valmont's reed-like figure was unmistakable in silhouette. The horses stomped and snorted. "I'll come quickly. The animals are restless."

Andre squeezed her hand, then lifted it to his lips. "As others are too."

She grinned. "The sooner you let me go, the sooner I appear in your studio."

He pressed a lavish kiss to her open palm. "Leave me before I abduct you."

She stepped down into the street with the aid of Andre's groom. Climbing the steps, she heard another carriage pull up and paused to watch Uncle Killian's town coach approach. He emerged, his black hair ruffled by the wind, his top hat off, his evening cape flying behind him as she caught up to her. The two of them entered the hall when Foster opened the door for them. The butler took his master's cape and waited for her to give him hers.

"I'll take mine upstairs, Foster. Thank you."

Killian arched one long dark brow.

She understood that he wanted news of the night. "The girls had a wonderful time. I did, too."

The butler disappeared down the hall.

"Remy pulled it off, eh? Good. I understand he asked his friend the *Comte du Maine*."

"He did," she said as unbuttoned her summer jacket. "Both men enjoyed themselves."

"Not a total chore for *Maine* then. Fine, fine. I like him. And I know Remy had a fine evening." He gave her a lopsided grin. "Ada behaved?"

"Impeccably, sir."

"What about those two friends of hers? How were they?"

"No *faux pas* this evening." *Even if they're up to something.* "Well, I'm off. Good night, Uncle."

She was halfway to the first landing when he called up from the foot of the stairs. "I see Valmont across the street."

She halted. *He couldn't forbid her from going. Not now. Not after she'd waited so long and been so attentive to Ada.*

Killian put an elbow to the balustrade. In his black cutaway and starched white cravat, his inky hair swept from his brow, he looked like a sleek jaguar she'd once seen in a circus sideshow.

"He waits for me."

Killian nodded once. "Enjoy yourself, my dear. You deserve the right to every moment."

Like water over a fall, her doubts drained from her. She wanted this. Needed the satisfaction of a *rendezvous* with a man she cared for. Cared for deeply. "I will, Uncle. I leave by the kitchen door. I'll see you at breakfast."

"I'll instruct Foster not to lock the doors just yet and to unlock them early tomorrow. At dawn, shall we say?"

"Dawn would be right, yes."

With a winsome smile, he turned on his heel and made his way toward the servants hall.

# CHAPTER 8

The coach was cool. Valmont had opened one of the windows and the night air was a refreshing breeze upon her heated skin.

She closed her eyes, at peace with the decision that had been conceived in instinct and—after all these months and so many occasions—was borne in conviction. She adored *Monsieur le duc de Remy, prince d'Aumale*, Andre Claude Marceau. In that realization, she rested secure and happy.

The streets at this time of morning were quiet. Though the *bon ton* traversed the boulevards, to and from the theaters, the cafes or the boudoirs of their loved ones, their sounds were muffled, discreet. The clop of matched horses. The whisk of a coachman's whip. The footfalls of pedestrians on their way home denoted that all was well.

Her journey would be short. A good thing since her heart was unable to beat a steady tattoo since she'd entered the brougham and sunk to the plush squabs. Inside the cozy cab, Valmont had strapped a silver ice bucket to the tiny drop-down table. He'd poured her a full measure of crisp champagne into the crystal flute upon the inlaid polished wood.

She took one drink, unwilling to cloud her mind for the scintillating experience she welcomed with all her heart.

She alighted at an impressive home, two stories high. In milky Parisian limestone that gleamed in the lamplight, the house reflected Remy's personality in its elaborately carved robin's egg blue front door and the multitude of huge paned windows that marched along the first and second floors. She put out her hand to knock upon the varnished wood and it fell open.

A half bare mighty arm reached out into the night and drew her in.

She giggled.

Andre caught her up in his arms and whirled her about, laughing himself. In his foyer, the chandelier above blazed in tiny lights. She could see him. See him as she'd never seen him before.

Wildly happy. With the broadest grin on his chiseled lips. The merriest twinkle in his incomparable eyes.

"You must put me down," she told him, her hand to his chest.

"Why?"

"You'll get dizzy. I am."

"I've been dizzy since I met you." Panting, he stopped and fell back against the wall. "If I want to make you as light-headed as I am, you cannot blame me for trying."

She put her palm to his cheek. His strong jaw lay in her hand and she marveled at his perfection. "I'll blame you for my joy. An exhilaration I haven't had since I was a child."

One side of his mouth hooked up in a rogue's grin. "I'll take that, *ma chou*."

She winced. "I do not approve of being your cabbage."

"Very well. My star. My moon. My sun."

"Use them all. Why not? Now put me down before you injure your back. Show me the house."

He set her to the floor and put his hands on his hips. "What would you like first?"

She pointed toward the road. "Actually, I could do with the rest of that fabulous champagne."

He snapped his fingers. "I have more. Come with me to the kitchen."

He took her hand and led her down the massive hall, adorned with brightly colored paintings on the walls. They depicted ordinary women and men at parks, dancing, drinking, picnicking on verdant grass. "Do you like them?"

"Very much. I like you more."

He wiggled his brows. "I dismissed my maid for the night. My assistant too."

"We're alone." She was pleased, struck to the quick once more by his kindness.

"We are." He stopped in the middle of the long hall. "You like these?"

"I do. Who painted them?"

"My friends whom you met last night. Renoir for this one. Du Bois, this one. And this—" He stood beside her as she marveled at the simplicity of a painting of a blond-haired baby, fat and jolly, rolling in his lacy crib. "You like this one?"

"Oh, I do."

"This is by another friend of mine. Louise Antoine. If you wish, I will take you to meet her."

"Do others like her work? They should. I can almost hear his burbling about how he loves his fat little toes."

"Louise exhibited with us last April and sold a few paintings. Enough to pay her rent and buy a few rounds for us all at the Agile Rabbit."

"Did you ever starve for your work, Andre?"

"No. I am fortunate." He picked up her hand and kissed the back. "Starving the body is not always the best way to find a path to your true self."

How well she knew that. "Starving is never the best way to do anything."

He circled his arms around her, his impressive hard body a firm reminder that she was not here for the remembrance of bitterness. "I want you to be happy with me here."

"If you don't give me that champagne, how can I proceed?"

He hugged her and took a few steps into the kitchen. It was a cavernous room lined in big white cupboards, a huge trough for a sink, and a long wooden worktable in the center. "*Viola!*"

"You could feed an army from this place."

"Never will. Not my intention. This is for the cook. Or cooks. I've had perhaps ten friends at most to dinner. And never as formal as what you'll have when you come to the house in Rue de Rivoli."

She didn't want to talk of friends or dinner parties. "I'd just like my champagne, good sir."

"*Pardon e moi, Madame.*" He bent to his task of opening a bottle, popping the cork and pouring her a large draft. Before her, he plunked down a mug. "Are you hungry, too?"

"No."

"Then let's go up." He grabbed the bottle of champagne and hooked his other arm around her waist. "*Madame* must see the rest of the house."

Along the corridor, he pointed out his tasteful salon. Then he led her up the granite stairs. "When I bought the land here, I decided not to excavate the hill, but to use it to my advantage."

"What do you mean?"

"This appears to be a second floor here in the rear of the house, but it is in fact the first floor. I had the builders pour a firm foundation because I needed stability in my studio floor to support the marbles." he said as he paused before a massive door. "And I wanted wonder of the universe each time I walked in to my studio."

He flung the door wide and the glory of the starry night fell over her. She put down her mug on the nearest bureau, needing no wine to intoxicate her with the moment or the man. Her head back, she could not get enough of the black sky, the flickering stars in the firmament, the infinity of the universe. Tears obscured the view.

Andre was beside her, his arms around her, his lips tracing the whorl of her ear.

She spun into him and choked back the clog in her throat. "You'll have to help me disrobe."

Wordless, he began with the crocheted frogs at the collar of her coat, his gentle fingers sliding open the closures, sliding the garment over her shoulders, down her arms and draping it over a chair. He came back, his pale eyes afire, and walked around her, his tender ministrations counterpoints to the pounding of her pulse. The cooler air rushed in to lick her skin as down, down, down he opened her simple day gown and pushed it to the floor.

She stepped out of the pool and bent.

But he said, "No," and picked up the piece to place it upon the same chair as her other garb.

Planning for this moment, she'd not donned a chemise. Only her most comfortable corset, one petticoat, her finest stockings, garters and shoes. Drawers she'd left home, too. Boldness was an adventure, one she'd ignored for more than a decade. Tonight, she wished to show this assertive man she could be his equal. If only for one night.

Behind her, he pulled and tugged at the lacings to her corset. Made of soft white cotton, the garment was cut low, skimming the swell of her breasts. The whalebone could cut into her flesh, but before supper she'd ordered her maid to lace her loosely. To dance with Andre, she'd needed breath. To make love with Andre, she wanted speed.

The corset undone, she inhaled deeply.

He swept it away. Her breasts fell free and she sighed. He unhooked her petticoat tapes. Her last modest covering slid to her feet.

He sucked in air, the sound at once invigorating and soothing to her senses. She waited for his next move.

But he did not.

She gazed down at her naked body, her nipples pointed, aching for his hands, his lips, his tongue. She swayed and he caught her by the shoulders.

She turned to him.

He gazed only at her face. His expression was reverent, matching her own emotion.

"I've imagined this rendezvous for months," she told him, her own voice surprisingly even, if raw. "Each time, I began by admiring you. As I do whenever I first glimpse you."

He raised a hand, shaking, to release two combs that held up her curls. Her hair fell around her shoulders, a few strands draping over her breasts. He still did not look at her body, a twitch to his left eye told of his tension.

"May I undress you?" she asked him, her tone shockingly one of a schoolgirl asking favors.

He held out his arms, his breathing deep and fast.

Tonight to the Moulin de la Galette, he'd worn casual clothes. A dark linen jacket, cream linen trousers and a soft white shirt. Upon return here, he'd discarded his coat, kept the shirt and changed to loose dove grey pants. These, she surmised, were his work clothes. This was who he wished her to see. The sculptor. The man with ambition and substance.

She stepped toward him and undid the ties at the neck of his shirt. She gathered up the material, loose and giving in her hands, and pulled it up over his head. She spun and placed it atop her own clothes in the chair. When she turned back to him, his gaze flowed over her hair, her mouth, her nose, her eyes. His pants were secured round the waist by a leather belt, the fabric gathered haphazardly to keep them up. With her gaze holding his, she undid the leather, a loop of supple leather, and pulled it away. The garment whooshed to the concrete floor. As he had done, she did not fill her eyes with his nakedness.

With both hands, she framed his face. "I spent nearly two years of my life tending the wounded and the dying first in my own home and afterward in a Rebel hospital. They came in, walking, hobbling, some on stretchers. Filthy, starving, ragged, they were torn by bullets and ripped by bombs."

Andre ran two hands through her hair, his expression pained and reverent.

"I learned the human body in my parlor and that church. That the perfection God created can be blown open, desecrated by other humans in the name of some cause, some purpose. I saw that blood can rush and muscles cramp, that arms and legs can be blown away, and the result is a man, deformed and reduced, sobbing for his mother. I never wish to see that or hear it. Never again."

Did he have tears in his own eyes?

She stepped against him, her skin on his, warmed by his body heat. "I want to memorize your body, feel your strength, absorb it if I can."

He brushed his thumb over her bottom lip. "My darling, whatever you wish is yours."

She felt suddenly young, terribly young, as if she'd never despised her cowardly husband, never suffered war, never nursed any man through amputation or blindness or madness. "I want to admire how perfect you are."

He pressed his thumb to her mouth and stepped backward.

Beneath his skylight, the moon washed pale rays over him. He was big. She'd relished that from first sight of him. He was tall and stately, standing as he was nonchalant, but intent on her, a tender smile upon his lips. His neck was thick, strong, his blond hair, white in the moonlight, curling around his nape. His chest was wide, corded with muscle from the years of chipping stone and lifting marble. Tapered and rippling over his ribs. His arms were long from shoulders that bunched with movement, to massive hands and elegant fingers, the nails short.

His hands hung lax at his side and she was tempted, so very tempted to slide her gaze to his groin. Years of etiquette caught up to her. His thighs, heavy and roped with long hard muscle, sent ripples of excitement to her stomach. His legs were shapely, his ankles lean. His feet, bare, were long and broad.

This was a glorious man. A noble man. Huge and powerful in form and spirit. One who had breeched the confines of his own class to become what he wished.

And there at the juncture of his massive thighs was the essence of his manhood. The element of his body she craved as much as she needed his smile, his laugh, his touch. And he wanted her. Desired her with a passion living in his eager assessment of her.

She strode up to him and plunged her fingers in his hair. Thick and silken, his heavy mane filled her hands. His scalp was wide, his forehead high, his temples pulsing with desire for her.

She caught his gaze, permissive of her folly to define him with her touch. She etched his pale expressive brows, brushed the edges of his blond lashes and ran both her forefingers along the Gallic arch of his nose. His cheekbones were broad, the hollows beneath them deep. His mouth—his wide appealing sensuous lips—curved up as she traced the outline.

His chin, his jaw, a square declaration of his heritage. Warrior, Norseman, Celtic, king, emperor—they'd all been his forebears and he represented them with a noble visage.

But his throat was sure symbol of his strength. His shoulders, cut with cords of honed muscle, put her in mind of Atlas who held up the world. He had a sculpted torso, ribs prominent, hips too. She traced the line of his thighs with the flat of her hand and strolled around him, her fingers skimming the indentation of his waist and the leanness of his hip. His back was broad, more impressive than his chest, his bulging muscles rippling with tension as she splayed her full hands wide to measure him. She glanced down. His derriere looked firm and when she smoothed her palms over him, he flinched.

She pressed her naked body flat to his back, her arms circling round him, her lips against his scapula, offering a kiss in homage to his strength.

He caught her hands against his stomach, his head arching back. Then with a sharp inhalation, he grasped her wrists and led her hands down to his penis. She squeezed shut her eyes, blocked out all but the feel of him. The thick hair of his groin and the long rigid form that was his manhood. And he was not shy about leading her to define all of him. He took her index finger and smoothed it over the tip of his cock. Drops of moisture beaded there, thick and hot.

Desire whirled through her, her loins pulsing, demanding. She held him and swooned a little, wanting all of him inside her.

He spun in her arms, a rogue's smile upon his lips.

His huge hot hands crushed her close. His skin was fire, his might the bulwark she'd always assumed it would be. He embodied protection against hell. Salvation in heaven.

He pulled back to cup her face between his hands and

took her lips in a slow sweet declaration of his need. "Come learn more of me as I do you."

"Yes, oh yes." She took a step.

But he caught her up in his arms and carried her to a large bed. There he laid her down so that when he loomed over her, she saw him as light within the black of night. He swept her hair from her cheeks, then lay along her length. Up on his elbow, he traced her brows, her nose, the outlines of her mouth with his fingers. His lips followed.

Mesmerized by his care, she lifted her knees and rolled into him. He snatched hair pins from her coif, dropped them to a night table. He swung back to kneel over her, hovering there, to grasp her hair in handfuls and drape it over her shoulders and down her breasts. Her hair tickled and she squirmed, arching her hips up and discovering the hot imprint of his penis and balls upon her core.

She groaned and he bent to take her chin between two fingers and hold her there as he kissed her and took all that her mouth could grant him.

"*Mon bijou*," he murmured and a thousand words more as he savaged her mouth countless times.

He stroked her breasts, round the bottom, along the tops, and bent to suck one nipple into his mouth and make her gasp. He cupped her other breast, his thumb rubbing her nipple until she bucked and cried his name.

Grinning, he rose and winked at her, then took the other nipple into his mouth with a ravenous pull.

She was lost.

He sat back on his haunches and whirled his palms over her breasts and her ribs. Bending over her prominent hip bone, he kissed his way down to the juncture of her thighs. He placed his mouth at the hollow of her groin and dropped a brief kiss there. She gasped in anticipation of his journey to her core, but he surprised her and ran one hand down her thigh to the garter of her stocking.

He sat back, a wicked crook to his mouth. With a sound of satisfaction, he lifted her leg in mid-air, flipped off her slipper, then toyed with her garter. He pushed her leg farther back and kissed the back of her knee.

She groaned, laughing.

He unwound her garter with one twist and peeled down her stocking. The next moment, his mouth was to the arch of her foot and then the fiend bit her.

She yelped.

He chuckled and reached for her other shoe, her other garter, undid it with practiced ease and stretched himself out atop her. His body was frightfully heavy as he pinned her to the mattress. "Before the dawn, I will taste each inch of you."

She grinned, her desire at once ravenous. "I will permit it."

"Will you now?" he teased. "Thought of it, have you?"

She pulled at a lock of his hair. "Every night. But know, I will have the same."

"I demand it."

She tipped up her hips, opened her thighs and his cock fell along her seam. He was so massive and rigid, so very hot, she quivered. He clasped her more tightly.

She clamped her arms around him. He considered her, his eyes narrowed, his brows knit. And then he moved against her.

In that second, everything she knew of a man with a woman was tested by this man, his tenderness. She'd lived for years hoping such gentleness existed in a man. Having waited so very long, she had been ready to abandon the dream.

*No need to run now.*

He curled against her, his lips against her cheek, the corner of her mouth. He fought for air, maybe sanity too, and flowed his cock against her, seeking, finding the opening to her core. He paused, took her lips in a tremulous kiss and slowly sank inside her.

And oh, he was huge. His girth stretched her. His heat blazed within her. She undulated, taking him deep, deep, deeper still. She gasped at the fullness of him. She saw the stars, the moon. But she closed her eyes, trusting that she could discover a new universe in his arms.

He moved inside her and she had her proof. With measured precision, he delved inside her. His movements smooth, his rhythm sure, he drove her up into a frenzy for some elusive goal.

Her breath stuttered. The rapture he brought her, the objective he dangled before her with each arch of his body, enflamed her. He picked up his pace, her heartbeat did too.

And then he slowed, hooked his arms beneath her knees and brought her legs up to drape around his hips. Smiling down at her, he began a deliberate joining of their cores as he gazed at her and lured her with a smile.

Until she could no longer look at him, no longer count or measure how he pleased her, until she tensed and he caressed her with his talented fingers and she burst apart, gasping and joyous. Calling his name.

He cradled her close, her shaking body seeking more of his, as he whispered words of delight and lost himself in the bliss they had created.

He drew away from her, loathe to stay lest he frighten her by how fiercely he wished to bind her to him.

Running a hand through his hair, he fought with his instinct to roar like a savage that he'd finally claimed her. Yet the past months' experience had taught him that to keep her, he'd need not brawn, but wits.

He found a blanket and draped it over her. She lay upon the sheets, her ivory skin more satin than any marble he'd ever polished, her lithe form so much more supple than he'd ever sampled. Her ardent response to him, so much more spontaneous than he had predicted.

That shocked him. But gratified him. She could make love to him eagerly. That she trusted him so much meant he had less work to do to keep her by his side.

He made to go.

She caught his arm, her exquisite face aglow with drowsy satisfaction.

"I return. I have a few things for you."

"Hurry."

He grinned, triumphant. Naked, he padded away. In the kitchen, he grabbed the elegantly wrapped paper tent, his purchase from the patisserie, and strode back upstairs.

"Sit up," he said to her when he was beside the bed.

Her brows wiggling in glee, she pushed herself back against the pillows, gathered the blanket to cover her breasts and stretched up to see his offering. "You baked!"

"As I do each day!"

She laughed. "*Certainement*! You have so much time for that."

Sitting beside her, he placed the package in her lap. "I'll get the champagne. You tear it open."

"Ohhh, thith is scrumthous," she said, her mouth full of chocolate *mille-feuille*.

Chuckling, he left then quickly returned to her with the wine and her mug in hand. He took a drink, thirsty for all the night had to give. "I'm happy to humor you."

"Messy." She put a finger to the corner of her mouth to gather cream.

Inspired, hungry himself, he put the champagne and mug aside. He took her hand, lifted it away and licked chocolate from her finger and then from her lips. When he pulled away, her eyes were closed, her mouth open.

He loved her.

The reality dawned on him, gentle as the silent starry night. But he'd known. He'd known months ago.

He'd been patient for good reason. The reward was this. Luscious Marianne Roland in his bed gloriously naked at last was now his enchanting *amour.* He tore his gaze away and poured more champagne into the mug. With satisfaction, he took a drink of the wine and watched her devour the pastry.

"What is that one?" She pointed to a crusty tart.

"*Tarte Tatin.* Apple. Try it."

She widened her eyes and picked it up to bite in. "Mmmm. You know how to please me."

*In pastries. In bed.* He arched his brows. "I have macarons in the kitchen. Would you like them now or—?"

She went up on her knees to cup his neck and kiss him on the lips. "For now, I'm content with these and you."

His body shot through with ferocious need. He wanted her again, now, so soon.

Her humor died. She met his silence with her own.

He held his breath.

She put the pastry to the floor and turned toward him. Still up on her knees, the sheets rumpled around her, she resembled a mermaid rising from a frothy sea. Her breasts were full, her nipples hard rosy mounds. She panted as she scrambled toward him, sank her fingers into his hair and kissed him with all the ardor he'd sought from her for months.

Ravenous, he seized her and brought her across his lap. Her body lay before him like a pagan's prize, her elegant throat, her full breasts, the slope of her stomach, the point of her hip bones, the golden thatch of hair over her *mons.* The crevice, the long dark line that led to the part of her he needed again, was a thin dark valley he longed to savor with his cock and his mouth.

He opened his hand and caressed all of her offered up to him. The chords of her neck, the sweet points of her round breasts, the succulent heat of her folds, the lush wet cream that coated her sex.

At his tender touch, she arched, her whole torso a gift. That she could allow him to satisfy his appetite for her astonished him. She was new to rendezvous. New to him and love. He could conclude only that she did indeed trust him. Implicitly.

She was his to pleasure.

He gently pushed her thighs apart, his fingers tracing the line of her *chat*. She made a little noise of contentment, her face nuzzling his chest. He watched his hand caress her, what he felt so much more electrifying now that he could see what he caressed. Her legs fell open. He caught his breath, proud in his conquest. Humbled in his hunger for her, he found her center and sent two fingers up inside her. She arched up off his lap, moaning. He gentled her with deft strokes, a massage to enchant her, an invasion to possess her. She whimpered, her lips upon his skin. He slid his fingers from her core to find her swollen nub. He pinched her and she bucked. He swirled his fingers around and round, her cries louder, her nails digging into his hips, her lips parting, frantic.

His body screamed for him to bury himself inside her. Yet he wanted to imprint himself on her in indelible ways.

He slid from beneath her so that she lay flat upon the bed. Bending down to her, he licked her lovely breasts, kissed her belly and opened her fragrant folds to lick her and kiss her. Her lips had tasted of wine and chocolate. Her breasts had tasted of *eau de* camellias. Her creamy *chat* tasted of thick passion and of him. And she let him have all of her, every bit he desired, unrestrained. She lay quivering, panting, crying to have him. And when she pulsed in completion, he pivoted around and sank his cock inside her to revel in the last throes of her climax. And then he gave her his own.

The moon was high, the stars merrily twinkling when she rose from their bed.

She'd slept a little, enough to sate her.

Andre snored. The manly abandoned sounds amused her.

She tiptoed behind a Chinese screen searching for a basin and towels to wash. Smiling, she saw what she needed. He'd prepared so well, charming her with every need fulfilled. She washed in the fresh warm water and picked up the robe draped across the nearby chair. It was of heavy ebony satin, lined in white wool. His, it was so large she had to roll back the sleeves and pick up the hem as she strolled around the room.

The heavens above had greeted her in his haven. But what drew her now, here on his earth, was the wealth of his work before her.

Much like the shelves she'd seen in the gallery in the Rue Dauphine last February, his studio was a treasury of his efforts. Large, small, clay, plaster, paint, brushes, pens, ink, lay hither and yon upon wooden or granite topped tables. The figures were scattered among them about the huge room. And much like the exhibition in the Rue Dauphine, in the center stood a monolith of white marble upon a massive plinth. This however had little shape.

Intrigued, she marched around it.

Across the room, she saw him push back to the headboard and smooth back his long hair.

"Do you know yet what this will be?"

"I have a few ideas."

"Do you have sketches?"

"Of this? *Oui*."

"Do you ever show them to anyone?" she asked, her hands sliding over the thin yellow veins in the Carrara, evoking images of what might emerge under his vision.

"Not usually, no."

She would not ask. She understood his need to privacy. She only ever showed anyone her best work.

She strolled away and on the top of his bureau, she spied his hair brush. Picking it up, she approached him and brandished it. "You first."

He rose from the bed, naked like a glorious Neptune, snatched the blanket from the bed and twirled it around his hips. He sat in one of the two chairs and pointed to his head. "Do your best."

It was a tangled mess. Knowledge that it was their romp in bed that made it so had her grinning as she drew the brush through his hair from crown to nape. The rhythm of it soothed her, the satin of his hair upon her fingertips arousing her hunger for him once more.

"Do you still draw me?" he asked.

"I do. Whenever I have a free moment. I get better. Seeing you each day affords me the chance I may one day get you right."

"Would you show them to me?" he asked.

"I could." *But when?* That made her pause. Had she made a hideous mistake to ask for only one night with him?

"Tomorrow night." He rose up, took the brush from her and put it down, then marched to the bed. There, he flung the blanket to the floor and sat. "Bring them."

If she came, what would she risk? If she brought them, what would she gain?

In the moonlight, she detected compassion in his smile.

"Come here, *ma cherie*." He beckoned her with waggling fingers.

She drifted across the room on her bare feet, the cold of the concrete floor chilling her dreadfully.

He reached out.

At once, she shrugged out of his robe. The heavy silk slid away and took with it her old resolve to find a lover who was temporary.

She put a knee to the bed and his hand stroked up her thigh, around to her core where his talented fingers drove up inside her. She melted to him.

"You must come tomorrow night."

She was floating in the wonder he created, his fingers beseeching her to surrender to the intimacy, the relationship. Agreeing with him should be the last thing she should do. "You persuade me unfairly."

Against her skin, he laughed lightly. "Don't object."

She hung in his arms, seduced. "I can't."

He laved her nipple. Nipped her, licked her to quietude. "Say you'll come, *ma cherie*."

"I think I do already."

He laughed at her double *entendre*, but the hilarity died. He massaged her feminine folds with a frenzy that drove her higher, made her needier. "We are not finished, you and I."

She burrowed into him, her nails digging into his shoulder.

"Well you know it." He kissed her between her breasts while his fingers did their magic. "First there is the matter that I have not brushed your hair."

Her lips curved in a grin. Her body vibrated with the first pulse of an orgasm.

"And then there is that matter that I have not yet kissed each inch of you." He tipped up her chin, laid her down beneath him and flowed inside her. "Nor you me."

She grabbed his hair, her need to have him finish their joining so primal that she groaned. He obliged her and brought her up to a strangled cry as she fell over the edge to quake in his arms. Within the next minute, he followed with a long moan.

As they lay there, he stroked her hair.

She'd acted boldly tonight and flourished. She could do it again—and perhaps grow. Conceding was not difficult. "I want to know what that marble will become."

"Bring your sketches. I will tell you."

She slid her head back into the crook of his arm. He was strong man, charming, romantic and a formidable opponent. "You lure me with prizes I cannot resist."

"May I be so wise as to find more of them."

## CHAPTER 9

T he sun rose rapidly as she scampered around the house to the kitchen entrance. Valmont had been at the reins waiting for her for much too long. Andre dressed, insisting to go with her. Lips against her temple, he'd wrapped her close for their journey from the heights of Montmartre butte down to the City proper and the Hannifords' house on Rue Haussmann.

Painful to leave him with her body so deliciously tender, she'd kissed him deeply and stepped down from the coach. Valmont assisted her out, and waited until she turned at the corner of the block and gave him the signal that she was in sight of the kitchen door.

As she pushed it open, she imagined the coachman was still there. He and his master took no chances that harm would come to her.

Inside the back entry, she heard voices in the kitchen. All the servants were awake and to their duties by now. Most, she expected, were taking their breakfast in the kitchen and she tiptoed to the back stairs. Up she flew, light as air, proud of herself, delighted with her night, her lover and her future.

At the second floor, she breezed down the hall toward her suite.

Her uncle's door opened and she froze, afraid his valet or some other servant might discover her.

But her uncle stepped out, securing the belt of his dressing robe around him. His silver gaze flashed over her. "You're well."

"I am," she said, hearing in his tone not a question so much as relief that she was indeed well.

"That's all I wanted to know. Good morning." Pivoting, he returned to his bedroom.

Inside her suite, she ran to the sitting room window and threw back the drapes. She twirled the latch and pushed open the double casement. In rushed the morning breezes, fragrant with springtime and rebirth.

She undid her cloak, letting it drop to the settee. She pulled open her desk drawer, fishing for her most recent sketchbook. It was lodged in the back and she tugged at it. Out flew two bound notebooks.

They dropped to the floor and she went down to pick them up. Then froze. Both had fallen open. One was her newest book, the other older. Frayed. She recognized it and shuddered.

Why had she saved it?

Her mind reeled backward to months, years, a decade ago. The drawings were old. Sixteen years old. She'd kept them purposely for many years to remind her of all she was determined to forget. But most of those from the period of the war and immediately afterward, she'd burned. Ashes to ashes.

This book she had saved.

She clenched her jaw. The man who stared up at her, his black eyes small, his nose thin, the nostrils pinched, his mouth wide, capable of lies and deceptions. *Nothing like Andre.*

She snatched it up and marched to the fireplace. Late July and there was no need for a fire. She looked for tinder, a match. No, no, there was nothing.

She ripped it, tore it like a determined, angry animal. Thousands of pieces, as small as her fingers could render, destroying his image. Innumerable bits of a man she'd not thought worthy of a moment's notice. Not for months had she recalled his sneers, his insults, his cruelty.

She marched to her waist basket, opened her fingers like fans, the bits of him discarded, floating away.

Pacing, she fumed at herself that she'd found him amid the fabulous drawings of Andre. Why had she not destroyed them? Him? Why bring him to Paris? He didn't deserve it. He was buried in Gettysburg. That was where his body laid, in the last place he took breath, the last place he'd failed others.

*I will not draw you again.*

*Ever.*

*Ever ever ever.*

To scrub him from her vision, consign him to hell, she strode back to her desk and yanked the drawer wider. There lay her other sketch books. There. There were the good ones, the new ones. Visions of Andre.

She opened one, riffled the pages, flipped to the recent pages and grinned. She did have him to rights. Here was heroic Andre. Andre, the gentleman. Andre, the artist. Andre, her lover. Except for a little more hollow to his cheeks, a few more emphatic shadings of his nose—his hawlike Gallic nose. Caught by memory of how he'd regarded her last night, she grabbed a stick of graphite and shaded his jaw the way it ought to be. Corrected the arch of his brow. The admiration shining in his eyes. She sat down on her *chaise longue* and refined the portrait of the man she'd always thought was perfection in the flesh.

Two hours later, that's where her maid found her. Dressed

in last evening's attire, sketch pad and graphite in hand, sound asleep in her chair, the drawings of Andre all around her.

"*Pardon, Madame,*" her maid said, awakening her and dropping a small curtsy. "I did not want to disturb you."

"No apology is necessary." She was refreshed, her husband gone as he should be, and would now forever be.

"Would you like a bath, perhaps?"

"*Oui, merci beaucoup.*" She would make nothing of the woman's discovery of her in her day dress, from the night before. "And then I'll dress for breakfast."


"Were you out late last night, Marianne?" Pierce stood at the sideboard, filling his plate with croissant, bacon and omelet. "You usually eat earlier."

"Yes, very late." She was caught off guard by his question, her fork halfway to her lips. Had Uncle Killian mentioned to Pierce her plans to meet Andre? "And you too."

"As you can see. We weren't the only ones."

"Oh?" Her concern for her own reputation evaporated. Unless he referred to his father, she was at a loss.

"Ada came in late." Pierce was a tall, dark elegant man with all his sire's devil-may-care looks and ruthless ambition. At twenty-six years of age, he also possessed a keen devotion to his family. "Tipsy, if you ask me."

Alarm rushed through her. "She was supposed to be with Ezzie Moore and Francine Lang last night."

"Hmm. Yes, well." He came round to sit opposite her. "They were at Ezzie's house last night. Doesn't mean they can't get into her daddy's stash of cognac. I asked Foster to ask the coachman. He confirms that's where our man drove her and where he went to fetch her at eleven. He waited, however, more than an hour for her to emerge."

"Not good of her to keep him out on the box like that."

Pierce met Marianne's gaze, anger mixed with concern. "I haven't seen Papa yet this morning but I plan to tell him. I've got a meeting or I'd give her what-for myself. But Ada should have more care for those who care for her. Especially our own servants."

"I agree. I'll speak with her."

He tucked back into his eggs. "Where's Chaumont lately?"

"She's been ill."

Pierce shook his head. "Must be a terrible malady. It's been weeks since we've seen her. Don't you think?"

"I've been worried and sent a few notes over to her, but she says she'll soon be up to par and be ready to join us for our trip to Cherbourg." Uncle Killian had decided that all of them would adjourn to the seaside resort on the western coast. They'd leave at the end of the week. Most of his business associates were off themselves either to their country chateaux or to catch the breezes off the Atlantic. He thought it best to vacation, too. Conduct business nonetheless.

"Cherbourg," Pierce sounded like he was mourning. "She'll come too? I'm not happy about that."

"Oh?"

He frowned and took a bite of his omelet.

"Why?"

When he rolled his eyes, she had to chuckle.

"Oh, no. Don't tell me she *likes* you, Pierce."

He squinted. "Shall we say, a lot?"

Marianne laughed at his challenge to disenchant the lady. But she pitied the woman. Poor Chaumont, she'd tried to entice Andre with her charms and failed. "She's a widow."

"As she is fond of telling me."

"And she's lonely."

He locked his gaze on hers. "How very lonely she is. And

so grateful to all of us for giving her a position which is respectable. She wants me to know that her home is always open to me. Day or night."

Marianne giggled, a napkin to her mouth. "Oh, no."

"Oh, yes! She'd like to show me her chateau. A day's ride, merely that, no less. And a lovely bit of stone, from the eleventh century when a tyrant named Folk Black raided and murdered his rivals. Butchered them, she told me happily."

Marianne cringed. "Folk Black?"

Pierce feigned amusement. "Oh, you know me. Awful French. That's what it sounded like."

"His name—" announced Ada as she waltzed into the breakfast room like a queen, "—was Fulk Nerra. Fulk the Black. And he built fortifications that became lovely chateaux. We should be grateful to him. He unified the nobles of the Loire valley, preserved the *chenin blanc* grape and founded a few *ecole*."

"And what in heaven is an *ecole*?" Pierce was laughing.

"A school, my dear illiterate brother. A school." She sat next to Marianne and the footman appeared beside her to pour her tea. She urged him away. "Coffee, please, Maurice. It's a school, Pierce."

"I'm impressed with your French, Ada," Marianne told her cousin.

"I've been studying, you'll be happy to note. I like Ezzie's tutor better than my own."

Pierce shot Marianne a look that spoke of danger.

"What's her name?"

"He is *Monsieur* Durant. Bernard Durant." Then Ada sighed, her lashes fluttering. "He's easy to work with. His pronunciation is..."

"Yes?" prompted Pierce.

"So—I don't know—understandable. He's kind and knows Americans speak in different ways."

Pierce stopped, his knife and fork to his plate, as he stared at his sister. "Handsome, I guess."

"Ohhh," Ada gushed. "Blond and tall, refined."

Pierce pursed his mouth and returned to his eggs.

"Oh! You see! Not a nincompoop like you." Ada stuck her tongue out at him.

Pierce sighed.

"You must meet him." This was directed at Marianne. "I want *Madame le Comtesse* to meet him, too. I know you will like him."

No one responded to her.

She huffed and pouted. "What's wrong with you two this morning?"

"Nothing," Pierce said.

But Marianne perceived there was indeed something amiss. "Why should the *Comtesse* and I meet Ezzie Moore's French teacher, Ada?"

She turned to Marianne full on and with her crystal blue eyes brimming with expectation, said, "I want him to become my teacher."

"I see." But what Marianne *heard* was that this tutor had more assets than his refined good looks and unusual ability to influence Ada to learn more French.

"Do you have his card?"

"I—what? Yes, his card. I do."

"Give it to me after breakfast. I will speak to him today."

"You will?"

Marianne tried to sound practical. "Why not?"

Ada's mouth hung open. And try as she might, she couldn't seem to close it. "Thank you."

"Don't thank me yet. Chaumont and I have to meet him, don't we?"

"Well, yes, you do. But *today*?"

The way she pronounced the last word put Marianne on guard. "Today is the best day."

"Action," Pierce said and sipped his coffee. "Best course."

"But today I'm to go to Ezzie's to finalize plans for her excursion to Rheims. You remember? We told you. At the cafe? Yesterday?"

Marianne did recall. "You can go to Ezzie's. You should not be here for my interview of *Monsieur* Durant."

"But I want to be."

"Why?" Marianne put her fork to her plate. "Can he not speak for himself?"

"Yes. Certainly. I only thought that...I could, well," she stopped to clear her throat, "introduce you."

"Thank you. If he can arrive before you must leave, do that. But if he must come later, then I will muddle through myself. No matter what time he arrives though, you can go on to Ezzie's as you planned."

"But—" Ada was exasperated.

So was Marianne. "I want you to go. I'd think you have a lot of planning to do. The cathedral deserves your attention. I must confess, I'm curious though. Why did Ezzie choose to go there?"

"The Rose Windows. She wanted to see them. And now that I've read about them, I know they are absolutely ancient. Don't you think it amazing that people seven hundred years ago had the ability to construct such large buildings and tinted glass?"

Marianne marveled at Ada's new interests, the tutor and the trip. She picked up her fork again. "You like the idea of the excursion. That's a change of heart for you."

Ada nodded, pleased at the compliment. "I admit, though I'm sure you'll both gloat, that it's useful to speak good French and have a sound understanding of French history."

"Pardon me while I fall off my chair," Pierce said.

"Oh, pooh, Pierce. You'd never believe I could have half a brain in my head."

"I'd love to try," Pierce said. "And you'd benefit. When you return from absorbing all that fine culture, I'd like to hear your assessment of it."

"Why?" Ada wrinkled her nose. "Do you want to put a new water system under the church?"

"You never know," he said. "Everyone needs water."

Ada rolled her eyes. "All you think of is making money."

Pierce's expression drained to a stark somberness. "I wish you were right."

Surprised at his turn of emotion, Ada startled and presently directed her attention to her coffee.

Marianne had not seen much of Pierce these past few weeks since they'd arrived back in Paris. He'd thrown himself into his business ventures, securing funds for his public works ideas. If he still thought of Elanna Ash, who was now the married Countess of Carbury, he did not mention her name. But neither did he seem to take an interest in any of the French beauties who were pushed his way.

Ada sighed. "I wish you'd let me stay to introduce you, Marianne."

She forced her attention to Ada. "Thank you, my dear. Please get me *Monsieur*'s card. I will send him a note and we shall see if he can arrive early. If not, do go to your planning for your trip."

"But if you don't like him—"

"Is there a reason why I shouldn't?" she asked her.

"No. He's perfectly respectable. A gentleman."

"Well, then. If having a different instructor has brought about your new interest in learning French, I will give him my fullest consideration." *If he looks like a wolf in sheep's clothing, then in short order, he will be shown the street.*

*"Monsieur* Durant, welcome." Marianne welcomed the slender young man with a polite smile and indicated the settee opposite her. "You may leave us, Foster," she told the butler.

*"Merci beaucoup, Madame Roland."* Bernard Durant was blond and tall, with bulbous brown eyes and the sinuous movements of an egret, bowing his head and sitting gracefully upon the red damask. "I am honored to be asked to call."

*Call? No. This is no call.* "My cousin, Miss Ada Hanniford speaks well of you, *Monsieur."*

"I have met her at her friend's home. She is a lovely girl."

"Thank you. I understand you met her in your capacity as tutor to Miss Esmerelda Moore."

"I did." He folded his long thin fingers together, his knuckles growing white with the pressure of his grip. "They are both excellent students."

Never had any of Ada's teachers said she was that. Flighty. Gossipy. Irreverent. Funny. Her most spectacular quality, her loyalty to her friends.

"I'm pleased you think so, *Monsieur."* Marianne smiled at him to ease his tension. "Do please describe your credentials, sir."

He launched into a well-rehearsed list of his schools, all Parisian, most names Marianne had heard of, culminating in the University of Paris. "And your decision to tutor young Americans comes from your love of language?"

*"Oui, Madame.* My teachers said I had a gift for it. I understand the formation of the tongue and lips, the functions of the muscles."

"I see. And how is that, sir, that you know this?"

"I have worked with the deformed soldiers who live at the *Invalides, Madame.* I try to help them talk again. Many have suffered shock. They have a palsy of mind and heart. Two have partial tongues and lips. Bombs can do terrible things to a body. Even bullets can rip open a jaw, take the entire cheek, the muscles beneath are exposed and the question is how to surgically repair—"

She stared at him, her breath gone.

"Oh, forgive me, *Madame*. You grow pale."

She clutched her hands together. "No, I am quite well."

He frowned, unsure.

Such a raw description of the horrors visited upon soldiers she had not expected in this afternoon's discussion. "That's very noble work, *Monsieur*."

"*Madame*, think of me differently, I beg you."

"How do you mean?"

"I teach because I must earn my keep. I enjoy the challenge, but with *Mademoiselle* Moore, it is no burden. With your cousin, I would predict the same ease."

"What will Mrs. Moore tell me of your work with her daughter?" Marianne tipped her head, the question quick and necessary.

"I do believe she is very happy with Miss Moore's progress. She allows her to order for her in French when they go to a cafe."

That was a point in his favor that Marianne could seek analysis from Ezzie's mother. "With your work with Miss Moore and the veterans, have you time to teach my cousin?"

"*Oui, Madame*. I could insert her lessons into my days. No more than an hour each day is required to become expert."

"I would demand a maid be present."

"Of course, *Madame*. I would be happy to do so."

He did not flinch at the prospect of a chaperone. "Very well. Let us begin in September."

"Ah. *Oui*. You go to Cherbourg for the month."

"We do, *Monsieur*. I will expect you here the second Monday in September at eleven o'clock. We will have you work with Miss Hanniford for a full four weeks and reassess her progress after that."

"I would be most happy. *Merci beaucoup*."

She stood.

He followed.

"At the end of each week you teach my cousin, please send an invoice for your services. I will give them to my uncle and his manager will promptly send you your fee. If at any point, should I not be pleased, I will terminate the lessons immediately, sir."

"I agree. You should. Thank you, *Madame*. I am most pleased."

So was she. He left her with an easier smile and a more graceful gait. Her instinct said he was no charlatan, no seducer of young women.

Her fears that Ada might be planning some antic dwindled. This man was as he said, a teacher, a technician. Charming too and for Ada, that was inducement to learn from him. All the better. But would he appeal as a lover?

Ada needed a man of discipline and drive. That was certain. She definitely needed a man whose looks arrested her. But she would never find appealing a man who was a scientist. A man devoted to the smallest fact, the finest tuning of a muscle or an engine. *Monsieur* Durant could teach Ada French, but that, Marianne was assured, was all he would do for her cousin.

❧

"What time shall I come back, *Monsieur le duc*?" Andre's maid pushed grey hair from her forehead, bewildered, that for the second night in a row, he'd given her enough money to take lodging in the best hotel on the Butte.

"Seven, eight? Whatever suits you, Nanette."

"Sir? I'm not ashamed that you have a mistress. I was kind to your last lady, wasn't I?"

"Nanette, you were. I send you to *the Hotel de Tertre* not because you've lost your manners but because my visitor wishes no one to see her."

The maid tipped her head and squinted at him. "She shouldn't be ashamed of you, sir."

Andre should have laughed at that. He couldn't. "That's not her challenge."

"If you say so, sir. But I shouldn't be accepting such gifts from you. You pay me well enough, sir, and I—"

He held up hand. "*Merci*, Nanette. If anything changes, I will be sure to end your nights with those soft sheets that someone else washes."

She scoffed. "Your mother would be proud you take such care of your lady."

*My mother is furious that I have not yet married my lady.* "Go! Enjoy yourself!"

He waved her off through the back garden gate toward the square, where musical notes from the violinists and guitarists floated down the hill toward him.

The clopping of a matched pair on the street had him racing for the front door. He arrived just in time to open it for her and take her up high in his arms.

She laughed, more joyous tonight and the sound reverberated through him like chimes on a summer breeze. "You got my note!"

"Valmont was happy to retrieve you at an earlier hour."

"He likes his rest?"

"He likes his snifter of brandy."

"Ah. Put me down, you brute. Save your strength for your marble."

"You are a feather, *Madame* Roland." To demonstrate he hoisted her high, his hands holding her above him, noting the leather folio in her hand, and then catching her over his shoulder. Like a caveman, he strolled with her along the hall and up the few steps to his *atelier*.

She giggled, then tickled his backside.

Growling, he slid her to her feet and twirled her around to face the windows and the skylight. The sun was setting, a bronzed ribbon along the horizon, the roofs of Paris glistening like tarnished silver, the dome of *Les Invalides* shimmering like an upturned bowl of molten gold. He curled his arms around her as she looked her fill.

She wore the fragrance of camellias upon her skin, her little hat lost in the foyer, her white gold hair falling from her loose chignon, no jewelry, either. Beneath his fingertips, he detected she wore few layers. A simple gown, lavender cotton, buttons up the bodice. Perhaps only a corset, or a chemise. His cock jumped, eager, rushing past the enchantment of the moment and his intention to slowly seduce her into his bed.

"Do you know that Pierce wants to invest in Parisian sewers?" She allowed him the freedom of kissing her ear.

"A worthy enterprise," he murmured, laughing at the topic and the addicting opiate of holding her in his arms.

"Paris seems so settled already," she said, her voice catching as he slid his lips along the delicate cords of her throat.

"We grow, change, every minute." He took her portfolio from her and placed it on his worktable. Then he sank his splayed fingers into the magnificence of her hair, turned her around and kissed her until he needed breath.

They broke apart with a gasp.

"I wanted you all day," she whispered and pressed herself to his length. "Kiss me again."

Her invitation ravaged every polite restraint he'd schooled in himself. He took her lips, his tongue invading, seizing from her all the passion she would give him.

"Are you hungry?" he asked, breathless, attempting to be a gentleman and not a satyr.

"Yes." She went up on her toes, her strong fingers cupping his cheeks so that she put her mouth to his again. Her kiss was sweet, short.

He hugged her and chuckled. "I have supper. *Vin blanc,* a veal of—"

"No, no, *Monsieur*. It's only you I want. Feed me that."

He secured her to her feet, his lips twitching. Urgency propelling his hands to unbutton her gown. Her own fingers unwinding his leather belt. His trousers purling on the floor. Her lovely lithe form, her lush breasts pushed up by the corset, her petticoat, cream and lace, untaped, gone to the floor as well. No stockings tonight. Only slippers. Pink satin that she stepped from. Her arms reaching around his neck, looping there as he picked up her, naked to his naked heart and loins and legs. Naked and his.

His cock probed her cleft. She was hot and very wet. He picked her up, tilted her hips and in one sweet slide, he sank inside her. Mindless and sweet. Where did he begin and she end? He could not say.

She gasped as he moved inside her, backed her to his worktable and set her there.

Glancing down, her eyes went wide and then closed. "Oh, Andre. Andre. Give me more. I am so greedy to have you."

And when he drove inside her to the hilt, his own rapture dissolving reason, he inhaled and withdrew to take her once again, deeper, faster, harder.

She clung to him, her skin his. Her cries, his own.

Their mutual satisfaction, one, wild, and vibrant.

But not enough. Each minute that passed meant the sooner she'd leave him. He had to treasure the seconds, forget the future.

He scooped her from the table and strode quickly to lay

her to his bed. The two of them panting, the minutes rolling past, he caressed her throat and breasts as their bodies cooled and the sun sank on a hot August night.

He pushed her wild hair back from her face. "I think you need food now."

"Cheese and bread." She traced the whorls of hair on his chest. "Some of that wine and veal. Where is your maid? She'll think we are animals."

"Not here. Gone to the hotel in the *Place du Tertre*. I gave her the fee."

"I am costing you good money."

He caught her hand and kissed it. "Spent in good cause." *My love. He'd almost called her that. Which would never do. She'd run. Run far.*

Clearing his throat, he rose.

She looked at him askance. "What did I say?"

"I have money for whatever I want in this world." *If only I could buy you, I'd beggar myself.*

"You are a fortunate man, in so many ways." She lay there, not a stitch on her, without a bashful hint of modesty. Letting him gaze his fill, as if he ever would have enough of her.

"I am. How is it that I can attract a beauty like you, hmmm?"

"You have what I want." She wiggled her brows suggestively. Her eyes fell to his cock. "Even now," she said on a raw whisper and let her gaze rise to his. "Every bit of you is inspiring. Strength and ardor, muscle and passion. Wit and compassion."

Flattered, he fought for humility. "Did you come to this conclusion easily?"

"No. I was blind to it. Only seeing that you were the epitome of man for me. And I ran from it."

*Don't you still?*

She sat up, throwing her long white hair over her shoulders. "I brought my sketches for you."

He strode to his wardrobe, pulled out one of his linen shirts and picked up his black robe. Walking to her, he said, "Lift your arms," and he pulled the shirt over her body.

Shrugging into the robe, he said, "Now, show me your work."

She'd not been shy to display her body to him. Her folio, however, she held in her fingers for a minute or more. Biting her lip, she slowly unwrapped the ribbon and extracted a notebook of foolscap. The edges of the pages were ragged. She'd not spent much money on it.

He strolled to his granite workbench, pulled out two stools and gestured for her to join him. Without looking at him, she came to him, sat near him and pushed the notebook unopened toward him.

He did not touch it. "How many years have you drawn?"

"Always. I cannot recall when I didn't. I drew ants and bees, a kitten I had once. Then I tried drawing our horse, an old nag my father said would die soon."

"And people? Did you draw them?"

"Once I began, I have never stopped. Our kitchen maid. Our porter. My parents. I drew them often and they encouraged it. I saved those. Most of them I did before I was married off."

Married *off*. "Did you draw your husband?"

"Yes."

"Why?"

"To remember that I must look to a man's character first. Always."

Her resolve, her sorrow gutted him. "Do you still draw him?"

One shake of her head. "No. I've learned my lesson."

Her answer was too quick. "I see."

"I learned by drawing him and many other men." She swallowed. "During the war, the Yankees came south, headed to Richmond, which was the capital. My land, my husband's and mine, was in their path. They took it, most of it, for their camp. Ate my chickens, slaughtered my pigs. Oh, they shared the spoils with me, but I couldn't absolve them for it. They made my parlor and my dining room their hospital. I drew them all. The Yankees on my carpet. Bleeding on my floor. Their surgeons piling legs and arms in a ditch beyond my barns. I hated those drawings and I threw them away."

Shock of what she'd witnessed riveted him to his stool. What he heard was her horror. "I understand."

"Do you?" She challenged him, anger in her tone, the first he'd ever heard from her. "Have you drawn men in pain?" she asked him, the shadows in her green eyes resurrecting her own suffering.

"Only Samson."

"Do no more. You don't need to. To feel it is to know and wish to forget. And the relief when it's gone is miraculous."

"But to face its existence even when you can't feel it, isn't that wise?"

"Is that what art is? To summon the pain of the past?"

"Isn't it to mark the human condition? After all, we are just flesh and blood."

"No." She shot up from the table. "I won't do that. Look at those, if you like. I—I'm going to examine your garden."

Hands at her sides, fists hard, she made for the far door. His garden had been a refuge for him when his work cast dark shadows on his ambitions and only the sun or the moon could shine a light into his energy and resurrect his insights. She walked out, a hand to her brow as the sun struck her. Through his unlatched window, he heard her muttering to herself and he knew enough of her anger not to follow her out or to ask, when she returned, what irritated her so. Some subjects were meant only for discourse with the soul.

Some. Yes.

He placed his hand on the notebook. Inside was the essence of Marianne Duquesne Roland. Once he looked at this, he'd know her more intimately whatever her skill. Her talent had never been a qualifier for him. She liked to draw. She did it often. His self knowledge told him that one who was compelled to draw or paint or sculpt was usually also obsessed to do it over and over again. Perfection was not the goal. Articulation was. And with the attempts to render came a polishing of the ability. Praise by the public or critics was not so much a goal as a nuisance. Many artists made a living by simply doing what they wished. God knew, he did.

He opened the first page.

The second.

The next.

And next.

He considered the far wall, an expanse of white plaster. The only blank wall in his studio. His screen. His *tabula rasa* for his visions.

He shut his eyes.

There, as on the white wall, he saw her portraits. Her Uncle Killian, the rogue, laughing like a boy, one aspect Andre had never seen in him. Her cousin, Lily, now a duchess, waltzing on the wind, in love in the arms of his friend, Julian. Ada, the child with an adult's intuition and a sharp tongue. Pierce, gazing sorrowfully at the back of a lady dressed in finery. Was that Julian's sister, Elanna? A young woman Pierce had met briefly and who had tricked him into kissing her in a garden days before her wedding to an older man she despised.

Andre flipped another page. There he was, gazing at himself. A portrait in grey graphite. Another and another in ink. His torso swathed in a formal cravat, stickpin, waistcoat, cape. The attire he'd worn to the opera months ago when first he became enraptured by her. The expression on his face was one of wonder. He ran a fingertip over the bold india ink of her impression.

He turned another page. Here he was as he'd met her last night in the informal shirt and pants. Here he was at ease, his eyes wide and appreciative of what he viewed. Her. She had drawn him as he was when he looked at her. His was the look of love.

*Did she recognize it?*

Panic drummed through him.

*Did she understand that how she saw him and how she'd drawn him where unique representations of the truth? Her own artistic truth? One she had the talent to use to make her life sublime?*

*No.* That was the answer.

No.

He stood. Paced.

How to make her see her full potential? As an artist? As a woman? He had so little with which to bargain.

He had to show her...not tell her...

He could not ask her to marry him, half free as she was. If she said yes, she'd come to him thinking she could remain only half of herself. The woman, the lover, the wife of the sculptor Remy. Happy as that might make her, it would be only half of what she could become.

And if he did not offer soon, would she not end their nights together? Of course, she would. Fear of gossip and fear of pregnancy plagued their future rendezvous. And yet if she was not with him, night and day, how could he illustrate what was possible for an artist who lived to her full potential?

He stood, strode to his window. She walked among the roses, devoid of their blooms, bending to inhale the fragrances of his chrysanthemums, roots he'd purchased years ago from a Chinese man in a tugboat along the Seine. In the shade of his tall stone wall fence, the plants soaked up the heat of summer and grew like tall green weeds. She inhaled their perfume. He wished to create a new fragrance of life for her.

She lifted her face and across the grass, their gazes locked.

He smiled at her. She responded with a grin and strolled toward the house and him. She might have experienced loss and depravation, but she was not mean. Nor did she dwell on their differences. She knew how to fight for herself, else she would not have survived her war so well. But he bet that she wished never to fight again.

"I'm hungry now," she told him when she pushed wide his garden door. "Can we have that veal chop and your wine?"

The next morning as the sun cracked the shell of night, she rose up on her elbows and stared down at him. Felling her gaze on him, he feigned sleep. He had loved her so well, so often last night, he was a bowl of mush. But he could rise again in an instant to show her how deeply he cared for her.

"You're awake!"

He opened one eye, then grinned.

She cuffed his shoulder. "Oh, you deceive me."

"I was letting you admire me."

She laughed heartily. "Ah, so you didn't like my sketches of the noble sculptor Remy?"

His failure to discuss her talents bothered her. She'd mentioned it often last night when he would not comment. He hooked an arm around her shoulders and drew her down atop him. "I did not say that."

"You did not deny that." She scowled at him. "What is your assessment of what you did see?"

He touched a fingertip to her nose. "Why?"

She twitched. Defensive and skittish, she sought to leave his arms.

"No. Stay with me."

"You know what I ask for," she told him, tense.

"I do."

"Well?" she prodded.

"I will tell you in my time."

That had her frowning. She pushed away and eluded his reach. "Time to go. Valmont will soon be here and I am not washed or—"

He shot from the bed and caught her around the waist. His hands stroking down her stomach to her neat little thatch, he pressed her back to him. "I will wash you."

She strained to get away from him. "No."

"Yes."

She stomped on his foot.

"Ow!" But he clamped her tightly to him. "Meet me at noon at the Purple Cow in *Place du Tertre*. I will introduce you to friends of mine."

"No, I can't come. I have errands to do."

"It won't take long. An hour. And I promise you, you will enjoy it."

"Why?"

He found the center of her seam, the tight nub that could unlock her petulance and make her the agreeable girl he adored. Circling her flesh, he heard the liquid sound of how her body flowed for him. All that she was betrayed her intentions to leave him.

She sighed his name. "You are not fair."

"I play to keep you." He let his lips slide along her bare shoulder. "I'll brush your hair, wash you everywhere, everywhere."

She made a feral sound and swayed with his touch. "You can't."

"I can."

She sank in his embrace, sweet surrender.

He caught her up and placed her back in their bed. "Don't go. I promise to reward you."

"You are devious," she accused him.

"And to your benefit," he said with a wicked arch of his brows. "I'm getting warm water and cloth and then your hairbrush."

"Evil man." She huffed, then spread herself out on the bed, arms out, legs parted, an indelicate goddess for his appreciation.

He chuckled and ran an open palm over her throat, her diamond hard nipples, her belly, her hot wet folds. She made him weak with want. Delilah to his Samson. How little he'd known of the power of a woman when he'd hacked that man from the marble. Understanding that, he tore himself away from her beauty.

He had the need to show her what she lacked in life.

"You'll return?" she asked, anxious.

"I will. Only a few minutes. Stay where you are."

When he returned, he had all his strengths in hand. Siren that she was, he had a point to make here and she would benefit from his reluctance to tell her what he truly thought of her talent. He rinsed the cloth in the warm water he'd boiled and cooled. He soaped it, beginning with her throat, the fragile clavicles that spanned her chest, her shapely arms and elegant fingers. He rinsed and soaped the other side of her. He returned to her breasts, each a firm mound topped by large chiffon nipples the color of peaches. He drew each into his mouth and sucked her until she whimpered and bucked. Then he scrubbed her with the cloth and made her groan in joy. He moved on. Her belly was concave, smooth as glass. One day, please god, she'd carry their babies there. And if she never did, he'd need her as desperately as he did today. He'd love her and keep her, delving inside her with his fingers and his tongue. He'd part her and kiss her tender little clitoris and make her squirm and beg and demand, as she did now, to have her, put his cock inside her, and cry to never leave her.

"Never," he whispered as she sank to the mattress her orgasm this time as fiery as ever before.

"Come inside me," she begged him, her hands sliding down his ribs to take him by the cock and drive his mind blank as she stroked him. "You must enjoy us."

He must. He certainly must.

The feel of her around him, soft as down, sleek, burning him, branding him, making him hers was once more his finest ecstasy.

She laughed. "You see, you can't wash me without making it necessary to wash me again."

"Who is the fiend now, eh?" he asked as he quickly washed from her thighs the traces of their raptures. He pulled her up and sat her in his chair. Naked, the sight of her lush body nagged at him. *Have me again. Kiss me there. And there. Put your fingers there. Oh, yes.*

But restraint was necessary. He left her, rubbed his hands together and returned to do justice to her hair. He took her long silken mane and flowed it over his forearm. Separating the mass into skeins, he brushed the waist-length waves until they shown and shimmered in the rays of dawn.

Beneath his ministrations, she had sat silent, flowing with his strokes, limp, mesmerized by his rhythm and his care.

He lifted her by her shoulders. He dressed her, lacing her corset, taping her petticoat, putting down her slippers for her to step into. "Time for Valmont to appear and take you away from me. Look at me."

She stared at him with languid wonder in her gaze. "Thank you."

"You're welcome. Now tell me you will meet me at noon."

"How could I refuse?"

That warmed him. This woman was no coward. "You won't regret it."

She looked away.

He caught her chin. "Now tell me you will return to me here again tonight." *Every night. For all our lives.*

"I've no way. Everyone would know." She fell into his arms, clutching him tightly. "I have obligations. A reputation to uphold. Ada to supervise."

"Think on it." He ran his open palm over the smooth wealth of her hair, down her back. The lovely lady who must let down her golden hair and leave the security of her castle for the life she should have. "I will see you at noon."

When she climbed up into his brougham, she did not look back at him. Did not wave goodbye.

"Noon," he repeated as if he were drilling it into her mind. *Noon. Come.*

# CHAPTER 10

The Place du Tertre bustled with people in the heat of the August sun. The main plaza of the Montmartre suburb of Paris sat amid a *mélange* of stately limestone buildings and a few tumbledown wooden houses. Cheap housing attracted the artists plus dancers, the singers and the laborers of the suburb. Andre's house and *atelier* was one of the few substantial edifices in the growing arrondissement.

Marianne had stepped down from her public hackney near the huge construction site of the church of *Sacre Coeur*. Workers heaved heavy stones, directing pulleys to deposit the huge blocks to the walls. They sweat profusely in the heat. A few stopped to watch her, a woman alone and frankly, more fashionably dressed than many others up here on the Butte.

Her walk to the square cleared her mind of her concerns about coming here alone. She should be home directing her maid for packing for the family's trip to Cherbourg. The lure of Andre and her curiosity about his method of revealing his opinion of her work drew her on, though. To be honest, she welcomed the escape. To be with him in the light of day and to make a choice for herself that was solely for her own enjoyment filled her with a new and welcome confidence.

A few café owners had wheeled out their awnings to shield their patrons from the baking heat. In the square, men with their easels and toolboxes of paints and brushes sat beneath the few trees. Many had brought their umbrellas and lashed them to their easels. Squinting in the sun, they worked and measured their visions against their products. Two women sat among them, painting as well.

Music spilled out in to the plaza, pianos and violins rippled in counterpoint to guitars and concertinas. The artists seemed not to notice. They did not sing or dance. No one tapped his feet or snapped his fingers. Each was intent on his work. Some slathered a background onto a canvas in broad brush strokes. Others refined more finished works with their own techniques, some of delicate dots, or heavy daubs of impasto.

Marianne strolled along, caught by an artist's landscape of the plaza, done in peaches and greens, the illusions of the bustle around her gay and palpable. She walked on, to pause at last before a portrait of a little girl. The child was two or three years old, with intent blue eyes and pink chubby cheeks, the world she surveyed simple and jolly.

"Does *Madame* wish to buy this?" A painfully thin man with the avid look of an ascetic stood before her.

"I do like it. *Oui, Monsieur.* But I cannot carry it now. Perhaps if you are here in an hour, I could return?"

"I would remain here for you, *Madame*."

"*Merci beaucoup.*"

"Do you not wish to know the price?"

"*Oui.* Certainly."

"Ten francs."

"*Oh, Monsieur*. Ten is much too little. Your work is worth more than that."

"That is precisely what I have told *Monsieur* de Salle for many years." Andre bid his friend hello. He took her arm with one hand. In the other, he held her portfolio. She'd forgotten it this morning and was relieved he'd brought it for her.

"You are so right, *Monsieur le duc.* Quote me another price," she begged de Salle.

"Twenty."

Andre arched his brows at her. In the brilliant sunlight, his long waves glistening. Today, he was casual, loose shirt and linen trousers, sans hat. She was so proud of who and what he was. In any light, in any room, in any landscape, to her he was irresistible.

She opened her reticule and her tiny leather purse. She took out three bills and placed them in de Salle's hand. "I will return for the painting later."

"She will indeed, De Salle. She lunches with me in the Purple Cow." Andre motioned across the square.

"But *Madame*," de Salle said and frowned at the money in his hand. "This is too much."

"I believe a work of art has its value for the artist, but another for the admirer, *Monsieur.* I like your little girl. Please keep those francs."

He bowed. "As you wish, *Madame*."

Andre led her away, a grin gracing his lips. "*Madame* Roland, you have made that man very happy."

"I make myself happy." She walked with him into an intimate cafe that smelled of garlic, fish and beer. "When does one meet this Purple Cow?"

"He arrives after you've had a few pints of Flemish beer." He caught the eye of the garçon and the man appeared at their side. "Two beers, Paul, *s'il vous plait.* And to eat, what will you have, *Madame*?"

Rustic meals were simple affairs she'd rarely enjoyed since

arriving in Europe. Stripping off her gloves, she noted most in the dark restaurant ate mussels from a steaming pot. "The same as those patrons there."

Their waiter hurried away, his shouts to the cook at the rear of the bar, ear-piercing orders that had Marianne flinching. "Is he angry?"

"No. He's nearly deaf. Once an artillery officer in the French Legion. He thinks he speaks in a normal tone."

"How does he get the orders if he can't hear?"

"He reads lips."

"Inventive. Thank you for returning my drawings." She put out her hand.

But he shook his head. "At the end of lunch."

"You'll give them back?"

"I have a plan for them."

Anxiety crept into her good morning. "What is it?"

"You'll see. Ah!" He leaned back so that Paul could place their beers before them. "*Merci.*"

"What plan?"

Another man appeared at their table. Dressed in a gentleman's afternoon walking suit, he appeared quite businesslike.

"*Madame* Roland." Andre got to his feet. "May I present a friend of mine, *Monsieur* Edouard Montand."

"*Enchante, Madame.* I am pleased to make your acquaintance."

Andre pulled out the chair next to him. "I'm delighted you've joined us."

"My curiosity was announced by your note to me. Of course, I would come."

*Monsieur* Montand was a white-haired gentleman of middling height, ample girth, with a substantial winged mustache, pointed goatee and the sharp eyes of a man about town. Why had Andre invited him here?

"Do you live close by, *Monsieur?*" she asked him.

"No, *Madame*. I live above my gallery in the Rue de Provence."

*Not far from Rue Haussmann.* A very respectable part of town. "A gallery?"

"*Monsieur* has a very profitable business, *Madame*," Andre told her, then hailed the waiter to attend them.

"What sort of gallery do you own, *Monsieur*?"

Paul appeared at once and their guest ordered a German beer. "The Flemish is too weak for my taste," he explained. "I buy many paintings and sell them for a commission. Do I detect that *Madame* is an American?"

"I am." She tried to smile at him, but nerves were crawling up her spine. She could tell precisely why Andre had invited Montand here—and she worried at the result.

"I have many American patrons. English, too. But Americans are more liberal in their approach to art. They have a willingness to look beyond the classical to see *la vie douce*."

"The sweet life," she translated the term she'd read in the newspapers. "We've lived through war to prosper."

"Much as we have in France, *Madame*."

"Would I know any of the artists whose work you buy for your clients?"

"I wonder. Monet? Manet? Sisley?"

"Those 'impressionists', yes. I've heard of them. I've seen a few of their works."

"And?"

"I like them." She didn't hold back her grin. "They improvise. They are inspirational."

The agent tipped his head. "How so?"

"I draw."

"Well, then you appreciate the new, the *avant garde*."

"She does," Andre said with nonchalance. "She, too, is an artist."

She held her breath. If this man appraised her pieces and

found them wanting, she would recoil from the blow. "I have not shown my work to anyone. I do it for myself."

"She has," Andre said to Montand, "but she needs an opinion that is not mine."

Montand was quick to glance from one to the other. He smiled, the glow in his eyes giving her to understand he knew the two of them were connected by more than appreciation of art.

"I have a sample of her sketches here with me, Montand." Andre glanced at her briefly.

"You think them worthy of a look?"

"I do."

Montand reached inside his coat and extracted a tiny leather glasses case. "Shall I assess them, *Madame*?"

She must employ new boldness. "Please."

Flipping open his case, Montand extracted a folding pair of spectacles and perched them on his nose. He grasped the portfolio, removed the sketchbook and turned the pages. Silent, he examined one than another. Occasionally, he returned to a previous sketch. Once he compared an older rendering of Andre to another she'd finished last week.

Marianne drank her beer. Gripped her fingers tightly together. Looked away, bit her lip and took another sip of beer. Her spine tingled. Her eyes watered.

Paul came with Monsieur Montand's beer. The agent did not drink, but continued his perusal of her works.

At last, he closed the book, rearranged those pages that escaped the confines and handed the book over to her.

"Tell me, *Madame*, how long have you been drawing?"

"Since I was very young, three, four years old. It was a pastime for an only child."

"What did you sketch then?"

"People. Men and women. My parents. Our servants. Our field hands. Our dog. The barn cats. Occasionally, flowers."

"No landscapes?"

She shrugged. "They do not interest me as much as human beings."

"I wish to see more of every subject."

That shocked her. "I have few of those with me here at home. I came to Europe with my family last autumn and I did not pack my older works." *Or most of them. The inclusion of those of Frederick was a gross mistake.*

"You are abroad with your family?"

She shifted in her chair. To reveal that she was one of the Hanniford family might mean this man could repeat the fact in society. She'd be talked about. Her work discussed. "I am."

"I detect a need for discretion," he said.

Marianne heard the clipped efficiency of a businessman. So like her uncle's. "You do, *Monsieur.*"

"I am not in the habit of discussing my clients' private lives with those who purchase their works."

"*Monsieur?*" She was not his client.

"*Madame* Roland, let me be plain. I want to see more from you. In what other mediums do you work?"

"Ink, occasionally chalk. Watercolors, now and again."

"Do you have any I might view?"

"I do."

"And those of *Monsieur le duc*? Have you more?"

"*Oui, Monsieur.*" She sat taller as invisible chains fell from her shoulders. "Dozens."

"Newer? Older?"

"This collection is the latest set."

Montand leaned forward and extracted her most recent portrait of Andre. "The last one here?"

She cocked her head. "What about it?"

"I want it."

"*Monsieur?*"

"If you will allow me, I would sell it."

"Of *Monsieur le duc*?" She did not understand.

"Remy becomes a rage. You must know this, friends as you are."

She nodded.

Andre wrestled with a grin.

"Allow me to frame this. Sell it for you. Please bring me others, too. You could go to another agent. But I'd be happy to oblige you with the exposure."

"I—I hardly know what to say except I am honored."

"Permit me to be honored, *Madame*. And you, Remy?"

"*Oui,* Montand?"

"Nurture her."

"Ah. Montand, if she will only permit me."

Marianne listened but heard little.

Her entree came. She ate. Drank.

Andre and Montand spoke to each other. To her. They spoke of Andre's latest commission for the City. Andre demurred and said the marble in his *atelier* was unformed in his mind. He had been, he said with a glance at her, preoccupied lately. Montand discreetly said nothing. She chatted with them about mundane, simple things. About her assessment of Andre's works. The Samson. His Delilah. The laughing baby he'd carved.

All the while inside her, she noted the brewing of a storm. Winds of change ruffling her hair, showers draining away clouds of her own making.

Then Montand rose, kissed her hand, and hoped she would bring the portrait to him the next day.

"I will," she promised. She'd do it before she left with the family for Cherbourg.

"Excellent." Montand bid them both good day.

"Another beer?" Andre asked her as she watched the dealer walk away.

"No. *Merci.* How am I to thank you?"

"Oh, well." He scanned the interior of the dark little cafe. "I need none."

She grinned. "And if I insist?"

He wore a dashing smile. "I leave that for you to decide."

*Yes.* Of course he would. She leaned closer to him. "I am not used to such largesse."

"I know. But you should have it, learn its values."

"You could have told me this morning that you thought my work...good. Suitable." She lifted her shoulders and opened her arms. "Salable."

"If I had told you, would you honor my words as much as Montand's?"

"I do not think you capable of lying to me."

"I thank god for that, *ma cherie.* But I could not risk your reaction."

That took her aback. "You assumed I would take your approbation as my due because we sleep together?"

"I questioned if you would use it as a means to remain as you are."

"What?"

He glanced away and pursed his lips. Then he examined her minutely, as if he chose his words carefully. "Working and living in the shadows of your own talents. Your own goals."

Speech deserted her. His understanding of her roiled her. Even shamed her. But it stirred the storm inside her. She shot to her feet. "I must go."

He pushed back his chair, scraping the wooden legs against the rough-hewn floor as he stood. "Why?"

"I need to pack. We leave day after tomorrow. It's—it's Cherbourg for the month."

He took her hand. "Come to me instead. Live with me, Marianne. Here."

Oh, how she wanted that. The freedom, the raw pleasure of his company. But to become his mistress, anyone's mistress, was the very thing she'd promised herself she'd never do. Never tie herself to any man. Only physical pleasure was what she wished. Only lust. Never love.

"Forget Cherbourg, Marianne. Discover all we can be together. All you can be for yourself."

"I could dare to be so bold, but—" She would break every wall of her haven. Destroy every barrier between her and the unknown.

"Decide, *ma cherie*. What life will you live, Marianne? The life you think you want? Safe, secure from the chaos of the world. Or the life you choose for yourself? Rich in ambition, vibrant in reward?"

*Madame le Comtesse* bustled about the luggage as the Hannifords' footmen tugged it from the boot of their carriage. "I count only eleven. There were twelve, I am most certain."

Marianne walked around to Ada, eyeing her own standing trunk and the smaller valise that contained her clothes for the four weeks at the seaside. She had gowns, tea dresses, walking outfits for strolling along the promenade. A navy bathing dress. All intended for Cherbourg. *Without Andre.*

People eager to meet their trains bustled around them, headed for the station that took thousands each day from Paris to far corners of France and Europe.

"Should we send the carriage back for the other?" *Madame* Chaumont asked Marianne. The woman did not address Uncle Killian with such trivial issues. She knew better than to pester him so. "The maids should have checked the numbers."

"They did. I was there in the foyer." Marianne said, not caring about clothes or trains or trunks. She put a hand to her aching heart.

"We should have brought my maid and yours along," Ada

complained. "How do we know the servants we hire at the hotel will be worth their salt?"

"They are highly recommended," Chaumont said, justifying her own recommendation to leave the personal maids in Paris for the month.

"I should have counted them myself," Marianne said. She'd had no mind for such minutia, fretting about how Andre was taking her rejection of his invitation.

"*Monsieur* Hanniford?" Chaumont addressed Pierce with a flutter of her lashes. "What is your assessment?"

"I have one piece. Ada how many did you have your maid pack?" And on down the list, Pierce took a tally of what ought to be here.

Marianne heard only the voice of *Monsieur* Montand yesterday in his gallery. She replayed it in her head like a melody that obsessed her.

Over and over, she heard him. "*Madame* Roland, I am grateful to you. From this portrait of Remy, you will see a profitable beginning."

A profitable beginning. A *beginning*.

"I never sought to sell any sketch of mine, *Monsieur* Montand."

"Then I suggest you think of your art in new ways, *Madame*."

"Why would anyone wish to buy my sketch of *Monsieur le duc*?"

Whether Montand could not believe she was that naive, or if he simply wished to educate her in the way of the art business, she had no idea. But he said, "Your view of Remy shows his character, *Madame*. Thousands hear of him, few know him, fewer still may ever meet him. And what we see in your sketch is more than a *carte de visite* could show. You care for him. And here, as he gazes back at us through the page, we see how he cares for you. You have captured him as a man of flesh and emotion. He is all too human."

*All too human. Real.*

She'd glanced at her sketch once more and pulled back at the sight of Remy's portrait. She saw him through Montand's eyes.

'You care for him.' Montand had said.

*I do.*

"What's the problem?" Killian strode round to the rear of their carriage.

Marianne stepped backward, away from Killian and Pierce, Ada and Chaumont.

Pierce told his father the summary of his tally of the luggage. "*Madame le Comtesse* thinks we have misplaced one item. I still count only eleven."

"Does it matter that much?" Killian barked, sweeping off his straw boater and tucking it under his arm. He'd been in a terrible mood the past few days. Out late at night, surly with every one during the day. "If we're missing clothes, we'll go naked. Or buy what we need."

Ada fidgeted. She'd been irritable since she'd returned from Rheims with her friends yesterday. "Oh, please. Let's just go."

Killian fished out his pocket watch. "The train leaves in fifteen minutes. The conductor waits for no man. Take in the bags," he ordered the footmen.

Marianne stood, rooted to her spot, staring at Killian.

"What's wrong?" her uncle asked her. "Do you remember what's missing?"

"I do," she told herself more than him. "I'm not going with you."

"What?"

"I can't."

"Why?" Killian asked, skeptical.

She took his arm and led him a few steps away from the others. "I would like to take my vacation elsewhere."

"Marianne—"

"Please don't chastise me. Please don't bargain with me."

"I'm not. But—"

He peered at her. "You're not going home to Rue Haussmann, are you?"

She shook her head. "To Remy's *atelier* in Montmartre."

He flinched, came closer and lowered his voice. "You're a grown woman, my dear, but I fear for you, if this goes wrong."

"I know you do. But I must go. I am ever grateful to you."

Killian trained his gaze on the circle of carriages drawing up to the front of station. "Gratitude won't save you from physical consequences."

"I understand." She hadn't been careful about bearing children as a result of her intimacies with Remy, but what she'd never shared with anyone, what none of them knew was that she doubted she could become pregnant. During her married life, she'd never experience a halt in her monthlies. Frederick's hasty, feral couplings with her were so fierce, she'd been glad of her barrenness. Believing herself incapable of bearing children, she'd never worried about it. Never had reason to worry...until now that she had a lover whose caresses drove her to a sweet oblivion. "But I must have this time to myself. If you wish to disown me, you may."

"Disown?" Killian gripped her hand. "Never think it. You are my darling child as much as my other three. My sister would disown me on Judgment Day if I ever did that. For what she did for me, my girl, how she never disowned me, do you think I'd have the heart to do it to you?"

Tears sprang up.

"Don't cry, please." He took a handkerchief from his vest pocket and tucked it in her hand. "Take the carriage."

"No. People will know where I go. The scandal could affect you—"

He put two fingers beneath her chin and raised her face to smile at her. "We'll hold our heads up and laugh at them."

She put a hand to the brim of her hat, so she could see him more clearly. As he truly was, generous. Kind. "You are an extraordinary man, sir."

He barked in laughter. "Tell that to my rivals, will you?"

"Why, sir, I did not think you had any."

"Get on with you, you minx. Take the damn carriage. Remember the door to Rue Haussmann is open to you, if you need or want to return before we do. We are your family, come what may."

"*Merci beaucoup, Monsieur* Hanniford." She gave him a small curtsy and bussed his cheek. "I will return to the house at the latest on the day you return from Cherbourg."

"Go, before I change my mind!"


With great thanks for his solicitude to drive her to Montmartre before returning to Rue Haussmann, Marianne bid the Hanniford coachman *adieu*. He'd offered to wait for the owner of the house to open the doors so that he could take her trunk and valise inside for her. But she had not wished to cause him any delay.

A thin young man opened the broad blue door for her, then stood there bewildered. He pointed to a sign hooked to the knocker. '*Ferme!*' "We receive no one, *Madame*. My master is at work."

This must be Carré, Andre's apprentice, about whom she'd heard little, save his existence.

"*Monsieur*, I do believe if you tell *Monsieur le duc* that a *Madame* Roland is here, he will permit my entrance."

The youth's gaze traveled over her with curiosity. "He is not tolerant of interruptions, *Madame*."

"*Monsieur*, I will tell him you bear no blame for allowing me to call on him."

"That's not the problem, *Madame*."

"No?"

"He awoke late and he is...unpleasant. He does not receive anyone today. My strict orders are not to let anyone in."

"Then would you give him a message for me?"

"Very well." Carré glanced over his shoulder. "What is it?"

"Say to him, 'Marianne did not take the train'."

"I will tell him. Good day." And he slammed the door shut.

She folded her hands and waited. Up in the square, a violinist was tuning his instrument. A huckster barked his wares. *Mussels! Shrimp!* An old woman appeared in the upper story window across the street to peer at her and shake out her bed linens, then drape them over the sash.

The blue door was ripped open.

"Marianne?" Andre stood in the portal, shirt askew, pants tied by one of his leather ropes, bare feet, hair on end and sky blue eyes bloodshot. "*Mon Dieu*. Carré, get her bags."

He reached for her hands. "Come in. Quickly. Let me look at you."

She smiled at his shock and dawning delight. "Good morning."

The apprentice scurried about, grunting as he hauled the trunk over the threshold. "Where should I take—?"

"The bedroom along the foyer." He pulled her near to him.

Andre meant her to sleep down here, away from him? "Andre, if you do not wish me here, I can—"

He had her in his arms. "I most certainly will have you here. The bedroom on this floor has a larger wardrobe than the one in my studio. A bureau, too. And I see you have brought enough clothes to show the *petite bourgeoisie* of Montmartre how a fashionable lady dresses."

Wincing, she smacked a hand to his chest and turned her face aside. "And I can tell you had a bit too much wine last night."

"*Pardon e moi.*" He stepped backward, still holding her hands. "I awaited a verdict. I could not work. So I drank."

Carré disappeared down the main hall, dragging her trunk behind him.

She pulled off her gloves, one finger at a time. "Do you drink to distraction often, *Monsieur le duc?*"

He cast her a sideways look. "What do I detect in your tone?"

She'd come here today ready to be open with him about so many things. This too she'd impart. "I don't like dealing with drunkards."

"I'm not. Usually not. I had reason the past few days, if you give me leave for it."

She tipped her head to and fro, testing him, forgiving him. "I can."

"What else should you tell me about drunkards?" He lifted her chin, his fingertip tracing the swell of her lower lip. "There is more. I hear it. Tell me."

"I saw what drink can do to men. One or two and they're happy. Three or four and they're mean. Five or six and they can be murderous."

"I can drink five or six and I am still happy. Until of course, the next morning."

"And the next morning, can you work?"

"After a bath and shave, I consider it."

"And this morning?" she pressured him.

"I can. Under one condition."

"Which is?"

"You keep me company."

She grinned at him. "That I can do."

He smiled and then the joy drained from him. "You're here for August? All of it?"

"All of it. They return from Cherbourg the first week in September."

"Was your uncle angry with you?"

"He was more understanding than angry."

"Thank God."

"He wouldn't have stopped me, I don't believe. He was no angel himself. A scrapper on the docks of Baltimore. Winning with his fists and his wits. A gambler who bet that he could run the Union blockade and make money at it. Now, if he tries to burnish his reputation, I can't fault him. He wants to buy the world for his family."

"Including you."

"He recognizes I am older and that I have..."

"What?"

"A different background than Lily or Ada, even Pierce."

"They did not experience the war, did they?"

"They were children."

"So were you, *ma cherie*."

"Let's not talk of that, shall we? I'm hungry and I need to get out of these hot traveling clothes." She spread her arms to indicate the heavy walking dress, the cumbersome petticoats and bustle. The corset too.

"Shall I help you?" He wiggled his brows.

"You must." She put up a finger. "Just don't breathe on me."

"Of course not." He grabbed her hand and tugged her along the foyer. "Come with me."

Within minutes she was released from her layers of petticoats and stays, the bustle and her corset. He had unbuttoned, unlaced, untaped all her garments and kissed bits of her revealed to him. Her loins flooded with wet desire as he slipped his hands over the welts from her corset, the straps of her chemise. And when he put his lips to her nipples and sucked her up into his arms, she moaned her approval. But he smelled and she smacked a hand to his chest. "A bath, please!"

He chuckled and left her to dress. Her old gingham gown was one she added to her collection for the seaside. But here in happy Montmartre it suited her with its yellow stripes and lime green trim. It had faded but pleased her. And it was cooler.

She buttoned up the front to the broad collar, but decided it was so warm, she'd leave it undone.

From afar, Andre had watched her pull on the gown. As she finished he pushed away from the bureau to cuddle her close, his smile at her reflection in the full length mirror one of chivalry and devilry. "Now we'll go upstairs."

In the studio, Carré bustled about, filling up a long porcelain tub in the far corner of the *atelier*.

"Does he do that every time you wish to take a bath?"

"Horrible, isn't it? But we up here in the butte will get pipelines soon. Down in Rivoli, we have running water. A tub big enough for both of us, too."

She blushed and sneaked a look at Carré. He did not seem to notice her discomfort. Instead, the tub full, he hurried away and closed the door.

"We'll go down to the big house in a few days." Andre stripped, climbed in the tub, naked, and submerged himself head, hair and all. He came up, sputtering, reaching for a thick bar of soap. "I have to check on the servants. My mother's butler is aging and I must look to see if he's taking his tonics."

She strolled to the window and the view down into the City. In the heat, the skyline looked as if it misted in a mirage.

"What happened with Montand?" he asked her. "You did go, I hope?"

"I did." She walked to the work bench were one of Andre's sketch books lay open. Balls of paper scattered about indicated the frustration he had. "I gave him the portrait of you that he liked. He believes he can sell it. I remain utterly astonished."

"You had no idea your skills were superb?"

"Does one hope for it? Of course. Can one compare one's work to what one sees? Naturally. But to be so enamored with one's abilities as to hope it is...what?...commercial? No. I did not."

Andre was thoughtful, quiet as he washed.

"My uncle allows me use of Rue Haussmann, if I wish it."

Her abrupt change in subject and tone had him pausing to meet her gaze. "Do you?"

She licked her lips and took a few steps to perch on a stool that faced him.

He sat forward, sloshing water to the floor. "Tell me, Marianne. I must know sooner or later. I thought you said outside that you wanted to stay here for the month. Now—"

"I have a favor to ask of you. A few, in fact."

He rose. His glorious body sluicing bath water, his beauty touched her. Brought tears to her eyes. She would draw him like that. More impressive than any man she'd ever known.

He picked up toweling that Carré had draped over the lip of the tub. Running his fingers through his long hair, he hooked the cloth around his hips and climbed from his bath. "Well?"

"First, I must thank you for the introduction to *Monsieur* Montand."

"You did once." He picked up both her hands and kissed her fingertips. "You are welcome."

"I know I would never have met him were it not for you."

"It's what friends do for each other. Colleagues who share the same challenges."

She liked that. "Friends and colleagues."

"And lovers, *ma cherie*. You are my talented lover." He winked, and strode to his shave stand where he took tooth powder and brushed his teeth. When he was done, he sat on a large stool on the opposite side of the room. Far away.

"What do you wish to negotiate, *ma petite*?"

"I want to enjoy you here. That means I must tell you a few facts."

His good humor died. And he waited.

"I want you to know that I doubt I may ever get with child. I had no fear of it when we began our affair the other night and I have none now. I don't want you to worry that I would become pregnant and use it as a means to trap you."

Andre glared at her. "That would be no—"

"Stop." She clamped shut her eyes. "Please. Let me finish. I want you to understand that I know I am incapable. I was married for nearly a year before Frederick took his commission and went off to fight. We were intimate. He was... frequently attentive. He wanted a child. A son. Badly. Still I didn't ever show signs I might have been pregnant. Even if I had, I wouldn't have wanted his baby." She clamped a hand over her mouth.

Andre's expression turned mellow. But he remained silent.

"That was awful to say. But it's true."

"I'm sure you had a reason."

"Reason? Oh, yes. Many. First among them, he was a terrible lover. I suspected it but affirmed that five nights ago here with you. He knew nothing about tenderness or rapture like you do. He was crass and quick and—" She swallowed deeply, loudly. "I was glad there was no child. Glad. If that makes me a monster, so be it."

Andre narrowed his gaze on her, as if he concentrated on what she said beyond her words.

"I have had no lovers. Only you. So I am unable to tell you, if there is something wrong with me. If I am deformed or—"

In a second, he was on his knees before her, his fingers wrapped around her wrists. "My darling, you are perfectly formed. There is nothing wrong with you."

"But...but inside? It's possible."

"Why would you think that?"

"Because I—he—"

"Go on."

"He was cruel. He was clumsy. Crude. He liked doing it harshly. Often. On a whim. Anywhere. I was his property, he said. Just like his slaves."

Andre stood and attempted to take her in his arms.

But she pushed away. "After that wedding night, he took me so often, so quickly that I bled. I think I was torn. It was painful to have him inside me."

"Marianne—"

She put up a palm. "I was glad he went to war. Glad? No, that's too mild. I rejoiced when he was gone. So did our slaves. The field hands that he whipped until they bled and could not walk. The maids and our cook were liberated from his lewd attentions. He had them too, you see. Had them over and over, so often that they bore his children. Five of them. Five, I counted. Maybe there were more by the time he rode off to join General Lee. I could see they were his children. They looked like him. Every one. Blue-eyed. Sharp noses. Distinctively his."

Andre still stood, arms folded, his gaze full of sympathy.

She must be blunt. "You cannot expect any children from this."

"I want only you."

She bit her lower lip. He could and would say that. He wanted her that much. She felt it in his touch. Good thing then that this interlude was just that. Temporary. Fleeting. A love affair that would be an elusive butterfly, quick, charming, borne on a lightness of air. "I must have something else."

"Name it."

"You must not to do anything as you did with *Monsieur* Montand to introduce me to anyone who will advance me."

"Very well."

"If I have any talent, I want others to see it as they will. Not because you promote me."

"As you wish."

"And finally, I would ask that when our four weeks are over, you let me go without argument."

He set his jaw, the cords in his throat working in strain. "Why?"

"I cannot stay."

"You can if you wish, Marianne."

"No. I do not wish." *A lie. And yet not one.*

"What are you afraid of?" he asked her, his voice rough with anger and hurt.

She put two hands to her chest. "I am not afraid!"

"*No?*" He challenged her.

"This was not a good idea. It couldn't work." She rose and stepped toward the door.

He caught her back against him. "I don't know yet how to kill the demons that haunt you, my darling, but someday you will show them to me."

She shook her head and to her shock, tears were rolling down her cheeks.

"Stay. Live with me. Let me buy you wine and feed you chocolate. Let me watch you sketch. Let me give you the freedom you have never known and need to grasp. Let me make love to you at night and in the morning sun, in the garden on the dewy grass and on the floor."

She gave a laugh in spite of herself. How alluring was the life he offered as if it were her due.

He turned her around and thumbed the cascade of tears from her cheeks. "Stay. Don't leave me. I need you, *mon étoile*. The night is long and day is sharp. But love makes it a miracle."

CHAPTER 11

S he'd never lived like this. Without a schedule. Slaves
to direct. Servants to supervise. Cousins to chaperone. Calls to make. Breakfast at sunrise when she was
a child and a bride. Then as an adult, only in the dining room
between seven and nine. Corsets, chemises, petticoats to don
and always the damned bustle to tackle. Tea was had once a
day in America or often in England when someone called.
Sometimes even at eleven. Luncheon was as formal as dinner.
Clothes were changed three, four, five times a day. Gloves for
this. Shoes for that. Hats, hair pins. Jewelry. Stockings.

But here in Andre's *atelier* none of that prevailed. Rules
were gone. Banned.

"I like you without your stays," he said one evening as he
stripped her of her day gown. "The bones marred your flesh.
You are too perfect, *mon amour.* Those ugly things are meant
to change what needs no changing."

She sighed as he nibbled on her throat and sent mad
shivers down her spine. "If you tell that to *Monsieur* Worth
and *Madame* Rousseau, they would lose half their income."

"They deserve it. Transforming a woman into a creature in

a cage? It's what they do. Why? When this—" He kissed her nipples, each in turn, and had her hanging deliciously limp in his embrace. "This is perfection."

He carried her to their bed. His hands skimming her ribs and her hip, he let his mouth follow. And when he was inside her, and she arched up to feel the full power of his possession, he said, "I want the world to view what a glory you are when you make love to me."

She undulated, the luscious girth of him inside her, caressing her.

"Say you'll let me."

She cupped his handsome face and tipped up her hips. "Yes, anything. Just make love to me."

The next morning after Nanette had left them to their peaches and cream and baguette, Andre tore off a piece of bread and asked the question again. "I'm not sure you heard me, *mon amour*."

She noticed how he was calling her that lately. Since she'd accepted his invitation to live here with him this month, she'd become his 'love'. The words thrilled her to the bone. Though she could reciprocate, she did not and felt guilty. Why, escaped her. Or rather, she pushed the question aside. Her examination of that could wait. Must. After all, had she not told herself that she dared not love? Dared not give herself completely into someone else's power ever again? Especially a lover who could use her love of him to bend her to his will.

"Did you? Hear me?"

She chewed her bread and nodded. "Yes. Given your...ah... position inside me last night at that moment, I was not certain if your remark was politesse or romantic chivalry."

"I assure you, *Madame*, it was neither. I appreciate the female form. But yours?"

She tossed her loose blonde curls over her shoulder. "*Oui, Monsieur le duc?* What of mine?"

He threw down his bread and a heated but whispered curse escaped his lips. In a thrice, he was up and around the trestle table in the kitchen, took her wrist, and led her off to the far bedroom where he shut the door with a thud. "Let me show you."

He proceeded to remove every stitch of clothing she wore and turned her unceremoniously to the cheval glass. Behind her, he stood with his blue eyes blazing hotter by the moment with desire. She demurred, noting how her nakedness cooled her skin and his attentions heated her blood and her belly.

"Look at yourself."

She raised her eyes slowly.

"Examine the proportions of your head, your neck."

She followed his instructions.

"Put up your hand to your face, palm to chin, middle finger to the top of your forehead. Good. Now put your palm to your forearm, elbow to wrist."

She'd never realized that her hand was as long as her forearm. Or her face.

"Now put your forearm to the length of your thigh. Yes. And again to your lower leg."

"I never saw such proportions existed."

"In you they do. Now sit there in the chair."

She primly took a seat.

"Lift your foot and place your foot to your forearm."

She smiled at him.

"Most humans are proportional in at least three aspects. You have them all. Now stand up. Come here." He beckoned her with his fingers to stand again before him and face the mirror.

A blush rushed from her chest to her cheeks.

He put his whole hand, fingers splayed, gently against the

curve of her throat to her shoulder. Against her ear, he said, "Now look at your breasts."

She did. Why not? She'd looked at men in their naked-ness, their bare pain, hysteria. She'd glimpsed them lax from morphine or screaming to have more of it, eaten up with terror of a saw. She'd watched them bleed. Held their hands while their last breath slipped between their lips. She'd seen their muscled arms, their lean ribs, their thighs. Yes, their bare groins. She'd understood how one muscle interplayed with another. Shrapnel and bullets and bombs did not discriminate, showed no discretion for etiquette or propriety. This was God's perfect creation, the complex symphony of blood and muscles, nerves and brain. She had sketched men, women, children, her family, and Andre, over and over. She'd viewed them as personalities. She'd failed to experience them at their primal form. Failed to understand them inside out. She'd become a much better artist if she were able to render them as physical entities, similar to each other in form, dissimilar in small details how they moved—and how they acted.

She confronted the example that stood before her in the glass. To draw others, did she not need to know herself first and best?

Of course, she did.

She was her first best model. She had to portray herself well before she attempted to perfect others.

The curves of her breasts were subtle, her nipples smooth, pink and hard. His gaze excited her. His praise dissuaded her from the erotic influence of his presence.

She put her hands beneath her breasts, lifting their weight, marking the change in shape from moons to spheres. Stepping to one side, she marked her profile and the outline of her form. She arched up and noted the lift, the extension of her back, her buttocks, her legs. How the muscles rippled and coordinated, how they synchronized.

She faced front once more, extended her arms. The cords of her own muscles lent shape to her arms, her shoulders. The shape of her breasts changed then too.

She dragged the chair before the mirror. Seated, she was a different form. Leaning forward, twisting to one side and the other, she moved in a fluid dance, as unpremeditated as anyone who walked the streets outside.

The sun hung low on the horizon when she barged through the door of the *atelier*.

Her hand to the door latch, she paused and stared at Andre. Carré was not to be seen. Not Nanette either. In anticipation that the two would still be here, she'd had presence of mind to throw on her clothes before she ran through the house up to the studio.

Andre sat at his worktable, the block of Carrara directly in his sight, his little glasses perched on his nose. He worked with a soft clay figure. His fingers deftly modeling the dark clay, he shaped the figure of a woman. She stood arching to the sky, lithe, nude, less than half as tall as Marianne. It was the first time she'd seen him at his work and she had no wish to disturb him. He was lost in his work, pinching here, smoothing there, taking a small knife and removing a bit of clay in another point. The woman seemed to emerge from the clay, stretching out to reach the sky...or perhaps even her lover. Marianne padded to the table, attempting no sound, but he had sensed her and turned to stare at her with unseeing eyes. Still flowing in the act of his own creation, he blinked. His vision cleared and he regarded her with an arched brow.

She rested her cheek on his shoulder. "*Merci beaucoup* for the instruction, *mon cher*."

He regarded her with satisfaction.

"I'm pleased to see you at your own work." The woman had long flowing hair, like her own. High cheek bones, like her own. Uplifted breasts. Her own. A flat belly, lean hips. She'd never carried a child. "Does she have a name?"

"'Dawn'. At this point, I would say that is her name. But she is only clay. Malleable. Tomorrow wax. Melting. Next month, perhaps, bronze. Forged to an altered form. Who knows if we will still like her once I take her from the marble?"

*Of whom do we speak, Andre?* "Could she change that much?"

"What one hopes to achieve can change with time and circumstance. *Oui*, she can change. Utterly transform and what we would have called one thing may well be the opposite."

She nodded. He was so wise.


The tempo of their lives together changed.

As avid as she'd been to be Andre's lover, the complement to the rapture of that became the obsession she felt to her art. She sketched, one after another, but on a moment's inspiration, a stab of erotic need, she'd go to him and kiss him, taste him, touch him.

As if one passion fed the other, she seemed always hungry, greedy in fact, to caress his perfect body. And with each delightful encounter, she starved for more of him—and more need to refine her art to do him justice in her work. She had no visits or notes from the agent, Montand, and she concluded there would be none. Perhaps the man had been too kind or purposely so to honor his relationship with Andre. Perhaps no one wanted an amateur's sketch of the famous sculptor. They would much prefer a piece of his art. She justified her disappointment on the sale of the sketch, by understanding that she had a long way to go to become an artist whose works showed emotion or the essence of the human condition. That was fine. She was in no hurry. She was with Andre and the experience was so revolutionary, so intense, so heart-rending, she wished to savor each moment. Commit it to memory.

He asked her to model for him. The clay figure of Dawn was inadequate, he said, to the reality of who she was. Yes, he told her, Dawn was intended to be she. But he needed to see her naked as his subject to perfect the figure.

Would she do that for him? Allow him to view her, touch her, understand her every muscle, her every movement as a living breathing entity?

Yes, of course she would. She welcomed the risqué freedom of it. She had her own time to work, to leave him, and this new adventure of baring herself to him for his own purposes appealed to her as an artist. Dispassionate for hours as she stood at his command.

And when he dismissed her, ended his work session, she would take his hand and lead him to their bed, strip him and offer up the rest of herself to him. He would bless her with his mouth and hands and delight her with his reverent body and his heavy cock. She sought to return the favor and one night, inspired, driven to display how she adored him, she took him in her mouth and paid homage to him until he broke away and possessed her.

Later, as he clasped her close, he asked her if she had enjoyed her erotic foray. She had very much, she was unashamed to say.

"May I explore you in the same way?" he asked her, his bright eyes heavy with lust. "You did not comment when I did so last week."

"Please love me however you wish," she said with all her heart.

The next night, he had kissed her to distraction and spread her thighs wide. There he played for many torturous minutes while she whimpered and moaned her approval of his ministrations. When he finally came inside her, she climaxed immediately, violently. He put his fingers to her intimate flesh and she burst apart again, a star exploding. She clung to him for long minutes afterward.

The next morning, he was not in their bed when she awakened. Pulling on her robe, she rounded the screen and there he stood, his back to her, at his table. She walked over, kissed his shoulder and peered at his work. There she was outlined in grey pencil splayed upon his paper, her head thrown back, reminiscent of Dawn, but more erotic, more enraptured, her legs wide, her frilly folds spread open. He dipped his brush in a watercolor of palest human pink and washed her flesh in the moment of her ecstasy. Her rosy mouth parted, her fingers to her lips, her body glistened with the searing moisture of her desire. That he had seen her like that filled her with awe. That he could duplicate her like that astonished her. How she admired his talent. The artist. How she admired him. The man.

As if he feared she'd disappear from his sight, he began to reach for her four, five times a day. His appetite for her was insatiable. He made love to her against a wall, on a chair. She came, ready, willing, needing him as fervently as he did her. He had only to smile at her with that wicked gleam in his eye or put two fingers to her breast and she dissolved in a sea of sensuality. To make love to him during the day was delicious. In the evenings, upon retiring, and then again later in black magic moments, they would reach out, each to the other, and consume all they had to give. Every nerve in her body sang with romantic use. Every thought was of him or her work. Intense and fulfilling, this life could not last.

She knew it. And fought the mourning. That would come soon enough.

But she grew restless.

One evening after they'd made love on his bed, she was unable to sleep. She rushed out into the humid night air. Naked in the high-walled garden, she whirled about. She could dance here and no one would say she couldn't. The stars shown down on her and she marveled that she'd never been so truly happy.

Oh, as a child, yes, her days had passed in the cocoon of her parents' fond regard. Their prolonged illnesses and the beginning of the war had severed her from her childhood serenity. When they had decided to have her marry—"for her protection" her father said—she had no ability to object. The boundaries to the North were cut. Her parents were too ill to travel and attempt to run the battle lines. Communicating with her mother's brother, Killian Hanniford, was as impossible as crossing the lines to take her to him. They'd married her to Frederick, twenty years her senior, a widower, wealthy with a fine plantation, slaves—and in need of wife and heir. Within the space of six days, she changed from a young girl with loving parents to an orphan, then wife to a man who took her to his arms and his bed with a brutal indifference. His regard for her person was as the vessel of his release, the means of his progeny. That she was the object of his desire repulsed her. But she'd borne with him and his attentions. Within seven months, he went off to war. His duty, he called it. Her reprieve, she named it.

No wonder—she halted to stare at the inky satin sky above her—no wonder she'd drawn people without the divinity they possessed. All these years, she'd drawn and perfected her love of the human body, but had not attempted to portray the glory of emotions beneath the skin.

She whirled to run in and tell Andre.

But there he stood in the doorway, the moonlight limning his classically chiseled body, his dark robe framing his firm torso and his well-hewn thighs. "You love the night."

"I love this night." *I love you.*

He opened his arms.

And she, resisting tears at her silent confession, went to him and accepted his embrace. He smelled of the wine they'd shared over supper—and his own distinctive fragrances. Soap, lime, the masculine scents he used in his baths enveloped her. He smelled of chalk too. How that was, since he washed the dust away each day in his tub, she could not say.

He dropped a kiss to her hair and spread his robe to wrap the lengths around her. "I don't want you to take ill."

She shook back her hair to smile up at him. "I've hardly ever been sick."

He cuddled her close, her breasts rubbing against the wall of his chest. "Stay well."

Portending as that did the time when she would leave him, she turned the subject. "I want to go to the square tomorrow and take my pens and easel."

"Ah. Courageous. I am pleased to hear it."

She kissed the place above his heart. "You can work in peace."

He tightened his grip. "What do you mean? I work in peace with you here."

She bit her lower lip. "I worry I am a distraction."

He leered at her, a charming devil. "I am tempted to rest inside you each minute of every day."

She blushed and pressed her face into his chest.

He pulled back, his gaze—lit by the stars and moon— dropped down her naked form. "Truly, my dear woman, you are no distraction. You are more inspiration."

That she took as more compliment than substance. He still had not shown her his drawings for his marble. She had not coaxed him either. Some habits were sacred and she would not offend him. "I want you to be as productive as you have made me."

"I am."

"But I see no progress."

"*Ma cherie*, marble does not give up its secrets easily. Or for me it does not. I think on it many days, months if necessary, before I take up a hammer."

"I want you to work." Her tone struck her as the harping wife who urges her man to the fields. "You have the commission for the City and Montand thinks you are delaying."

"I'm not and he's wrong."

"Have you a theme for it yet?"

"I do. And I don't mind if you go to the square without me." He cupped her derriere and hoisted her so that his cock drove high inside her. "Only promise to always return to me."

# CHAPTER 12

A few mornings later as they finished breakfast, a courier knocked on the kitchen door. Carré went to answer and returned with a package under his arm. Wrapped in old newsprint, it looked to be oblong and light in weight. He gave it to Andre.

"Finished your cocoa?" he asked her. *"Oui?* Then come upstairs."

In his studio, he pointed toward a stool. "I ordered a present for you. Sit there. Close your eyes."

Dutiful, eager, she perched on the seat and waited.

Andre tore off the paper.

"What are you doing?"

"Put your hands out."

She did.

Into them, he placed a lightweight box. She slid her hands over the finely sanded, varnished wood.

He strode away and returned. Against her leg, Andre rested a heavy object.

"All right. These are gifts for you. Open your eyes."

In her lap sat an oblong box, a scribe's toolbox. Beautifully carved with acanthus leaves, the oaken box had a drawer. She pulled it open and inside was a set of four pencils, black and white chalk, and a dozen or more ink nubs to attach to wooden pens. Each nub was a different thickness. Against her leg rested a folded stool.

She rose to kiss his cheeks. "Everything but the ink. Oh, thank you."

He grinned at her delight in them, one arm going around her waist. "Not jewels or silks or lace. But what you'd like more than those."

"I do. Even the stool. For me to use in the square, I presume."

"Quite." He strode over to take her wide-brimmed straw hat from the hook and came back to place it on her head and tie the long sashes. "Now, make me four promises."

He'd demanded so little from her.

"Of course."

"Promise me to wear this hat so your skin does not burn."

"Done."

"Promise to come home each day with one new work you are very proud of."

She tsked. "A hard task-master."

"Promise me to take the very best one of all to Montand the day after you return to Rue Haussmann."

The reference to his agent was not in violation of her own demand of him. But this was the first he'd spoken of their separation that was to come. She'd dared not to think of it before, but now she could barely speak. "I will."

"Ask him his assessment, but don't let him badger you into letting him sell it. In fact, ask him for the address of his competitor." Andre finished tying a huge bow beneath her chin.

"Why?"

"Because you want to hear another dealer tell you what he thinks of your work."

"Don't I want another artist to give me their opinion?" she teased him.

"Never!" He turned her toward the door. "Now *au revoir, mon amour.* Do not return until five."

"Isn't that the fifth promise?"

"Out! Out! I must work and you must too!"


An only child, Marianne had always been friendly. But in the square, she was reluctant to be forward. She walked about, found a spot under a shady beech tree and set up her stool to observe. For the first few days, she simply sat and observed others. Not everyone who came to the top of the Butte was an artist. Many Parisians ventured up from the City below to observe the view, the long sweeping panorama topped by the golden dome at the church of Les Invalides. There, Napoleon Bonaparte rested in his porphyry coffin, home, surrounded by reminders of his victories in war and worshiped by his countrymen.

Marianne understood little of French politics. She did not wish to know. In the square, many debated the issues but she was more intrigued by the contours of a Frenchman's face as he argued with his friend. More enchanted by the jab of his finger or the open handed exclamation of dismay. Less drawn to the men than the women.

The women were a varied lot. Most of them were work-ers. By their attire, she could tell some tended bar in the cafes. A few, she became acquainted with, took in wash, or mended for their clientele. They tended to be poor them-selves. Living in Montmartre near the old walls of the City, the rents were cheap. Buildings were mostly wooden, ramshackle. Indeed, Remy's sprawling studio upon the crest of the hill was one of the very few that had solidity, style and any ornamentation.

"*Bonjour*!" A lady who sat painting under an adjacent tree asked her one day. "*Comment ça va*? Do you not paint?"

Marianne smiled and bent to get a finer view of the woman's rendering of the red restaurant on the far corner of the square. "*Tres bien, merci*. I draw. And I like your painting of *Le Coq Hardie*."

"You are kind, *Madame*. I am new at this." The lady spoke fluent French and yet Marianne thought her manner more carefree, more American. She was red-haired, red-faced and elegantly coiffed. Her gown covered in a white butcher's apron, she wore the latest style and she had an open manner to her that said she'd lived in Paris a long while.

She wiped her hand absent-mindedly on her apron and offered it to Marianne. "Patricia Farmer from Chicago. And you?" she asked in English.

Marianne shook her hand. "Marianne Roland from Virginia."

"Wonderful to meet another American who has the urge to be different and join the men! Have you been in Paris long?"

"I arrived with my family last fall, but we've traveled since then to England and back. Are you here on vacation?"

"Oh, no." The woman pushed her straw hat back from her forehead and wiped her brow with a handkerchief. "I live here with my sister in the Rue Clichy. We took a house at my insistence. I like the air of Paris better than Chicago or New York. More freedom for a woman. Especially one who attempts to enter a man's profession."

"Have you been painting for a long time?" Marianne asked and hoped she was not being intrusive.

"Since I was a child. And you?"

"Yes, drawing since I was young. During the war, I stopped. No heart for it. No paper, either."

"Were you in Virginia during the fighting?" Patricia asked her.

"I was."

"So many battles were fought there. Did you suffer?"

"Our land changed hands too many times to count. So, yes. My home and barns were a skeleton of their former selves by the time I left."

"Oh, that must have been horrible for you." Patricia grew still. "To be in the thick of it, I mean."

"I had both Union and Confederates on my land. What one didn't trample, the other took. Still, the wounded suffered equally. I nursed them all." Marianne inhaled, remembering the bleeding men who died on the floor of her parlor. "When the lines permanently passed on south, I was able to leave. I walked north to my uncle and his family."

"Alone?"

"Yes." *There was no other choice.*

"That must have been terrible."

"All of it was." *It became the defining event of my life. More than my time with Frederick. More than his cruelty and disregard.* She sat forward, struck by that truth which she'd not identified before. "I was young. Determined to get out of there. I had a little money."

"Confederate?" Patricia was surprised. She put down her paint brush and sat, examining Marianne with curiosity.

"No, thank heavens. That was so worthless. Before the war, my husband had hidden a few gold pieces in the bedroom floorboards. When the first Yankee soldiers arrived, I sewed them into the hem of my skirts. Almost two years later, when I had the chance and heard that the lines north were broken, I walked free and used two of them to buy food and lodging."

"You're very courageous."

"Not really." Marianne demurred. "I prefer to think of it as necessity."

Patricia nodded toward Marianne's sketch pad in her lap and her empty easel. "And do you draw what you saw?"

"No." *Never.*

"You could make an impression. A woman illustrating war."

"I lived it. It was terrible enough. I won't draw it."

Patricia pursed her lips. "What I hear too often from men about war is all bluster and bravado. How they think war is a game and adventure. It's not. It's hideous destruction of bodies and souls."

Marianne heard in her voice an inkling of her despair. "You lost someone dear to you?"

"My brother. He was sent home, an amputee. But what was missing was his will to live."

"I'm sorry," Marianne said.

"Tell me what you do draw," Patricia said, sitting taller and looking valiant in her attempt to change the subject.

"I am more interested in portraits. Realistic portrayals of people who have no idea how unique they are."

"Good. Because here?" Patricia lifted a hand to indicate the crowd. "Most give us scenery. Pastorals in the changing light. I'm one of them. And I begin to think there are too many. If you will give us those who walk those lands, that would be refreshing."

For days afterward, as Marianne became closer friends with Patricia, the American's words repeated in her head.

She had always drawn people. Those whom she thought intriguing.

If she was more than an amateur artist, if she was to be more than a dilettante, the question she had to answer was who would she draw. Who would she illustrate? To render

Andre had been a past time. Part of her desire for him. Her love of him. But she could not, must not continue that. She'd not make a reputation by using his to boost her. She must show others. Others in their element. Others in their habitat, their condition. Others whose portrayals an audience would buy not because the subject was famous. But because the human was a true portrait of his or her life.

He was losing.

Losing her every day. Losing her to her quest to find herself. What irony to aid her in that, only to find he loved her more as he lost his hope of their future. He knew not how to bring her back to him. Logic told him—as did his promise not to influence her—that he should not even try.

That day last week when he'd made her promise to return home to him, he'd let slip the panic that shot through him whenever he glimpsed his life without her. That night as the deep of night fell to dawn, he'd made love to her there in the garden, spreading his robe on the thick grass and loving her amid the fragrances of flowers and the sound of birdsong.

It was as if each new day she became a new incarnation of her self. Oh, still gracious Marianne. Sweet naif that she was, she was also now a fierce practitioner of her work. If she was not lying in his arms or squirming in the tub allowing him to love her to moaning madness, then she was drawing, sketching, irrepressible as a fiend.

Yes, yes. He'd lured her from her past. Unveiled the artist. Presented her with the potential of her fullest self. And she'd met the challenge of self knowledge—and then left him.

Not physically. That was still to come. God help him.

But spiritually, she was gone. Gone to the square. Gone the rapture of new bliss. Understanding her talents. Acquiring new friends. A female artist whom she brought home with her the other day. Likable, assertive. American, too.

Perhaps he should invite the woman to tea and pry out of her what was the uniqueness of the American animal. Male, female, they were a species unto themselves. Aggressive and naive. Inquisitive and strangely acquisitive. Without the cage of ancient manners, they could be crude or charming. Ferocious beasts to try to tame.

*Was that his problem?*

He wished to tame Marianne?

Oh, never.

He had endeavored to set her free. And now that she saw the horizon of that land open to her, she rushed toward it. *If only she'd want me with her....*

He'd never thought he could adore a woman so completely that he'd need her presence to make him feel whole. His art had sufficed. His family—his mother and cousins and friends—had fed his human need for fond companionship. For all his many years, he'd been self-sufficient. Now in a blaze of desire with her, he lived in ecstasy each moment she was near. Could she discover her own delights in her art and still want him?

"*Monsieur, pardon e moi*," Carré approached him from the stairs. He bore a letter in his hand. "A visitor is downstairs and this letter has come for you."

"Who has arrived, Carré?" he asked and reached for the cream parchment. The elegant handwriting told Andre his mother wrote.

"*Monsieur* Bonnet. You requested he call today, if you remember?"

The man who casted his bronzes. "Ah, *oui*. Show him up, Carré."

As Carré fetched the man who took his clay figures to forge them into bronze, Andre tore open the envelope.

His mother wrote regularly of nothing of note. Still her health, fragile as it was, concerned him.

He read her words and smiled. She was well. Her cousin was well. The tenants were well. Very well, indeed, and she asked for news of his progress on his commission.

He shook his head. "Slowly, *Maman*. Very slowly."

Then she asked of other news. What were his plans? Would he stay in Paris? Come south perhaps for the harvest? The tenants asked of him. Hoped he might come south and bring his friend. What might he tell her of his plans for that?

By that, she meant his plan to present his lady to her. His plans to keep her. Marry her.

*What could he say to her?*

"Nothing. Nothing that would please you."

He crushed the letter.

Carré stood at the door, worry lining his brow. "Bad news?"

"No, no. Where is Bonnet? Ah, there you are, *mon ami*. Come in. Come in."

The man who fired his figures in his bronze furnaces was the third generation in his family to have the art. He'd served Andre well now for two years and had cast two of his works in various sizes, bringing in thousands of francs for both of them.

Andre went to grasp the big man's meaty hands. Nearly as tall as Andre, Michel Bonnet was a bear of a man and was jovial in complement to his size.

"*Monsieur le duc*, I'm happy to be summoned."

"Wine and cheese, Carré, for our friend. And three glasses. You will join us." He met Bonnet's glance of surprise. "One day you will be casting Carré's works, I am certain."

"Oh, no, no." Carré demurred with a wave of his hand.

Andre tipped his head at Carré, but feigned a grimace at

Bonnet. "I have taught him much but not yet have I schooled him in arrogance."

"Oh, ha!" Bonnet chuckled in his booming bass voice. "Carré, don't learn that from this oaf. He shows enough for all of us."

The joke hit Andre like a rock. He'd meant it as a jest, but also a suggestion that in an artist, pride was a vital element to success. Was he too prideful? With his work, for one. But with Marianne for another? Did that warn her off him? Was he wrong to assume that because he loved her totally, she could and should love him with a longing that superseded all else?

He ran two hands through his long hair, smiled at Bonnet and offered him one of his stools at the workbench.

Carré hurried away to the kitchen in search of three glasses, a jug of wine and some Camembert. Bonnet examined the two figures upon the table, both were his best versions of Marianne as Dawn.

"I'm afraid these are the only works I wish to discuss," he told Bonnet after a minute or more of silence.

"A small number, *Monsieur le duc*." Bonnet pursed his lips as he studied them. "Not your usual abundance."

"I am not at my full capacity, my friend."

"May I?"

Andre opened his palm.

The caster picked up one. The woman reached for the sky in an elegant arch of her body. "She is quite breath-taking," he said after many minutes. "Will she emerge from that marble as well as my furnace?"

"I think on it," Andre said, his eyes traveling to the white block. "I hate to commit to it until I can see her more fully. I was too quick with my Diana last year and lived in a private hell for it. I will not bring in my assistant sculptors until I have this view firmly in my mind."

"But this—and this?" Bonnet put down one and picked up the other clay figure. "They are ready?"

"They are two progressions of the same woman."

"As I see," said Bonnet with a reverence to his tone that Andre had caught when he'd shown him the clay model for his Samson.

"I hear what you think of them, Bonnet." Andre leaned on his elbows and pointed to the facial features of both female figures. "But the expressions. Speak to me of what they tell you."

The man was a gruff Breton. Big, burly, but at Andre's request, he blushed. Then he slid one toward Andre. "She can be a young woman awakening from her rest to greet a new bright day."

Andre nodded.

"Or her lover."

*Just so.*

"And this one? The same woman. Clearly. The large eyes, the arched brow, the abundant hair and the perfect breasts."

Andre watched as his friend swept a fingertip over the allusion of the face, the waves of the hair and touched the full cup of the breasts. Andre's vision blurred. He could taste her, his Dawn, his Aurora. Taste the silken sweetness of her nipples and the cream of her core as she flowed for him.

"This one," said the Breton in hallowed tones, "is a woman in the throes of her passion."

"Is she complete?" he asked her and wondered at the complexity of his question.

"She writhes in her climax, but she looks away from her lover. The hand to her brow, palm up, as if next she will push him away."

Andre shot from his stool. That's what he'd known within himself. What he'd not dared to admit. "Do you think her worthy of bronze?"

"Worthy? Oh, *Monsieur le duc*, she is exquisite."

Upon the small easel in the corner stood the watercolor and pencil drawing of Marianne that he'd made in a whirl of emotion the other morning.

"But this—?" Bonnet went to stand before the drawing. "This takes my heart."

*As she has taken mine.*

"Will you show this to Montand?"

*Could he part with that?*

Never.

*Could he part with her?*

He had to, didn't he? Not because he wished it, but because she did.

Within the next hour, Bonnet made to go, taking both figurines with him in a wooden box he'd ordered Carré to make for that purpose. Andre walked Bonnet to the front door and when he opened it, Marianne reached for the door knob herself. Home from the square, her little patch she'd claimed as her own under a beech tree, she had her sketch book under one arm and her wooden items in the other.

"Oh, pardon!" She laughed up into Andre's face and smiled at Monsieur Bonnet.

"Allow me to present my friend, Monsieur Bonnet."

Bonnet's grin was warm and winning. The man knew how to charm the bark off a tree.

"How do you do, *Monsieur*."

Bonnet offered a polite bow. "*Enchante, Madame* Roland."

Andre saw the spark in Bonnet's eye. Indeed, the man recognized the lady who was Dawn. The two of them chatted, the polite dialogue of those who meet for the first time. Andre informed her that Bonnet had collected two figures to cast in bronze for him. She exclaimed how wonderful.

"I see you are also an artist." Bonnet indicated her tools.

"I am. Not as talented as some I know. But the contrast keeps me on task. Hoping, you see, for lightning to strike. "

"Lightning can be dangerous," he said. "I would hope for a less harmful way to emerge from the confusion of the mind."

Nonetheless, Marianne grinned and accepted it as a polite comment. "I agree."

Bonnet took his leave.

Andre closed the front door, reached to take her easel from her and headed for his studio.

Marianne followed him up the stairs.

Inside, Nanette was picking up glasses and plates from the wine and cheese service. Carré was putting away the clay in tempered boxes, the work of the day finished.

Marianne removed her straw-brimmed hat, pushing up stray curls into her chignon. She walked to Andre, smiling at him in expectation. "Monsieur Bonnet took your two Dawns?"

"He did."

"He liked them! Oh, fabulous. What did he say?"

"He always does like what I give him. These were no exceptions."

"Did he see the watercolor?"

"He did."

"Did he ask you to make a clay figure of that?"

"No. He knows better. Besides, that is mine," he told her. "Only mine." *As you should be. But may not need to be.*

She examined him, looking for hidden meanings that he would not utter. She knew him too well, enough to see his anxiety, but not enough, he prayed, to understand his sadness and his fear of losing her.

He caught her close and kissed her quickly. "So I think we must celebrate. We will make a night of it, eh? Nanette, do not cook dinner. Put on your best gown. Carré, finish quickly here. Take off your apron, man! We're going to dine in that cafe we all like in Boulevard de Rochechouart. Then we're all going to the *moulin de la Galette* to dance."

"Sir?" Carré looked aghast. "No! I cannot dance."

"Yes, Carré, one day you will be famous, rich and the ladies will hover over you. You must know how to dance."

"But, sir—"

"No arguments. Afterward we're off to the theatre to see the new troupe do the can-can."

He had to drink and dine, dance and sing. He'd show Marianne what they could be together. Or begin to return to who'd he'd been without her.

# CHAPTER 13

Marianne strolled into the *atelier*, home from her afternoon sketching in the square. At the front door, she'd taken the mail from the postman and the only piece was a letter for Andre. "Another from your mother, I think."

Nodding, Andre took the parchment from her hand and ripped the envelope. "Ah, *oui*. The third in a week. I imagine she asks again when I will go to the chateau."

Marianne noticed that Carré turned away, busying himself with the clean-up of the days remains of clay from the bench. She deposited her sketchbook and easel, her pencils, chalks and inks on the far table, then removed her hat.

"Have you thought about a date?" She expected Andre would go south after she left him. That was to be in three days. They didn't talk of her departure. She didn't want to start now. But still. This was his mother and the lady deserved an answer about his arrival.

"I have." He opened the letter, read quickly and then walked it to his rubbish bin. He dropped it in and turned back to the clay figurine he'd been working on for the past week. "When you leave."

*When I leave. When I leave...how will I manage to smile?* She caught a breath. "I haven't any letters from Lily lately."

"Not from Ada either," he said idly as he turned away.

She'd commented yesterday to him on that lack. "That's unusual from both of them. Well, actually, Lily is more to be relied upon than Ada."

He busied himself with the figure. "Lily is a newly wed woman. And a duchess with immense responsibilities."

"Her tenants have been ill and she's been nursing them. So I can excuse her. But Ada's lack worries me."

"If you think she'd get into trouble, Killian will stop that with one crook of his finger."

She laughed.

A pounding emanated from the downstairs hall.

The three of them halted.

The beating on the front door resumed.

She grew alarmed.

Carré stopped his cleaning. "I'll see who it is, *Monsieur*. That Eugene Saubert across the street gets more drunk every day. Probably him again."

Whoever it was banged with such might that the sound pulsed up the stairs and into the room where the sun was sinking in the west horizon.

Moments later, a breathless red-faced Killian Hanniford stood in the middle of the room.

"*Mon Dieu, Monsieur*! Wait!" Carré scurried behind her uncle. "*Monsieur le duc*, I could not stop him. He—"

"No apologies, Carré." Andre held up a hand. "I know this man. We both do. This is *Madame* Roland's uncle, *Monsieur* Hanniford. Killian, what in hell is wrong?"

Marianne had seen her uncle dismayed, distressed, even grieved. She'd heard of his rages with adversaries, his disagreements with his subordinates. She'd watched him bark at underlings and urge others to higher standards. But she had never seen him in a state that burned all before it.

"What's wrong?" She hurried to him, a hand to his sleeve. He was wide-eyed, wild. Someone was hurt? Lily? Ada? Pierce? "Tell me."

"You must come home with me."

"What's happened?"

Andre stepped to her side.

"Come home, Marianne."

"Why?" she urged her uncle. "What's wrong?"

"It's Ada."

"What about her?"

"She's ruined herself. I need you to talk some sense into her. She's locked herself in her room and won't talk to me."

Marianne shook his arm. "How did she ruin herself?"

"She went with those two idiot girls night before last. They met three men who took them to a cottage along the beach. They fed them wine or liquor or god knows what. Ada walked back to our hotel along the promenade. Alone! The concierge in the hotel says that other guests told him, she was singing bawdy songs as she walked home."

Marianne couldn't believe it of her. "Ada is foolhardy but she's not stupid."

"She doesn't have to be. That Francine and Ezzie are stupid enough!"

"Is she—? Did these men hurt her? The others too?"

"Ada says not, but then can I trust her?"

"Yes. You can. Ada is no liar."

"She was drunk!"

Marianne recalled how she'd feared something like this would occur. Pierce did too, when he'd stated weeks ago that the three girls had gotten into a little too much brandy. "She knew enough to find her way home."

"I should not have let her go."

This was very true. "Didn't they have a chaperone?"

"Ada told us—Pierce, Chaumont and me—that Francine's mother was to be with them."

"Was she?"

"No! It seems that paragon Mrs. Lang has taken a lover for the summer. She left them to their own devices."

"Who are the men?"

"Ada won't say."

"Why not?" Marianne asked.

"She doesn't wish to hurt anyone's reputation. Meanwhile... Meanwhile! What of her own?"

"I hear you, Uncle. She always was a carefree girl."

"Carefree? She's always gone for the lark. The fun of it."

Marianne bit her lip. That was true.

"I'm sending her back to Baltimore."

"Oh, Uncle Killian. She can't go back there. She'll surely be ruined then. People won't see her and that'll fan the rumors. Even assume she's with child!"

"I told her if she crossed me I'd send her home and I will."

"Let's learn what happened first."

"No. Everyone in Cherbourg knows about it. She sang, for Christ's sake! Nothing like announcing you're a tart."

"And where were the other two girls?"

"I don't know. I don't care."

That was ridiculous. She glared at him. "Of course, you do, Uncle Killian. You're the man who saved ten African men off a sinking slaver ship at risk to your own. Do not tell me you do not care about those girls."

That calmed him. But he winced. "I need you to come home. I need you to talk to her. Find out all the details."

"I will, of course. I'll come tomorrow."

"Now."

That offended her. He'd never demanded anything of her.

But then, she's always given what she could which was, literally, her companionship, her love, her devotion. Could she do that again? So liberally? "You promised me, sir, you would not force me home before my time here was done."

Andre took a step forward.

Killian frowned at him and told her, "This is different. It's Ada."

"She is most likely very upset. At herself. At her own lack of judgment. At your displeasure with her. She doesn't need me to point out her foibles or emphasize—"

"Of course she does. You were her mother after she had none. You were the one who kissed her scraped knees and helped her with her Latin. You were her voice of reason—"

"I may have once been her substitute for her mother. I may have once been her voice of reason. But she is of age and she must learn to steer her own path."

"She steered it onto the shoals," he said through gritted teeth.

"She made a mistake. But she must face the results. Before she marries."

"No one will have her now," he said, his brows knit, his tone mournful.

"I doubt that. She's lovely, charming. If she's also carefree and honest, many men could benefit from that in a wife. It will take time, but people will forget."

"I doubt it. I've seen proof they don't."

He meant his own black reputation as a ruthless businessman and before that, as a Confederate blockade runner whose stealth had made him notoriously rich—and universally feared.

"They do not know everything about you, sir. When they learn, they amend their views. And the gossip ends."

"Does it?" he challenged her, his tone anguished. "I can't wait. I'm sending her home."

"To do what? Be under lock and key?" She was appalled. "Be reasonable."

"She's going home."

"No!"

"And I want you to go with her."

Her world tilted. Righted. "I cannot do that."

"Why not?"

*Because...because I don't want to.* "Send *Madame* Chaumont."

"Fat lot of good Chaumont can do," he muttered.

"She likes to serve. She needs the money. And she's a better chaperone than none. "

Killian stared at her as if he'd never seen her before. "You're serious?"

"Quite so."

His silver eyes flashed with anger. "We had an agreement, you and I."

One year to see Lily married. Another to see Ada launched. Meanwhile, her own life slipped by. A life that now was so different from the one she'd had within his fold. "You have been good to me, sir."

"I need you to do this, Marianne."

She raised her chin. "I will speak to Ada, but I do not approve of you sending her home. It would stain her permanently. And I'll take no part in that. I'll go and talk with her, but that is absolutely all."

"You defy me?"

"I do."

"And our agreement?"

What was that agreement compared to her dignity? Her independence? She could live. Somehow. Use her own money. She'd pine for her family but Killian could not buy her compliance. And she must not let him. "I end it."

"You joke?" He was shocked.

"Not at all. I'll come to talk with Ada tomorrow." She

strode toward the door to the stairs. This was the end of their discussion.

Andre walked behind her.

Carré who had remained by the door, yanked it open.

"Tomorrow," she told her uncle. "I'll arrive at one. I'll speak to Ada alone and learn what precisely happened in Cherbourg."

Killian jammed his hat on his head. Defeat was an evil he'd never known. "I'll send my carriage."

"No." She shook her head. "I'll hire a hack, Uncle. Good evening to you."

Ada was deathly pale. She shot to her feet to greet Marianne the moment Foster opened the salon door to her.

"Hello, sweetheart." Marianne went to her and kissed her cheek, took her hands and pulled her to sit with her on the settee. "Sit beside me."

"I'm so glad you've come. Papa is being horrid. Where is he?"

"In his study. I told him I preferred to speak to you alone."

"He agreed?"

"He did." Her uncle had never forced her to do anything. Given her refusal of him yesterday, Marianne predicted he wouldn't start now. Not about this. Not about accompanying Ada home to America.

Ada glanced at their entwined hands. "I realize I've shamed everyone and I'm so sorry. But I really didn't know that Mrs. Lang would abandon us. Francine did, I think. Francine arranged it all and I'm very angry with her."

Marianne patted her hand. "I'm sure you understand why your father is so upset. And I am quite certain you know what this means for your immediate future."

"He says he'll send me home. I can't go back, Marianne. I don't want to. I never would've said I'd go with Francine if she'd told me the full of it, but you know Francine is devious and—"

Marianne put up a hand. "Stop please. I give you the benefit of the doubt that you weren't fully aware of Francine's plans nor her mother's duplicity toward you and Ezzie."

"Thank you."

"I told your father that I think you foolhardy, but not stupid. I'm sure you know how this episode has caused a stir."

Ada bit her lip and hung her head. Her sleek golden brown hair was caught back in a severe knot. For a long moment, she gazed at her tightly clapped hands. Her knuckles white. Then her shoulders shook. She cried quietly.

Marianne waited until the small storm passed. When Ada was little, Marianne had often hugged her close and soothed her tears. But both of them were older now and affection might salve her wound, but it would not heal it. Not when it was self-inflicted. "You must tell me all of what occurred. I can't help you in any way if I don't know."

"Yes, of course." She dug for her handkerchief in her skirt pocket and blew her nose. Then, unlike the little girl who had often clung to Marianne's hands, Ada rallied, rose and walked to the mantel. She whirled to face Marianne. "We were to attend a private party at a cottage along the promenade. Mrs. Lang was to be our chaperone. Francine said it was to be a little supper for all of us. But then three gentlemen arrived. I was surprised but tried to be gracious. Ezzie was keen to leave. We should have. But I stayed on."

Marianne noted her hesitation. "Why?"

Ada rolled her gaze around the room. "I didn't want to be a nay-sayer. And you see...well...one of the gentlemen was *Monsieur* Durant."

"The French tutor?" That was surprising. Marianne had

thought better of him than to seduce a young woman who was to be his client, no less. "Why would he go to Cherbourg? Doesn't he have students to tend to?"

"He does. But it's August and he was on holiday. Sort of. You see, he's a *vicomte*. Poor, but still. I learned that at the party. He told me. His estate is very small and he must work."

"Why did he think it proper for you to be there? For him to be there?"

"He didn't. The other two gentlemen asked him to come along. They needed a third to fill the party. He said he heard I was to go and he wanted to come to protect me."

"I see. A fine sentiment. But he failed." Marianne nodded. "Tell me about the behavior of Mrs. Lang."

"She was there with Francine. I was relieved we had her there, but then in a few minutes, she left. And I panicked."

"Did you think to leave?"

"I did. I did. But by that time, I'd had a glass of wine."

Marianne tilted her head in question.

"Actually, two."

"Did you like it?"

"The first glass was fine. I was nervous and drank it quickly. Too quickly, I'd say. I've tasted good wine, though and the second glass was terrible. Red. Dregs. Awful. But by then, the taste didn't much matter."

"So Mrs. Lang left. Then what happened?"

"Francine had more wine than any of us and she began to sing. She's a truly awful singer. Anyway. Ezzie got scared and came to me. She said she didn't care for the man who was partnered to her. She wanted to leave. I told her I'd think of a plan. And so I piled a few bits of dinner on my plate. Cold, it was. I had only the cheese. And then I thought of what to do. I told Ezzie we should pretend to be ill. From the wine, of course."

Marianne nodded. "And?"

Ada brightened. "I went to get Ezzie and told her to pretend to be ill from the wine. We saw Francine as we left. She was...um..."

"Where?"

"Outside with the man she'd paired with, kissing him."

"Do you know that man? His name?"

"I do."

"And the man who was paired to Ezzie?"

"Yes."

"I see." Uncle Killian had asked her to get the names of the men who were at the cottage. Marianne had no doubts he would confront the men and Francine's mother for their behavior. The repercussions would be ugly. "And did Ezzie's gentleman—I use the term loosely—accost her?"

Ada shook her head. "No, she swears not. She wouldn't let him."

"And *Monsieur* Durant?" Marianne asked her, hoping for the best. "What was his behavior toward you?"

"A gentleman. I assure you, Marianne. A complete gentleman. In fact, he saw that I was upset and wanted to leave. He watched me, stood beside the back door when I led Ezzie out of the house."

"What did you and Ezzie do next?"

"I walked her to her hotel. She was so upset. I told her she mustn't cry and attract attention. I took her around to the hotel's servants' entrance. Then I hurried to our hotel. By myself."

"Along the promenade?"

"Yes. It's a short walk but I thought it took years."

Marianne had once walked from chaos to safety. The journey had taken four days. Three days running and hiding in the woods without only a bit of bread and a canteen of water. One day on a rickety train from Washington City to Baltimore. She covered her mouth with her hand, forcing back a groan. She hadn't thought of her walk from Confederate territory across Union lines in ages. She straightened and brought herself back to the issue at hand. "And what was your behavior?"

"I was not singing, if that's what you mean. Papa said someone told him I was singing. That's a lie. Whoever said that is mean. Why would I call attention to myself when all I wished to do was get inside to our suite and crawl into bed?"

"Where was Pierce? Chaumont? Uncle Killian?"

"All out. Thank god. Or so I thought at the time. No one saw me come in."

"No hired maid was in the family suite?"

"None. No one saw me."

"And you met no one along the promenade whom you knew?"

"None."

*Might this be an incident society never learned about?*

"Well, my dear," she told her cousin. "You are to be commended for your solution to a thorny problem. It remains to be seen if the world knows of it. But Ezzie should thank you. Her mother too. As for Francine and her mother, I think that your father will have a few harsh words with them. Francine may suffer worse if the man she was with showed her any more affections than his kisses."

"It would be awful if she was to become...well, you know."

"Pregnant?" Marianne used the boldest term to signify the worst results and to jolt her cousin to reality.

"Yes. Pregnant."

Marianne had compassion for Ada. For any young woman led astray when confusing lust with love. "Even so, my dear, Francine might be made to marry him. Perhaps that was even the plan. We shall learn from Mrs. Lang for certain."

Ada quivered. Tears reappeared in her eyes. "Oh, that's awful. To marry a man who treated you badly? That's..."

*A crime.* "Yes. I hope you see for yourself what errant behavior can do to a woman."

"Of course I do." She ran to Marianne and sank down, clutching her hands. "Please don't send me back to America. I know I'm awful and I deserve to be punished. But please don't do this. I like it here. I like being with all of you again. School was horrible. All those girls fighting over hair ribbons and arguing like cats."

That was a surprise. "I thought you liked it there."

"I hated it."

"But your letters?"

"I told you it was grand because that's what all of you expected of me."

Marianne understood that practice far too well. She'd done that through her marriage and through the war. "It's true?"

"Yes. I smiled and was polite but I couldn't wait to leave and sail off with Pierce to join all of you. Now Lily's married and you're with Remy. Papa is wonderful but he dotes on my every move. Pierce is...a man. And Papa doesn't need to breathe down his neck. Please, Marianne, don't let him send me back. I'd be so lonely."

Marianne knew what prices loneliness extracted. She hadn't been lonely since Killian had welcomed her into the Hanniford fold at the end of the war. "It's not for me to decide, Ada. But truly, I agree with you. The worst possible result would be for you to return to Baltimore."

"Papa says Texas. Just because I said it, he threatens me with the ranch."

"I doubt he'd do that."

"You won't let him. Say you won't."

"I'll try, Ada."

"But if you tell him *you* don't want to go to Texas. Not Baltimore either. He'll listen you."

"I doubt that, Ada. You see, if he sends you home, I told him I won't be going with you."

Ada drew back. "What will you do?"

Since last night when she'd said the same to her uncle, Marianne had asked herself that often. She'd walked into Andre's embrace as Killian left the house and Carré shut the door upon them. But she had no answers. No real answers. Enchanted with Andre, she wanted the dream to continue. But could she hope for that with him when she'd argued against it so often?

"You'd stay here in Paris?" Ada asked her, her crystal blue eyes bright with worry. "Would you live with Remy?"

*Would I? I'd asked him not to question me about my plans for the future.* He'd honored that promise. Her choice was, as it always had been, hers. Hers, alone.

"I haven't decided." She pushed a tendril of Ada's hair back from her cheek. "But like you, I want to stay in Paris. I want to live here. I want to work here."

"Work? Oh, no. What will Papa say of that?"

"He won't approve." Marianne was certain of that.

"But how can you do it if he doesn't?"

*I can and should if his view is irrelevant. If my choice is for me, by me.* But to answer that aloud would be to fuel Ada's rebellion and she mustn't do that. The girl had made poor choices. Now she must make better ones. By herself.

A knock came at the door.

"That might be Papa."

"I doubt it. I told him I would see him in his office when we were finished here."

"Come in," Ada called in response to another rap.

Foster, his droopy eyes uncharacteristically wide with shock, appeared before them and on his heel, stood Julian Ash, the Duke of Seton.

"Julian!" Marianne shot to her feet to greet him. He wore

a wild expression similar to that of Killian's last night. "What's wrong?"

"Is Lily here?"

"What? *What?* She's not with you?" Marianne asked him.

"How can that be?" Ada shook her head.

"Is she here?" he asked, his voice rough.

"No," Marianne blurted. "No!"

"We've had so few letters from you," Julian said. His eyes were red and weary, his attire disheveled. He must not have stopped at the train station to even comb his hair. "When Lily didn't return to me, I thought perhaps she'd come here and told all of you not to write."

"Where has she gone?" Marianne couldn't believe her ears. Horrified, she seized his arm and led him into the room. Stabbed by guilt she hadn't written to Lily let alone thought about her these past few weeks, she told him what he needed to know. "The family has been in Cherbourg. On vacation—"

"*Julian?*" Killian charged through the doorway. "Foster told me to come at once. What's wrong? What are you doing here and where's—?"

"Lily. I came to find her."

Marianne clutched her hands.

Ada sank to the settee.

Killian went white. "What do you mean?"

"She's left me."

"What?" Killian's outrage rang through the room. "How? Why?"

"We've had our challenges," Julian said, meeting his father-in-law's stare with determination.

Killian snorted. "I'll bet. My first guess would be your mother."

"I've taken care of her."

"By what? Sending her to deepest Africa?" Killian fumed.

"I might try that," Julian responded.

"What happened to Lily?" Killian demanded.

"Without a word, she has left. No note. No indication of where. I've tracked her from the countryside by coach. I've been to Willowreach and Ashford. I've checked in London. I've put my solicitor on the job to trace her. There is nothing. Nothing. So if she's not here, would she have returned to America?"

Killian, Ada and Marianne checked each other's expressions.

"No," said Ada.

"I doubt it," said Marianne. Lily loved this man. What could be so horrible that she would she leave him?

Julian winced and shook his head.

"Our Lily is no weakling," Killian declared. "But to be alone? Alone? What happened? You can't come here, drop this on us and not give me some rationale."

"I didn't cure our mutual problems early enough. She grew...away from me. More than that, I'm not certain. I've had so much to do to take on the duchy that I ignored her and I...I lost her."

"Christ." Killian went for the bell pull.

"I'm right here, sir," Foster said, stepping forward. He'd never left the drawing room.

"Brandy. Get us a bottle. Tea, too. Food, please. Here." His gaze ran over Julian. "You look like hell."

Julian inhaled and nodded.

"Have the maids prepare a room, Foster. Did you bring luggage?" he asked Julian.

"Only my satchel. A few shaving items."

"Sit down. Tell us details. All of them again. What you've learned. Where you've looked."

"I'll bid you good night." Julian made his apologies to the

three of them and went up to try to sleep. He'd talked himself out and planned to depart in the morning, returning to London. He'd told Killian he'd hire a special solicitor whose specialty was searching for missing people.

Killian said he'd send telegrams to New York, Baltimore and Corpus Christi to his friends to try to track Lily.

"I'll retire, too," Ada told her father and Marianne, then climbed the stairs to her rooms. She too was undone with stress and worry.

"Please come talk to me, Marianne," Killian said to her.

She followed him to his study, expecting he'd wish to hear about her discussion with Ada as well as her views of Lily's disappearance.

Rarely did she come into Killian's office. It was a large, quiet masculine room, lined with mahogany bookshelves, a huge globe and reading table in the middle of the room and Killian's massive desk in the center.

She sank into the large wing chair in front of his desk. Her head back against the cool leather, she sighed.

"You don't think Julian hurt her, do you? Physically, I mean."

Blinking in shock at his question, she shook her head. "Absolutely not. He's not the type."

"Where could she be?"

"I know her well. And I'd say, she's not far. But gone somewhere to think. And wherever that is, she's safe."

He surveyed the bookshelves as if secrets hid within. "Lily was almost ruined for her escapade with Julian. That he married her saved her from scandal, but now we've come to whatever it is she's doing by running from him. Ada has made a mess of her own debut."

"And my affair with Andre has not added any luster to the Hanniford family reputation. For that, I'm sorry Uncle."

"In truth, my dear, these past weeks, I've heard nothing of

you living with him up on the Butte. I think he warned his friends not to breathe a word."

"That would be so like him." Warmth spread through her at the very thought of him. "He never intimated to me that he did."

Killian slumped in his chair. "This is all my fault."

Never had she heard any such dour sentiments from the infamous blockade runner and robber baron, Black Irish Hanniford.

"Don't take all the blame, Uncle. That would be unfair. We each make our own decisions. We profit or we fail by them. Hopefully, we learn from them."

He met her gaze. "My example has not been sterling."

"Ruthless, irrepressible, driven, yes, you are all of that."

He grimaced and looked away.

"It's true, you worked against the law. As a boy. As a ship's captain. Even, perhaps, as a business man."

Hearing her assessment, he seemed unmoved as he looked upon middle space before him.

"But as a man, you were a loyal husband and are a loving father and a fine parent to all your children and to me. If you're demanding, that's your nature. If often you are not diplomatic," she said and sent him a consoling smile, "that too is part of your character. It's what makes your children honor you."

"But not obey me."

She lifted a shoulder. "Sometimes, people must stumble to learn how to walk upright."

He folded his hands in his lap and studied her. "You have always walked upright, my dear."

"A compliment to hear you say it. Thank you. But my upright stance has put me in a trance. I've been so safe. So secure that I haven't learned how to work for what I want and take it."

"What are you telling me, Marianne?" He looked beaten.

"I'm not returning here day after tomorrow."

He nodded once. "I'm not surprised. I've seen how you care for him. I should have accepted it."

Her uncle assumed she'd stay in Montmartre. Yet Andre hadn't asked her to remain and she had made him promise not to ask her to.

What had she done? In her effort to be bold, had she barricaded herself behind an impenetrable wall?

Killian grabbed a breath. "I apologize for my behavior last night. You're a grown woman and I should never have treated you as any less than that."

She waved it off. "I forgive you."

"Do you?" he asked sadly.

She sat forward, urgency to be gone from here nipping at her. "You'll forgive me. As you have Lily. As you will Ada. Even Pierce if and when he defies you, and he will."

Killian snorted. "A fine family this is."

"It is. And you have made it so." She got to her feet. The need to move quickly, decide her own future driving her from the haven of her family to the heaven she'd created with a man she loved. "I'm leaving. I'm sure you'll help Julian find Lily. I'll want to know your progress."

He stood behind his desk. "I'll send a messenger over to Remy's house if and when I know anything."

"Thank you." What could she say that would not alarm Killian? *I may not be there. If Andre doesn't want me, I could be anywhere. Anywhere.*

"I want you to know that if you choose to live with him, I won't object. I will accept it as if it were a marriage."

"Thank you, Uncle. That's good of you."

"To prove it, I'm instructing my solicitor tomorrow to deposit into your bank account the sum total of money I've saved for your dowry. I would have given it to you upon your marriage. It's yours."

"Uncle Killian, thank you. You are gracious."

"You deserve it. I should have given it to you years ago. You need it. A woman needs her own money. More than the pin money I've given you. And if you ever were to part from Andre, you'd be glad to have it. Use it or let it grow interest. Up to you. Totally up to you. But I'll deposit it there for you tomorrow. A line of credit from the Eutaw Savings Bank in Baltimore to Rothschild's here."

The sum freed her. Gave her independence, heart and hope. "I'm very grateful."

"Use it in health and happiness. The amount makes you an American princess worthy of your wealthy prince."

"Oh, don't be funny."

"I'm not. He's shockingly rich, my dear. But with your own savings—yes, I know you have them—and this, you are a prize for him."

She ran to him and kissed his cheek.

As Foster summoned the Hanniford coachman to the front door to take her back to Montmartre, she stood in the foyer and bid goodbye to what she had been here. Safe. Secure. Loved. Protected.

What she had been for too many years was cocooned. Dependent. Passive.

But no more. As she descended the front steps and climbed up into the carriage, she asked herself how she would change to embrace a future she valued for all the right reasons.


The Hanniford coachman helped her down from the brougham, doffed his cap and waited until Nanette answered the door to let her inside.

Across the street stood the crested Remy town coach, two matched grays stomping in wait. *For whom?*

Had Andre's mother come to visit? Had the coachman been sent up from the Remy Palais on the Rue de Rivoli with news of Andre's mother's health?

Picking up her skirts, she rapped on the bright blue door.

It was past ten o'clock, the windows in the house were dark. The gas turned low. Nanette let her in and she breathed in relief.

In the far corner of the foyer, stood a small leather traveling case. A man's.

*Had a visitor arrived?*

Panic raced along her spine.

"Where is *Monsieur*?" she asked the maid. Perhaps Andre might have gone to the square or to visit one of his friends.

The woman, normally jovial, even at this hour of the night, glanced up toward the stairs. "In the garden. He said he waits for you."

"*Merci*, Nanette." She hurried toward him, through the starlit *atelier* and out into the fragrant night. In one corner, Andre sat in a wicker chair, his eyes on the doorway as she appeared there. He had a wine glass in his hand, half full, the green bottle on the table next to the remains of his *al fresco* dinner.

As she approached, he rose, gallant as ever before to position a chair for her. She rose up on her toes and kissed his lips that tasted of the *vin rouge*. "Are you well? Is your mother? I saw a valise in the foyer just now. Do we have a visitor?"

"I'm well as is my mama. No, we don't have a caller. Sit, please. Tell me about your visit. I assume Killian had his coachman bring you home."

"He did," she said, grateful at the news to sink into the chair he offered and accept his gesture to fill a glass for her.

"I thought he would. Best at this time of night instead of a hack. Did you have supper?"

"Yes. We all did. Julian arrived this afternoon."

"Julian? From England? Why?"

She bit her lip. "Lily has left him."

"*Mon dieu.*"

"He doesn't know where's she gone."

"He must be out of his mind."

"He is."

Andre took a drink of his wine. "Has he any idea why she's gone?"

"He does. And as you might expect, he keeps it to himself. But he says he was slow to solve some of their problems."

"A pity." Andre took another sip and swallowed slowly. "They do love each other. It could even be a grand passion, despite the circumstances of why they married."

"He returns to London tomorrow. He sends his regards to you and asks you to forgive him for not calling."

"Unnecessary." Andre brushed it off with wave of a hand. "He must find his wife. And what happened when you talked with Ada?"

Marianne took a sip of wine. "Well, that turns out better than we anticipated. The situation is much less severe than we thought. She's very upset and promises to be more intelligent about her choices of friends from now on. She apologizes and hates herself."

"And will Killian send her home to Baltimore?"

"No. She'll stay. To go would cause more problems and she prefers to be here with her family."

"A good choice," he acknowledged. "And what of you, *ma cherie*? Did you and Killian discuss how you will return to his fold?"

"No." She summoned her courage, happy and yet skeptical of how he'd receive her decision. "I won't, you see."

He arched both blond brows and in the moonlight, he appeared wary...but not surprised. "No? Why not?"

"I must sort a few things out for myself before I do anything."

"What does that mean?" Anger tinged his voice.

She gulped down the urge to fling herself into his arms and declare her love for him. But he deserved better than that. He deserved a full accounting of her resolutions and her failures. "I will leave here tomorrow morning. That's for a brief—"

He looked away. "It's for the best."

Her thoughts rushing, crowding out logic, all those sentences she'd planned skipped away. She hated the feeling of being surrounded, closed off. And she'd never felt it with him. "It is."

He inhaled sharply as if she'd struck him.

"I must take a few days by myself." She'd always craved solitude, too much at times. But she needed it now to sort her thinking and to fortify herself for the new decisions she must make.

"I see. A holiday, is it?"

She hadn't planned where to go. Only why. "Not a vacation. No."

He stood. "It's as well. I cannot say I didn't expect you to leave. I depart myself now."

"What? Now? That's why your coach is here?"

He nodded. "The house is yours. Leave at your leisure."

To her shock, he turned abruptly and left her there in the garden. Her mouth open. Her heart aching.

She understood his feelings. His hurt. But what could she explain to him if she hadn't fully sorted it out? If she knew a piece of her self-knowledge was missing, how could she understand her love for him?

She ran to him. Caught up to him. Took his arm. "Please let me explain. I don't want you to think ill of me."

He gazed down at her, his blue eyes dour in the moonlight. "Marianne, I don't think ill of you."

"I must sort my thoughts. I have so many faults. Lacks I must repair. I see them now. And if we are to be good together, I must winnow and sift. You have given me so much but I must find all the pieces of myself."

"You change. We all do."

"Yes, but even now, I'm not complete." She had to tell him the parts she had discovered about herself. She rushed on, without reason, thoughts spilling from her lips. "I've been a coward. Hiding from myself."

He cupped her cheek. "Oh, my darling, you have not a cowardly bone in your body. What's more, you've become brave in ways you never expected."

"Not totally. Not yet." She took his arm. "I want to come to you, whole."

"My sweet darling, don't you see? I have valued you as you were and saw you as you might be. I valued you more than my own sanity. More than my work. More than my friends. Even my mother. There is no higher value than that. But I cannot wait any longer. I despair and that is new and terrifying to me."

"I don't understand. You lo—"

He slanted a finger across her lips. "I cannot work. And in work have I always found myself."

That she understood. So had she found herself in her own endeavors.

"I am lost. Lost without you."

"But I'm not gone—"

"You are. Still. To yourself. By your own admission here tonight. And I cannot pass my own life waiting for your revelations." He swept one hand up into her hair. Her pins fell like raindrops and her tresses cascaded over her shoulders like a shroud. Lifting her face, he bent down to bestow a kiss. She stirred in his embrace as she always did. Pressing against him, she gave her all to the emotion of making love to him again and to her astonishment, he finished his sumptuous exploration of her mouth—and stepped back. "Go with my blessing. But do not return to me."

She sucked in her breath.

He put up a finger. "Promise me."

Tears burned her eyes but she would not shed them. "No."

He smiled sadly. "Then I promise you, if you should come to me, I will not receive you."

# CHAPTER 14

Two days later, she took a hack from Montmartre down to the Rue de Provence. Since she had left his house, she had not slept. She had not eaten. And she had not allowed herself the luxury to cry.

Under her arm, she carried a large portfolio that she had purchased in the Rue Clichy yesterday. Patricia Farmer and her sister had recommended the shop that sold artists' supplies and Marianne was delighted with her choice. Half her height and as wide, the leather case was big enough to hold her largest sketches. Quite a few of them, too.

She entered *Monsieur* Montand's gallery, announced herself to his assistant and passed the interim by strolling around his display. She noted a vibrant blue and white landscape done in the impasto style of one noted impressionist artist and grinned at the dramatic statement it made. In bold stroke and quantity of paint, the scene spoke of a violent storm on the Seine.

Next to that painting were two sketches in pencil and watercolors. Done in washes of pale pinks and creams, the drawings were ones she knew well. They were of she herself.

The studies of a woman in the throes of passion, her mouth open in a sigh, her back arched, her thighs together but bent at the knees, the two renderings showed not merely a woman in her climax, but a woman in love.

The euphoria of that moment—of thousands of moments in Andre's arms—washed through her. He had seen her in those minutes. Recreated them for others to learn what love looked like.

Ironic that it took his departure from her life for her to experience the torment of his loss and the beauty of what he'd bestowed upon her. Now she had to do the same for him. If she could.

Marianne had no need to read the signs of attribution. Still, she forced herself. Her gaze devoured the words—and she relived the ecstasies they portrayed. "Remy. *Studies of Dawn.*"

She caught her breath. Since she'd left Andre's studio soon after he had two nights ago, she'd become dizzy, angry, determined. Fired onward by the urgency to accomplish a few vital changes to her life before she launched her plan to win Andre back. If she could.

"*Madame* Roland!" Edouard Montand marched forward, his winged mustache and sharp goatee trim as ever, his dark little eyes aglow. He gave her a small bow, his firm hot hand to shake and then asked her to join him in his office. "I'm delighted to see you here, *Madame*. This way, if you please."

Inside his neat well-appointed office, she took the over-stuffed chair he offered. "*Merci beaucoup, Monsieur.*"

"You saw Remy's two watercolors, I noticed." He took a chair opposite her, instead of sitting behind his massive oaken desk.

She marked his wariness. Did he think she'd be embarrassed by their display? "I did. They're quite dramatic. I like them immensely. And I do believe you will be able to sell them for a handsome price."

"*Monsieur* Bonnet, who fires Remy's bronzes, was here this morning on another matter and he tells me that there is a third. Larger. More exquisite."

"He is correct." That one of her was so lifelike she shivered at the memory of Andre's hands on her, rapture incarnate.

"But he says Remy does not part with it."

"Is that so? Good to know." Come to think of it, she had not seen it in the studio on its easel that last night she was there. Had he taken it with him?

"Bonnet says that third one is extraordinary. That I could sell it for five times what each of the two will bring."

"Bonnet should know," she said with less tact than she wished. She was eager to get the niceties done. "He has an eye. As do you."

"Thank you. You are kind. But I am so happy you're here. I sent round a messenger to Remy's *atelier* yesterday only to have him turn back without delivery. He learned from Carré that *Monsieur le duc* was gone and so were you."

She swallowed her despair over that. "Yes. The *duc de Remy* has gone south for the harvest. And to visit his mother. He hasn't seen her in many months." *He's been too attentive to me.*

"I hope she is well."

"As far as I know, yes, she is." Marianne must end this dance around the real reasons for Remy's departure and her own to be here. "I've come here because Remy sent me."

"He did? Is there a business matter we did not conclude to his satisfaction?"

"No, no. And I would not dare to presume to discuss such matters with you." She patted the edge of her portfolio. "I've come to show you the best of my own sketches."

"Oh?"

"Indeed. As I think you know, I lived with the duc de Remy these past few weeks." She was not embarrassed to declare it, but proud that Andre had nurtured her, proud he and she had been lovers.

The man had the politesse to fix his gaze on hers and merely nod.

"He made me promise him that I would produce enough works to have a collection of those I considered my best. Those, I was to bring you and allow you to critique them."

Montand rubbed his hands together. "Marvelous. I must thank the duke when I see him again."

"*Monsieur*," she said, his charm luring a smile from her, "you haven't seen any yet."

"*Madame*, I saw the one. It whet my appetite for more. You see the reason I sent word round to Remy's *atelier* yesterday was because I wanted to tell you of the sale of your sketch."

"Of Andre?" Shock ran through her.

"Of Andre," he said with a teasing grin on his lips.

It struck her that to his art dealer, she called Remy by his given name, not his title. To be so familiar with a man of business was unheard of. Rude. Even wives did not always address their husbands by their given names. Such intimacies were truly that. But she had been Andre Claude Marceau, the duc de Remy's lover. For nearly one glorious month, she'd been his beloved. And she missed him with every breath, every heartbeat. She was not ashamed to admit it.

That she was in misery without him was a matter not to be alluded to here. "Forgive me, *Monsieur* Montand. I am remiss. To whom did you sell the portrait?"

"The mayor of Calais for the City Council."

She frowned. "Why would the mayor of Calais wish to own my portrait of *Monsieur le duc*?"

"They negotiate a commission with him for a composition in the town square in front of the *Hotel de Ville*. The mayor was in Paris on holiday, saw your sketch and wished to purchase it for the town hall. To commemorate Remy and his work for them. To hang there in its frame in perpetuity."

In Calais, they wished the great sculptor Remy to provide them with art for their people. Inside, her heart stumbled on a profound humility that she'd found a way to help them honor him. "I must say that's utterly wonderful."

"It is."

"Did the mayor take it with him?"

"He did."

"Remy will be honored. As for me, I'm overwhelmed. Thank you. I never thought to have anything hanging in a French city hall." Feeling teary, she wished to speed her interview. She could bask in the glow of her own success later. She lifted her portfolio. "I've brought these for your viewing. I hope you'll be frank with me about their potential."

He rose and took the case from her. "Let's put it on my table and let me get my loop."

She stood by as he removed her sketches and watercolors from the case and spread them on the table. He took out his various magnifying glasses, put them to his eye and bent over her works, one by one. And then he returned to examine each again.

More than an hour later, he went to his desk and sat down to face her, his expression blank.

"They're terrible. I can see it."

He shook his head.

"I knew the portrait of Andre was unique. And I'm pleased the mayor of Calais bought it. I'll take that as my one great success and be grateful."

"You do not understand, *Madame*."

"I do. I can see that sometimes a person produces an

outstanding work of art. I'm pleased...no, thrilled it was of Andre. Pardon me, to me he is Andre." *Andre*. She shot to her feet. "I'll collect these. Those others I gave you a few weeks ago, as well, and I'll not bother you again, *Monsieur*."

He stood. "*Madame* Roland. Please sit down."

She smiled through her pain and lifted a shoulder. "There is no need to be polite. *Monsieur*, please."

"*Madame*, I am not polite. I am in earnest. Your works are worthy of an exhibit of their own."

"Oh," she laughed. "What? No. Surely."

He chuckled. He tapped on finger on a sketch. "*Madame* Roland, your studies here of the laundry woman and this one of can-can dancer are realistic, yet evoke sympathy. Understanding. They are better than the ones you gave me weeks ago of the men in the Place du Tertre. But this one? The mother bathing the fat baby? Charming. Touching."

She sat down with a thump. "You're quite serious."

"I am." He sat, too. Folding his hands over his middle, he grinned at her. "I will take them all and sell them for you."

She flung back her head and laughed. Presently when she was more logical and less giddy, she said, "But *Monsieur* there is a problem."

"What is it?"

"Andre told me I was not to allow you to sell any of my works. I was to ask you for the address of your competitor and take my work there for him to sell."

"Like hell I'll do that!" he roared good-naturedly. "I'll have a word with your *Andre* when next I see him, *Madame*. He is too domineering. Beware of that."

"Oh, I am, believe me, Monsieur."

He leaned toward her. "I like your work, I've sold your work, and I can sell more of it."

They grinned at each other for a long satisfying minute.

"And so I suppose," he said to her, "I should tell you what the mayor of Calais paid for your sketch of your Andre."

She giggled. "Please do. All the details. I seem to have forgotten to ask for that bit of news."

Her hired hackney coach from the Tours railway station was an old, uncomfortable conveyance whose age, she estimated, to be twice hers and three times its proper retirement. The springs were non-existent, the squabs thin as a centime, the oiled window shades grimy and the horse, ancient and very, very slow. If the coachman was a happy lad, she took that as a good omen.

He was thrilled to be going so far as the Chateau de Remy. His eyes danced and he veritably licked his lips at the money he'd earn. "The sculptor's chateau? *Oui*, I can take you there, *Madame*. But the fare is heavy."

She didn't care.

"Charge me what you must, *Monsieur*," she told him. But as she dug her pocket watch from her reticule and checked the time, she silently acknowledged that the forty minutes it had currently taken her was worth the charge he'd quoted her. He should walk on.

Along the roadside, beefy dark brown cattle grazed in the warm September sun. In the valleys near the copse of trees, a hazy mist hung in the air and lent a foggy mystery to the rolling green landscape. Small farms clustered together here and there. Fat pigs gazed at the carriage through wooden pens. Chickens scooted around the yards. Children played stick ball and stopped to gaze at the travel coach as it passed them.

A border fence appeared along the road. Pale grey and white limestones hewn from the earth had been piled up three feet high or more to demarcate a boundary. Its sturdy structure announced to her the wealth of whoever owned the land it bound.

Then the coach slowed. The wooden wheels ground against cobbles, screeching loud as a scalded cat. She pushed back the curtain with one finger to see they turned into a wide lane. Before her was no limestone fence, but a ten foot tall brick wall that ran across the cobbled lane for a mile or more. Every three feet along the wall stood a white stone guardian, statues of men outfitted as Roman sentries.

Her mouth fell open and she rapped on the coachman's box with her fist. "Stop, stop!"

The man idled the coach and she pushed the oil cloth back to gape at the scene before her.

"Beautiful, eh, *Madame*?" the coachman called down to her. "A pearl. Cut from the same quarry as all of Paris."

The house glistened in the afternoon sunshine. She sat in awe of its color, snowy white. Its height, two stories as tall as Versailles with a high sloping slate mansard roof of dark grey. The entrance rose from the long cobbled driveway on wide stone stairs up to the main floor where three large porticos secured by huge iron grates greeted visitors. Behind them stood three black lacquered doors with brass fittings fit for a king. Or in this case, a duke who was also a prince.

This was no house.

She'd lived in a six-room farm house as a girl. A ten-room plantation house as a bride. Uncle Killian's two-story mansion in Baltimore on Charles Street. And the formidable luxury of the four-story townhouse in Rue Haussmann.

But this was no house. This was the aged and renowned Chateau de Remy, first built by the Comte de Remy in the fifteenth century, so Edouard Montand informed her when she told him that she was to travel here today.

But she, for all her cosmopolitan upbringing, could not

stoop to dub this structure a simple chateau. She could fit five of Frederick's house in here. Three of the Rue Haussmann.

Chateau de Remy was a palace.

She let the curtain fall and she sank back to the cushions. This was Andre's home and she had not predicted how formidable the house alone would be. To face him here, angry as he was with her, would require more than courage.

She'd need audacity to state her case and win him or leave with her head held high…if in the end, he threw her out.

She paid the man his fee and told him he could leave. He motioned to her traveling case and she nodded that he could carry it up the portico steps for her.

As she climbed the broad stone steps to the central door, a butler dressed in black frock coat opened the door wide. "*Madame?*" he asked, his manner kind but curious. "Have you an appointment?"

"No, I don't. I'm here to see *Monsieur le duc*, if you please."

"Your name, *Madame?*"

"Marianne Roland."

He lowered his eyes, bowed slightly and indicated with a polite gesture of his hand that she should follow him. She entered into a rotunda big as the Pantheon in Paris, a reception hall of extraordinary opulence. Surrounded by the same glittering limestone as outside, she moved in a circular trance to mark the sculptures around her in the stonework. Reliefs of Greek gods and goddesses topped the pillars that adorned the room. No furniture marred the symmetry.

Only the footsteps of the butler resounded in the room. "Wait here, *Madame*."

She could stand here for hours. Admiring the statues of Zeus and Psyche, Apollo and Athena, Marianne smiled up at the lifelike quality of their faces and forms. Andre had grown up here. No wonder he thought beauty lived in every day life. In here, was the essence of what an artist created to adorn his world.

She walked to the far doors and gazed out upon the landscape at the back of the house. The gardens, the elaborate *partiere* of boxwoods and rose bushes, evergreens and hollies stretched before her for a mile, perhaps more. To the left stood brick and stone houses that she would guess were barns. To the right, a large brick and stone edifice stood, its broad doors flung wide. Inside stood two carriages. One a silver and brown brougham. The other a large shiny black landau.

She bit her lower lip. Here was Andre's heritage, his past laid out for her. Such wealth she had not imagined for anyone and not him, either.

"*Madame* Roland?"

She spun at the sound of a woman's voice.

An elegant white-haired lady approached her from the far wing. The perfection of her oval face, the eloquent blue eyes and the careful refined manner proclaimed her as Andre's mother, *Princesse Amalie Sabine d'Aumale et Duchesse de* Remy.

Marianne steeled herself for this encounter and curtsied. "*Madame la Princesse*, I am delighted to meet you."

The woman clasped her hands before her at her waist and surveyed Marianne, head to toe. "*Pardon e moi, Madame* Roland," she said, her words were polite, her tone ice. "You recognize me?"

"I see the resemblance to your son, *Madame*."

To that, the lady leveled her eyes on Marianne. The look assessed, but did not welcome. "We had no notice you were to arrive."

"No, *Madame*. Forgive me. I do come uninvited." *As well you must know.* His mother would not make this easy for her.

She had to have her wits about her.

"Follow me." The princess turned on her heel, her skirts snapping to one side.

The woman strode down the hall from whence she'd come, Marianne trooping along behind her. In *en filade*, the rooms marched on. A library, shelves of thick mahogany, jungle dark and lustrous, rising floor to ten-foot ceiling, encumbered by hundreds of books, all sizes, all bindings, smelling of the years of dust upon their bindings. A bedroom, with the widest bed Marianne had ever seen, hung in rich burgundy and gold brocades, tapestries tall as the walls hanging there as kings and queens hunted stag and dogs swarmed to take down birds. A dining room, a table laden with gold plate centerpiece, a bust of Louis XIV on a pedestal in one corner, and in the glass-faced closets lining the walls, china from Sèvres, from Peking's Ming and Ch'ing periods, Aubussons of incredible pinks and greens and plums stretched out before her, a carpet in the spectrum of paradise.

The princess turned into a blue room, smaller than the others they'd passed. Upon the walls, stern-faced ladies in panniers and jewels, men in sumptuous satin coats and codpieces gazed down upon them. Here the princess indicated a settee and then, as the butler who had greeted Marianne bowed his way out, the doors were closed upon them.

"Please, *Madame*." The lady pressed the settee upon her. "I know how long that journey is from the rail station. What's more," she said in perfect English, "I have experienced the unique charms of *Monsieur* Villar's carriage. Only once, but it was enough to last me for decades."

"*Merci beaucoup, Madame*," she said and sat.

"I am pleased to meet you, *Madame* Roland."

Marianne wagered that kind sentiment was not to last. "And I you, *Madame*. I have heard Andre speak of you often and I—"

At the mention of her son's given name, the princess's blue eyes hardened to stone chips.

Marianne sucked in a breath, grabbing all her courage. *Very well. I may not be here long. Best to be bold.* "I came to talk with Andre."

"But you confront me first. If indeed Remy will deign to come to speak to you."

Marianne told herself that might well be the case. "*Madame*, I do not wish to argue with you."

"*Madame* Roland, I do not argue. I declare. And it is done."

Marianne stared at his mother. This was behavior she understood. Behavior she need not tolerate.

She stood. "I would hope you would tell me if *Monsieur le duc* is here. And where I might find him. Outside perhaps? If you cannot tell me, I will return to Tours and hire a messenger. He'll ask *Monsieur* to meet me in the Hotel de Vers there. Hopefully he will decide to grant me that and I can speak my peace."

The woman arched a long pale brow. "You would remain in Tours until Remy comes to you?"

"Yes. Of course. Why not?"

"You have the nerve to do so?"

She set her jaw. "I have the will to do so."

"And do you know what he told me to do if you appeared here and you wished to speak to him?"

"Yes," she barely got out the word. "*Pardon e moi, Madame.* I shall leave."

She pulled open the double doors and headed toward the rotunda. Tears burned her eyes, but she would not cry here.

"Wait!" The princess called to her. "Wait, *s'il vous plait*."

She paused in her tracks.

The swish of the princess's skirts punctuated the woman's approach. She rounded Marianne and looked her in the eye.

Shorter than Marianne by several inches, the lady had a stark look of despair about her. "I understand you are a widow."

What that had to do with this interview, she'd no idea.

"And that he was not a noble man."

Marianne chose not to add to that.

"That you have had no children."

The princess was concerned with her son's future progeny? No. No. That was not relevant here.

"And so I wonder if you have any idea what it is to have one child. One perfect son. A boy who grew in grace and beauty with each passing year. A child who became a man of principles and ethics. A talented artist who gives his all to his work and rises to the pinnacle for it. Da Vinci, Bernini, Canova. They are dead. But now for many there is this new genius Remy. No equal to him. No one who gainsays him. He could take any woman to him and tell her he loved her, and who among them would refuse him?"

Marianne swallowed her sorrow. "I do not refuse him, *Madame*. Have not, ever. You may wish to vent your anger at me here. I understand that. How do you love and not live to protect the one who means the world to you? You don't. Thank you for your time. *Au revoir*."

She sidestepped the princess.

"*Madame* Roland! If I am to summon Remy, I need your assurance that you will not harm him any more than you already have."

She faced the princess. "You think I came here to hurt him more? I came to apologize to him if he'll permit me to try. And if I can do more than that, I will do that too."

# CHAPTER 15

The wind pierced her coat as she hurried through the lower kitchen doors on the ground floor of the chateau toward the carriage house.

In the dimly lit expanse, she heard male voices emanate from the rear. She hastened along, her heels thumping on the solid earth, making little noise.

At once she was upon them, Andre and an older man both dressed in old cotton work clothes. Both of them stared at her, an apparition in the middle of the afternoon.

"*Bonjour, Monsieur le duc, et Monsieur,*" she bid them both and curtsied to Andre.

Andre frowned, running his bare forearm against his forehead. "What are you doing here?" he asked, his voice light with wonder at her appearance.

"I came to talk with you."

The older man made his excuses and backed away from them. Turning on his heel, he jogged away.

Andre looked outside, focusing on the cobbled path to the chateau. "How did you get here?"

"*Monsieur* Villar's coach from the train station."

Gaiety passed over his features like a ray of sun, quickly to vanish. "A nightmare."

"I've known worse."

In his hands, he held a farrier's rasp. "Did you dismiss him?"

"I did."

She saw Andre think of the possible reasons for that, reviewing them with a twist of his lips. "You should not have sent him off. Maurice!" He called to his servant. "Maurice, come hitch the gig for our visitor."

Marianne took a step forward.

"She's leaving," Andre announced and turned from her.

She took another step toward him. "Do not walk away from me."

He halted in his tracks.

She raised her voice, anger tingeing her need to stop him. "I came all this way and I will not be ignored."

"Then speak to yourself."

"I'll follow you." She kept pace with him. "Follow until you listen."

Maurice approached. "*Monsieur le duc?*"

She advanced on Andre, but she acknowledged the servant. "Very well, Maurice, you are my witness. Andre, I am here to apologize."

Dismissing her with a wave of one hand, Andre walked on.

So did she. "And to tell you that you are arrogant."

He whirled on her, his blue eyes aflame with hurt and distrust. "I? Am arrogant?"

She stood her ground. Chin up, she would win this argument. "All your life, you have had everything you wanted. Whether easily or not, I do not know. Not yet. But you have put your hand to anything you owned and perfected it, anything you wished and claimed it, shaped it and won it for your own. On your own terms."

He snorted. "That is no apology."

"And that is another character flaw of yours."

His brows arched high. "Pardon me?"

"You are impatient."

Maurice shifted from one foot to another. "Sir, I—?"

Andre raised a hand to his man. "Do go to your work, Maurice."

The man trotted off.

Marianne stood taller. Say this she would. "You have become so used to success you are blind to its effects on you."

His lips thinned. He fairly seethed. "I dare say, you are the one who's arrogant to come here and—"

"Yes. And it's about time, wouldn't you say? Or...well, you would have said. But in any case, you *should* call me arrogant. I need a strong dose of it to counter you." She advanced on him. "You are so confident that you are blind to your faults."

"Am I?" He fell back against the wooden wall and a flicker of self-deprecating humor passed over his features. "Explain that to me."

"You thought you knew me."

His lips firmed. His nostrils flared. "Didn't I?"

"Partly." She walked right up to him. So close she saw how exhausted he looked as if he hadn't slept in days. Thinner, as if he'd not eaten well either. If that was due to her, she could say she was gratified she meant that much to him, but dismayed that he could pine for her so dearly and affect his health. "You saw me as a victim of my circumstances, my parents' deaths, my early marriage and a bad one at that. You saw me as closeted, protected, secluded. Even cloistered. You saw me as a woman who had only an inkling she might enjoy affection from a partner who could nurture her sensual nature."

He frowned at her. "I saw your potential there. For more."

"Yes. With a man who could show me the erotic pleasures of an affair."

He grunted. "With a man who could show you the joys of love."

She pointed a finger at him. "Exactly. Even when you also saw that I might grow in professional ways, you gave me that as well."

His brows shot high. He was aghast. "And there was something wrong with that?"

"No! But to show me the path to that and then fail to allow proper time for what growth came from that? That was where your arrogance got the better of you."

"Did it?"

"Yes. And that's where your impatience ended our love affair too soon."

He stared at her, quietly searching her visage.

"You could not know me as the woman who nursed raving, dying wounded men. You did not know me as the woman who left the safety of her hospital one night and walked for days through strange towns and ugly forests alone. Who dodged remnants of Union lines, scalawags and deserters to trudge north across Virginia plains to the Potomac and buy her way across from fishermen with the gold she's sewn in her hems."

"Marianne." He blanched.

"You could not know me, did not hear me tell the tale of how frightened I was, how hungry, how desperate for sleep and warmth that I gladly accepted the safety of my uncle's home and family. That I declared I would never leave. And why would I? Hmm? What motive did I have?"

She poked a finger in his chest. "You failed to see me as a person who might grow and change to match you. Failed to see me as one who might declare her freedom from her cocoon, take her freedom in to her own hands and use those tools you gave me to draw a new life from my old one." She blinked back tears. "And yet it was you who showed me the way. You, always you. You who perceived the essence of me as you perceive images in the depths of your blocks of Carrara. I was there, bound tightly inside, and you carved me out, little by little, piece by piece, until I emerged, the creature I was, rough hewn but now liberated to what I can become."

Sorrow lined his brows. Anger supplanted it. "I did all that, and yet you stand there and tell me I do not know you?"

She inhaled and embarked on the more rational portion of her revelations. "Still not, no. You see the morning after you left Montmartre to come here, I packed my belongings and with Patricia Farmer's help, I found a vacant room in a flat in the Rue Clichy. I rented it for the remainder of the month."

That made him blink.

"I did not return to Rue Haussmann. And I won't go back except now and then as a visitor or a dinner guest."

He didn't say a word, but crossed his arms again.

"Yesterday, I went to visit Montand."

"Good for you."

"He sold my portrait of you to the Mayor of Calais."

Andre pursed his lips. And did he fight a grin? "I hope you got a decent fee."

"I did. And there is more. Montand likes my other works."

"Which?"

"The ones you told me to take to him. The best ones from each day. Remember you made me promise to take them to him and say he could not have them?"

His pride lit his features. "I do. Yes."

She swallowed and screwed up her courage for this last foray against his defenses. "With my fees, I want to venture out, take a holiday. I want to go south."

"What? Where?"

"Provence. I will rent a house. Patricia tells me it is so warm there, the sun is so close, the colors so intense, it blazes through you. Sears you, forges you into a different being. I want to go. Walk through fields of lavender and—"

"You earned this much money from the sale of your sketch?"

"No! But I have savings plus Uncle Killian gave me what was to be my dowry."

"How kind of him," Andre sneered and pushed away from the wall.

She caught his arm. "I want to take a house in the south of France where it's warm and sunny. I want—"

He glowered at her. "You want to be a naturalist?"

"Perhaps I do!"

"What?" He gazed at her as if he'd never seen her before.

"I want to stroll naked in the sun. And I want you to come with me."

He stared at her. Temptation rose in his eyes. His lips parted. But then he waved a dismissive hand and walked on.

She scampered after him. "Will you please stand still?"

"No!" He whirled on her. "You talk of my faults, your dowries and renting and the south. I thought you said you came to apologize. None of this is that."

"I'm trying to do it and you're acting like a spoiled child!"

"There you go again! Yes, I was a spoiled child. I am a spoiled child! Did not my mother tell you? I was everything to her, to my father, too. I was obedient and studious, reverent and got my proper education in the ways of the world when I went to boarding school and learned how to cheat and claw my way up."

"That's ridiculous," she said. "You are no cheat."

"No. But I know how to be. How to get what I want the best way I can."

"That's not what you did with me. You were the perfect gentleman. Perfect for me."

He watched her, a lion injured, hurting.

She could not relent. "So don't give me your regrets about your wayward ways, my prince. I know you as better than most. And best of all."

He grabbed her by both arms. "You know nothing of who I am or what I want."

"Oh, but you're wrong. I know you are the great Remy. The sculptor who will shake cities and continents with your perceptions of men. Carved in stone, fired in bronze, molded in clay, your works will stand for centuries for men and women to admire and imitate."

"What good is all that?" he mocked. "I'll be dead and gone."

"But what you have in life is what you'll leave the world too."

"You talk nonsense." He whirled away.

She hurried to scamper in front of him. There was a bit of humility in him and she grinned at its appearance. "They'll say this is the man we should admire. The one we should imitate. Not in his works but in his manner and his ethics. His dedication to his art and his students and his colleagues and those he loved."

He stared at her.

"Listen to me!" She stepped against him, her arms around his waist, her eyes adoring him. "They'll say he loved one American woman. She was no one. A Virginia planter's daughter. A widow of an unprincipled man, a coward and a bully. Niece to a robber baron and cousin to those she adored. But none of them meant as much to her as Remy. Her Andre."

He focused on her lips, but then raised his face. "I'm getting the gig."

"They'll say he loved this woman so much that she learned

how to live herself. He taught her how to tame her own art and to live with courage and joy."

"They'll say she refused him."

She nodded. "At first, she did. Yes. She was still so young to the charms of the freedom he taught her. She raced to keep up to him. She cast off her need to remain alone. That was to protect from the unknown, you see. She cast off her habit to reject her own desires. That was to remain safe. She cast off her fear of being a second rate artist to learn how to be a very good one."

She stood before him and hugged him to her. "She wanted to live with him. Love him. Share with him the rewards of what he had taught her to grasp."

His anger melted from his gaze. "And what did she do with all that desire?"

"She asked him to love her. To take her back. To live with her."

He considered her eyes, her mouth.

"She told him she loved him. Loved him and would until the day she died. And maybe longer."

"And if he refused her?" he asked on a whisper. "What would she do?"

She dropped her arms. "She'd say, I love you one more time. And then she'd leave."

He stared at her, the sadness in his gaze palpable.

She stepped away. She'd failed. Failed. She could not change him. Could not make him see her as she had become and as they were meant to be together.

She spun around, once more headed for the door.

"And if he told her he loved her?"

She halted.

His footfalls on the earthen floor were soft, almost imperceptible. "If he said he had loved her from the first moment he'd seen her in the Rue des Abbesses?"

She wanted to sob.

"What would she do with that?"

A great well of agony rose in her throat. "She'd say she loved his graciousness. His generosity. His great good heart."

"And if she could change the ending? What would she do?"

"She'd ask him to come south with her for the winter perhaps? A few months for a new beginning. She'd ask him to stay with her, all their lives, in fact, so that she might prove to him every day that he was the finest man she'd ever known."

She could not hear a sound in the old carriage house. Had he left her standing there?

Dear god. She'd lost. Lost. She squeezed her eyes shut, but picked up her skirts and—

He caught her around the waist and carried her, pressing her to the wooden wall. His lips to her nape, his arms gathering her back against his chest, he said, "I won't live with you. I won't be your lover."

She let out a groan.

"You won't be my mistress."

She shook her head, her heart cracking. "No."

He spun her in his arms and lifted her face with two hands cupping her cheeks. "You'll be my wife."

She laughed or cried, she couldn't tell which. This was the man who would not ask for her hand, but tell her she would wed him. "Yes. Of course. Why not? We are so conventional, you and I. Why shouldn't I marry my superb lover the illustrious, demanding, darling Remy?" She reached up and kissed his lips. "I love you."

He picked her up much as he had that first night she'd come to him in Montmartre and swung her up and around, giddy with laughter and success. Tears in his eyes, he kissed her with all the passion she recalled. "You will marry me."

"I will."

"And never leave me?"

"And never leave you."

"Because you love me," he said.

"Because you love me."

## THE END

# AUTHOR'S NOTES

My joy in writing historical fiction is attempting to paint a picture of the past that is as accurate as possible, but also as relevant to you, my readers.

Writing DARING WIDOW has been a delight for me, but it's also been a thrill to research! Days and nights in Paris and the countryside, I hope, live in these pages for you.

Paris in the late 1870s was emerging as the city of light. Baron Haussmann's civic improvements under the reign of Emperor Napoleon III had transformed the medieval town into a modern metropolis. Europeans from all nations flocked to the city for its gaiety. They came for the marvelous hotels catering to every whim, exquisite cuisine in ornate restaurants and entertaining night life in theaters and cafes. Nearby, up on the butte in Montmartre, raucous dancers performed a new risqué move, the cancan, many went to dance nightly in the *Moulin de la Galette*. As stone masons cut and positioned huge limestone blocks to build the new church Sacre Coeur, aspiring artists lived in tumble-down wooden shacks. Others who were earning a bit more money managed to live in more substantial abodes.

One of those houses still standing is now a part of the complex on the hill, known as the Musée de Montmartre. Renoir lived there briefly and over the next decades, so did quite a few other artists. The remains of one studio, with its fabulous *atelier* open the Paris sky, can take your breath away. This is the basis for the studio of Andre Claude Marceau, duc de Remy.

Remy, as you may have noted as you read, shows a few similarities to French artist Auguste Rodin. In body and spirit, Remy resembles the great sculptor with his dedication to his art and his capacity for great love affairs. One of those —some say the most tragic—is that of his relationship with sculptress Camille Claudel. Their affair was intense, fraught with Camille's competitive nature and volatile temper as well as Rodin's attempt to encourage her in her work. When she left him, Rodin was bereft, unable to work for many months. When he did resume his work, he continued to use her face and form as a model for many works.

Although Rodin never did live or work up on the hill in Montmartre, I chose to place Remy there to attempt to draw the full flavor of the artistic community that still thrives today. Even among the crowds of tourists, you can discern the qualities that attracted so many like DeGas, Manet, Utrillo and later Toulouse-Lautrec and Pablo Picasso. The fresh air upon the high hill above the rooftops of Paris and the sense of freedom from strict forms of etiquette still make this suburb of Paris a delight to visit.

Among the artists who lived and worked there were a few women. Some attempted the new landscape style of *plein air* art, but others—as Patricia Farmer tells Marianne—wanted to portray the ordinary people who lived and worked there. Barmaids, laundry women, cancan dancers and waitresses became their subjects. Like American painter Mary Cassatt and French artist Berthe Morisot, Marianne Roland finds her *métier* is portraying the daily lives of ordinary women and children. It is here, with the help of Remy and the art dealer Edouard Montand (modeled on dealer Paul Durand-Ruel) that she achieves her own individuality and her success.

The ancestral home of the *duc de Remy* and his mother, the *Princesse d'Aumale* and *Duchesse de Remy*, is my fictional representation of a chateau that charms me each time I see it. A few miles outside of Paris, accessible by Metro and local bus, Vaux le Vicomte is a treasure. While I leave you to research it online, I will tell you that the brick and stone gates, the striking entrance, the rotunda, the rooms, the carriage house and the enormous grounds with enchanting *partierre* are rendered in my text with a humility that can scarcely match its glory.

I hope you've enjoyed your journey back to Paris in the dawn of *La Belle Époque*. And I hope you join me for the next few stories in THOSE NOTORIOUS AMERICANS when Ada, Pierce and Killian Hanniford meet their matches!

*Cerise DeLand*

# ABOUT THE AUTHOR

Cerise DeLand loves to write about dashing heroes and the sassy women they adore. Whether she's penning historical romances or contemporaries, she's praised for her poetic elegance and accuracy of detail.

An award-winning author of more than 50 novels, she's been published since 1991 by Pocket Books, St. Martin's Press, Kensington and independent presses. Her books have been monthly selections of the Doubleday Book Club and the Mystery Guild. Plus she's won rave reviews from *Romantic Times, Affair de Coeur, Publisher's Weekly* and more.

To research, she's dived into the oldest texts and dustiest library shelves. She's also traveled abroad, trusty notebook and pen in hand, to visit the chateaux and country homes she loves to people with her own imaginary characters.

And at home every day? She loves to cook, hates to dust, goes swimming at least once a week and tries (desperately) to grow vegetables in her backyard in south Texas!

*For more about Cerise and her works visit:*

www.cerisedeland.com
cerise.deland@gmail.com

## ALSO BY CERISE DELAND

### *Regencies*

Lady Starling's Stockings

*Regency Romp Series:*

Lady Varney's Risque Business, #1

Rendezvous with a Duke, #2

Masquerade with a Marquess, #3

Interlude with a Baron, #4

Regency Romps Box Set, Books #1, #2 and #3

*Delightful Doings in Dudley Crescent Series:*

Her Beguiling Butler, #1

His Tempting Governess, #2, *debuts Winter 2018*

His Naughty Maid, #3,

*debuts Winter 2018*

### *Erotic Regencies:*

His Delectable Cook

Sense and Sensibility

### *Victorian Romance*s

Those Notorious Americans Series:

Wild Lily, #1

Daring Widow, #2

Scandalous Countess, *debuts 2018*

Outrageous Countess, *late 2018*

Black Irish Rogue, *late 2018*

### *Medievals*

*Swords of Passion Series:*

At Her Service, #1

For Her Honor, #2

With Her Kiss, #3

\* \* \*

### *Military Romances*

*7 Brides for 7 SEALs Series:*

You Were Always Mine, #1

No Getting Over You, #2

Only You, #3, *debuting 2018*

SEALs Going Hot, box set

Burning for Nero

Conquering Zeus

A Long Time Comin'

Hard Drivin' Man

### *Contemporaries*

Tall, Hard and Trouble, box set

Tall, Hard and Mine, box set, *Coming Soon!*

Tall, Hard and Fierce, box set, *Coming Soon!*

\*\*\*

Subscribe to Cerise's Delicious Newsletter!

**www.cerisedeland.com**